Caitlin –

Much love.

AMBER S. CLARK

ABOUT THE AUTHOR

GREG OLEAR lives in the Hudson Valley with his family. This is his first novel. For more information please visit www.gregolear.com or www.totallykiller.com.

TOTALLY KILLER

TOTALLY KILLER

a novel

Greg Olear

HARPER

NEW YORK • LONDON • TORONTO • SYDNEY

HARPER

HarperCollins books may be purchased for educational, business, or sales promotional use. For information please write: Special Markets Department, HarperCollins Publishers, 10 East 53rd Street, New York, NY 10022.

FIRST EDITION

Designed by Claudia Martinez

Library of Congress Cataloging-in-Publication Data
Olear, Greg.
Totally killer : a novel / Greg Olear.— 1st Harper pbk.
ISBN 978-0-06-173529-5
I. Title
PS3615.L426T68   2009
813'.6—dc22   20008051752

09 10 11 12 13   OV/RRD   10 9 8 7 6 5 4 3 2 1

For Stephanie

TOTALLY
KILLER

maxell **XL II**

POSITION
IEC TYPE II • HIGH (CrO₂)

TODD'S TOTALLY KILLER MIX
(FOR TAYLOR)

A DATE 11/2/91
N.R.   ○YES ○NO

B DATE .
N.R.   ○YES ○NO

Side A	Side B
SHINY HAPPY PEOPLE / REM	MEA CULPA / ENIGMA
GIVE IT AWAY / RED HOT CHILI PEPPERS	• GONNA MAKE YOU
(I DON'T WANT to GO to) CHELSEA /	SWEAT / CTC MUSIC FACTORY
ELVIS COSTELLO	OPP / NAUGHTY BY NATURE
LITHIUM / NIRVANA	LOVE HER MADLY / DOORS
LORELEI / THE POGUES	HEY HEY WHAT CAN I DO /
CARELESS MEMORIES / DURAN DURAN	LED ZEPPELIN
FEMME FATALE / VELVET UNDERGROUND	ADD IT UP / VIOLENT FEMMES
EVERYBODY KNOWS / CONCRETE BLONDE	JANE SAYS / JANE'S ADDICTION
HEAVEN KNOWS I'M MISERABLE	NOVEMBER RAIN / GNR
NOW / THE SMITHS	COLD ETHYL / ALICE COOPER
ALL I WANT IS YOU / U2	

PROLOGUE

I never loved Taylor Schmidt. Despite what you may have heard.

Love is more pure than the crude alloy of lust, fascination, and pity that formed my feelings for her. Baser metals, however shiny, do not gold make.

That said, I can understand, if never forgive, the confusion. I did have a hard-on for her something awful. Still do, and she's eighteen years dead.

Once in a lifetime, if you're lucky, you meet a woman who just *does it for you*. That was Taylor Schmidt. The chick oozed pheromones. She was sex. And not just for me. Everybody she ever met wanted to sleep with her. *Everybody*, not just every guy.

In time, this became a burden on her, same as if her preternatural sex appeal were some grotesque deformity—a pig nose, a harelip, a port wine stain on her cheek. She complained about it all the time. Her plight suggested one of those Greek myths with the ironical endings: girl isn't so hot, girl wishes for great beauty, girl becomes so alluring that it's impossible for her to have a nonsexual relationship with anyone. Men want her body. Women either want her body, hate her as a rival, or both. She can't win. She's Queen Midas, and sex is her gold.

I'm mucking up my metallic metaphors, but you get the idea. Guys wanted to bone her, is the point, and more often than not, she indulged their desire. Surrendered to their lust. Passively, but recklessly and utterly (and sometimes, it's been alleged, for money). Was she a nympho? Depends on your definition. What Freud would consider nymphomania and what some drunk guy at a bar would consider nymphomania are very different. Me, I think it's a cop-out, tagging her that way. Nymphos are easy, aren't they? And Taylor was not easy. In her all-too-brief life she'd bedded seventy-eight lovers—I know this because she kept a detailed list of her sexual partners; names of every ethnic configuration, in different shades of ink, with little misshapen hearts dotting the *i*'s—but she wasn't *easy*. She had standards. She turned men down all the time. She turned me down all the time. Well, almost all the time. She turned me down because she liked me. That's what she told me, at least.

Taylor was my roommate. She became more later on, but that's how it started.

She moved in on the Fourth of July, 1991. Historically, this was right after the dissolution of both the Warsaw Pact, at a meeting in Prague held largely as a formality, and my yearlong relationship with Laura Horowitz, at a meeting in our apartment held largely as a formality.

"I'm in love with someone else," my soon-to-be-ex-girlfriend explained, before collecting whatever things she hadn't already packed and hightailing it to Brooklyn Heights with Someone Else, a defense attorney at Legal Aid named Chet.

The ramifications of the breakup went beyond my broken heart and wounded pride. See, Laura and I lived together, and thus were, in Tama Janowitz's then-current phrase, slaves of New York. My pittance as an API photo librarian couldn't cover my eight-bill rent. I either had to move, or else find someone to occupy the second bedroom; and whatever I did, I needed to act pronto. An acquaintance at work—this photo stringer named Jason Hanson who knew her from high school—sent Taylor to me. To me and my small but legit two-bedroom apartment on East Ninth Street.

All the way from Warrensburg, Missouri, she appeared on my doorstep (or stoop, as it were) as if by magic, bearing two suitcases, an oversized knapsack, a month's supply of antidepressants, and five crumpled hundred-dollar bills wadded up in the front pocket of her pink denim miniskirt.

When I opened the door and let her in, I actually pinched myself. Jason hadn't warned me. Her mascara was smeared, her hair was a mess, there were dark circles under her eyes, but all I could think of, watching Taylor cross and recross her tanned legs on my torn vinyl sofa, was how badly I wanted her, what an amazing stroke of good fortune her presence in my living room was, and how this whole Laura-moving-out thing might have a happy ending after all.

Certainly the stars seemed perfectly aligned. Think about it: if Laura hadn't met Chet during the lone happy hour her workmates dragged her to . . . if *I* had moved out instead . . . if Taylor had opted for *Less Than Zero* Los Angeles rather than *Bright Lights, Big City* New York . . . But life is like that. A series of seemingly random twists and turns that winds up just so. How could I not have believed in fate? Some things, clearly, were meant to be.

"This is all the money I have," she told me, producing the wad of bills and setting them on my footlocker-cum-coffee table. "If there's any way I could, like, pay you in a few weeks, you know, after I get a job?"

"That's fine," I told her, although that would mean scrimping on my part. I figured my investment would pay off in the end. If neither of us had money, it stood to reason that we'd spend more time hanging out in the apartment, just the two of us. "Just, you know, pay me when you can."

Taylor broke into a smile so radiant it affected me on a molecular level. "Thanks, Todd. Jason told me you were a nice guy. He wasn't lying."

Nice—what a designation to live up to! How apt that in July of 1991 Bryan Adams's "(Everything I Do) I Do It for You" became the biggest-selling single since "We Are the World"—it was pretty much my theme song. For the next six weeks, I was basically her pro bono personal assistant. I went above and beyond. I foraged the East Village for discarded furniture for her room. I took her clothes shopping at A&S (pronounced "anus") Plaza. I cooked dinner for us almost every night, and when we did go out, I paid. I went through the *Times* employment section every morning with a pink highlighter, while she was still asleep, curled up on her futon beneath the collage of Absolut Vodka ads. I let her use my television, my tape deck, my phone. I told her which bars were cool (Phoebe's, Peggy Sue's, Pyramid Club, and, if you felt like braving the broken-needle gauntlet at four a.m. to get to Avenue D, Save the Robot). And what did I get for my efforts? Other than the pleasure of her company—and the corollary pleasure of being *seen* in her company—not a damn thing. My cat started sleeping with her, but did I? No sir. I never even made a move on her. Not once. The only way to win over a woman that hot is to pretend you're immune to her charms and let her come to you. Or so I reasoned. I never was good with the ladies.

The funny thing is, Taylor, she wasn't even that hot, per se. She was Missouri hot, maybe, but not New York hot. She had flaws. Lots of them. The most conspicuous being the bump in her already-prominent nose that evoked Streisand, or a pre-rhinoplastic Jennifer Grey. Her legs were too short, her skin too oily. Contrary to popular reports, she wasn't even blonde; her hair was dishwater brown, and she wore it long, with uneven bangs. Plus she dressed like she was Molly Ringwald and it was still 1985—all padded shoulders and bright lipstick and oversized earrings and pink. Everything was pink.

If you came across her picture in the freshman facebook—that was the one they ran in the papers, usually—you'd probably flip right past the page without even noticing her. But then, what can you tell from a snapshot? You might as well be looking at a painting of Lucrezia Borgia, or a marble bust of the Empress Livia. Babes of the first rank, both of them, but you'd never know from extant depictions. With Taylor, same thing. To appreciate Taylor—to really *dig* her—you had to grok her in person. In the flesh. You had to observe the bead of sweat on her upper lip, the stubble-bumps under her arms. You had to smell her, you had to *taste* her. She was a flavor all to herself. That's one of the reasons it's taken me so long to write this; I didn't think I could convey the essence of that woman with mere words. I didn't think *anyone* could.

Hold up—that reads too sentimental, too lovelorn. So let me reiterate: I did not love Taylor Schmidt. Not romantically. I did love her as a friend, I suppose. Certainly there were things *about* her that I loved. Her name, for one thing. Nowadays, half the girls in the country are named for some lesser president—I saw a little girl in Tompkins Square Park last week whose name was Carter—but back in '91, it was unheard of. Remember Daryl Hannah, in *Splash*? She wanted to be called Madison, and Tom Hanks said that's a name for a street, not a woman, and everyone in the cinema cracked up. *Splash* came out in 1984. Eighteen years later, Madison would be the second most popular name for baby girls in the United States. (Taylor would check in at number eighteen.)

But in 1968, when Taylor Schmidt was born, the twenty most popular girls names were, in order: Lisa, Michelle, Kimberly, Jennifer, Mary, Melissa, Angela, Tammy, Karen, Susan, Laura, Kelly, Amy, Christine, Patricia, Julie, Elizabeth, Tina, Cynthia, and Pamela. Traditional names, mostly. A chick named *Taylor*? She was on the vanguard. Her name added to her mystique.

And the way she pronounced it! Not *TAY-lore*, like a hick would say it. *TAIL-ur*. Like Prince Charles was calling her, or Laurence Olivier. Rolled right off the tongue, that name. And it suited her. A name like that should *fit*, right?

Another thing I loved about her: the way she'd look at you

with Miranda-like awe, steel-blue eyes open and yearning, as if whatever you were saying was the most interesting thing she'd ever heard. Like she was having a spiritual experience. Like she'd found religion in your words, your eyes, your smile. She was like that in bed, too. She made me feel like John Holmes, James Bond, and Casanova, all rolled into one. The boudoir was Taylor's métier. She did things with me and to me that no one else has ever done, will ever do. . .

But this is not a long-form letter to *Penthouse Forum*. My purpose here is not to brag, or worse, to reminisce. Higher aims have led me to the typewriter, I assure you. Lust is a private thing, but what happened to Taylor . . . people need to know about it. People need to know, people *deserve*, the truth. And I'm in a position— I'm the *only one* in the position—to provide that truth.

See, like Taylor, I was a client of the Quid Pro Quo Employment Agency. I, too, met with Asher Krug and with Lydia Murtomaki, and I know what went on in those stern oak-paneled offices. This is critical to understanding what transpired. Absolutely critical. And while I can't claim to be her closest friend—there were others who knew her better than I did: Kim Winter, her best friend from college; her mother, Darla Jenkins; even Jason Hanson—I was her roommate and, as such, her confidante. Taylor loved to gab, to confess her sins, so to speak, and I was fortunate enough to be her sounding board. That she mostly thought of me as priestly, a eunuch in the harem, helped loosen her tongue—that and the cheap chardonnay she drank copiously most nights.

Most importantly, Taylor was, like her idol Anaïs Nin, a dedicated diarist, and I had access to her diary. True, she didn't *know* I had access—mea culpa, I'm a snoop—but my Hardy Boys activities, albeit shameful, furnished me with glimpses into a Taylor Schmidt that no one else knew. Not Kim Winter, not Jason Hanson, not her wretched mother. No one.

I regret that I can't write more than I've presented here. That I can't spend the rest of my life studying hers, the way monastic scholars of old dedicated themselves to Christ. Would that I had the resources to author an unabridged biography—to interview acquaintances from elementary school, to spend time with Darla, to learn more about her late alcoholic father, to track down my seventy-seven fellow Taylor alumni. None of this, alas, is germane to my purpose. We'll touch on her backstory—we'll have to—but what concerns us here are the last days of her too-short life: the interval between the day she left her mother's rented prefab house in Warrensburg, Missouri, for the greener pastures of New York City, and the day she returned to that same hovel, in a black plastic box, four months later.

Taylor Schmidt, dead at twenty-three.

Hers is a big story, with far-reaching ramifications, and it's critical to cast it in the proper historical context. Everything that went down went down in New York City in the summer and fall of 1991.

Seems like only yesterday, 1991, like not that long ago, but it's 2009 already. Babies born in 1991 have already gotten drunk, smoked pot, lost their virginity. To put it in perspective: Emma Watson, the fetching nymphet who plays Hermione in the Harry Potter franchise, was born in 1990; Jamie Lynn Spears—already a mommy herself—in '91; Frances Bean Cobain, Kurt's Love child, in '92.

Admittedly, the nineties are not a decade that inspires much in the way of nostalgia. But there will come a day when the significance of the first year of that apocalyptic decade will become readily apparent. The great pitch and moment of that annus mirabilis cannot be understated. As my friend Walter Maddox once remarked, 1991 was my generation's 1969. In those twelve fleeting months, everything fell into place: culturally, politically, socially— the whole ball of wax.

You had Operation Desert Storm, the banner headline. A Gulf war that we thought, in our prelapsarian naïveté, didn't have the ratings to spawn a sequel.

You had Jack Kevorkian. You had Rodney King.

Jeffrey Dahmer was apprehended, Clarence Thomas confirmed, Terry Anderson released.

Robert Maxwell, the British media magnate who owned the *Daily Mirror* and the New York *Daily News*, drowned after falling from his yacht off the coast of Grand Canary Island—or so the coroner's report stated. His own daughter suspected foul play, to say nothing of the conspiracy theorists.

Oh, and the Soviet Union—the Big Bear, our Orwellian enemy for a half a century—broke up. Just *broke up*, went its separate ways, like it was a fucking rock band. Like it was Mötley Crüe or Journey. And on Christmas, no less, capitalism's holiest of holy days.

In 1991, my generation—the MTV Generation, the slackers, *shin jin rui*, Generation X—reached a creative zenith. You had the Richard Linklater film *Slacker* and the Douglas Coupland novel *Generation X*, both landmark works, released in July and March respectively. Bret Easton Ellis published *American Psycho*. *Seinfeld* hit its stride. In September, the grunge movement arrived with Nirvana's *Nevermind*. (Here we are now! Entertain us!) Three years later, Kurt Cobain would off himself—our Altamont. (Oh well, whatever, nevermind.)

The aforementioned works best exemplified the X zeitgeist, the so-called slacker subculture, one that baby boom pundits misread as indifference but was really a disinclination to participate. A generation of Bartlebies the Scrivener: we preferred not to. Coupland's antiheroes deliberately wasting their educations tending bar in Palm Springs. From *Slacker*: "Withdrawing in disgust is not the same thing as apathy." The cheerleaders from the "Smells Like Teen Spirit" video: black-clad, zoned-out, going through the motions—cheering, but not really cheering; cheering *ironically*. Irony, more than anything, was our hallmark. The sarcastic singing of the sixties anthem "Everybody Get Together" on *Nevermind*—the intro to track number seven—sums up the collective feeling at the time: *We are laughing derisively at your hypocritical idealism, you baby boom fucks.* Is it any wonder Prozac was so popular? I was on Prozac, and so was everyone I knew, Taylor included.

At the root of all our discontent was money. Understand, we were the poorest generation in memory, with little hope of financial salvation. Poverty was so inevitable, it became chic—hence the flannel shirts and dungarees and work boots. As William Strauss and Neil Howe noted in their magnificent study *Generations*, my cohorts and I were on course to become the most impoverished group of babies since the shat-upon Lost Generation of Fitzgerald and Hemingway. To be fair, *Generations* was published in 1991—that is, before the Internet exploded and my too-smart-for-their-own-good compeers took advantage of our parents' Luddite tendencies, thus leveling the playing field somewhat. At the time, though, who could have foreseen such a radical uptick in fortune?

The point is, 1991 was an especially bad year for money. It was a bad year to be unemployed, and a *really* bad year to be a wet-behind-the-ears college graduate with a sparse résumé and student loans to repay (student loans, I might add, that wouldn't be tax deductible until the Clinton administration). How bad was it? George Bush *père* enjoyed a record-high approval rating in May of 1991, at the end of the Gulf War. Eighteen months later, he lost his bid for reelection. The reason for his Cubs-in-'69 choke, as famously explained by James Carville? "It's the economy, stupid."

In short, the summer of 1991 was the worst moment in a generation to be in the position Taylor Schmidt was in.

And that's where our story begins.

PART I

Pink Slip

CHAPTER 1

Thursday, August 29, 1991. Dog day morning.

Ninety-five in the shade, the latest entry in a summer of record-shattering heat and humidity. Baking kiln-hot heat, bus fumes like fireball gusts, the stench of boiling urine. The day before, a clutch of elderly women in the Bronx had died, overcome by fragile health and high temperatures, and the twenty-ninth was even hotter.

Twenty-three and jobless, Taylor Schmidt stood on the lusterless stretch of East Fortieth Street between Fifth and Madison, the purgatorial half-block that most of the city's employment agencies then called home, nursing a lukewarm cup of street vendor coffee (she would have to wait three more years for Starbucks to worm its insidious way into the Big Apple). The bead of perspiration on her upper lip reappeared as soon as she wiped it away. Her Liz Claiborne interview suit was a black funeral special, bought on special at Marshalls, and wool. A suit for winter, not for a scorcher like today, but her only other one was at the dry cleaners.

She entertained the idea of losing the jacket, but decided that once it was off, it would have to stay that way, and her blouse was too wrinkled for that. Ah, the blouse. Its white faux silk clung to her shapely frame, her Victoria's Secret brassiere (34 C, a darker shade of white) plainly visible. On her feet, new Nine West pumps of hard leather, black like the suit, the heels adding two inches to her five foot three. Band-Aids applied to her heels did not stop the chafing, and there was nothing to be done about the blisters on her toes. Her feet swelled in the humidity of the miserable New York August, and those shoes were unforgiving.

Taylor ditched the coffee and peeled the plastic wrapper from a brand-new pack of cigarettes. Back then impoverished recent college grads could still afford them and smoke them just about anywhere. She smoked Parliament Lights—what was then, as now, an old fogy brand. She was aware of the irony. Others were denied the privilege, because she carried her smokes in a monogrammed cigarette case of filigreed silver, a gift on her last birthday—literally her last birthday—from Kim Winter, her best friend, who lived in Miami and claimed to have been at Au Bar the night William Kennedy Smith did whatever it was he did. Taylor fired up a smoke, put the pack in her slender handbag. Checked her reflection in the mirrored window of one of the glass-box buildings. The humidity had wreaked havoc on her hair, and her makeup could not conceal the unctuous shine on her cheeks. *Shit*, she thought, although I saw her when she left the apartment that morning, and sweaty or not, she looked good.

Taylor loitered in front of the building, people whizzing by all around her, puffing on the cancer stick. She tried to relax; to forget the fact that this would be the ninth time this month that she'd been to an employment agency, and the reality that there were no good jobs to be had; to construct, painstakingly, the house of cards that was her ego; to visualize the day when she would don her waxen wings and fly into the sunshiny world of steady employment.

Key word: steady. By now, she had found, and lost, work at several restaurants, most recently the newly minted Planet Hollywood, where she served as hostess. In the summer of 1991, the concept of sexual harassment was new. *Disclosure* had yet to be written. The Clarence Thomas confirmation hearings, with their pubic hair on the Pepsi can, did not go down till October, and when they did, the consensus was that Anita Hill was an uppity bitch who should know her place. In the food service industry especially, sexual harassment was the rule, not the exception. Without fear of reprisal, guys did what they pleased. Poor Taylor, not surprisingly, was a magnet for such lewd behavior. And boy was she sick of it. This is why she left, or was asked to leave, jobs at the Bottom Line, Tropica, and Planet Hollywood. In the latter case, it was a Schwarzenegger look-alike who goosed her ass and suggested a rendezvous ("Maybe you could join me in duh hot tub, Tay-luh"). She smacked his smug imitation-Austrian face and was promptly eighty-sixed.

Now, standing in front of the building's sooty mirrored glass in the dragon's-breath cauldron of summer in the city, she banished these dark thoughts from her mind.

"This can't last forever," she told her reflection, taking a last drag on the Parliament. "Somebody has to hire me, sooner or later." With that, she flicked the butt into the gutter, applied fresh gloss to her lips, and went inside.

Today's appointment was with Fraulein Staffing, a now-defunct competitor of Mademoiselle (the placement specialists, not the magazine of the same name). She'd been to Mademoiselle already, and Katharine Gibbs, and Rand, and Manpower, and four others besides, hands outstretched, begging for the alms that were job interviews. Those efforts had been in vain. Taylor couldn't even land temporary work—not even a job prettying up a reception area in a law firm or something. That's how bad the market was.

As soon as Taylor hit the lobby, the air-conditioning bowled her over. Through the wool blazer she could feel the sweat on her back freeze. It was a shabby lobby—no security guard, no doorman, no sign-in sheet. She walked directly into a stuffy, un-air-conditioned elevator with four other people, and prayed to a God whose existence she didn't acknowledge that the thing wouldn't break down. Her prayers were answered, or maybe it was just dumb luck; at any rate, the lift got her where she needed to go, loudly and slowly, but surely.

Fraulein's offices were on the seventh floor. As Taylor strode into the well-air-conditioned lobby, she noticed the same uncomfortable foam rubber couches, the same gray carpeting, the same pastel prints on the same eggshell walls that she had seen in the eight other agencies she'd been to. Uniform phones rang off the proverbial hook, were answered, in time, by automatonical receptionists ("Debbie? I'll transfer you. Please hold.") and rerouted before the caller could request to leave a message. Even the other job-seekers were familiar: the same polyester suits, the same résumés, the same look of abject desperation in their eyes. She watched them squint at yellow legal pads, leaf through magazines, stare hopefully at the receptionists. *I can't believe I'm here*, she thought (and would write in her diary that night), *with these fucking losers*.

Taylor checked in, sat, filled out her paperwork: the application, the I-9, the copy of her Missouri driver's license, the W-2. She'd filled out all this shit eight times already. How many exemptions . . . ? What did it matter! Let the government exact its pound of flesh, just give me a job already!

"Here you go."

"Super. Please take a seat. Someone will be right with you."

With great reluctance, Taylor joined the undulating swath of lesser humanity in the lobby. She sat, crossed her legs, and kept still as an ice sculpture—the sweat on her back had pretty much frozen her into place. Only her cold eyes moved, studying the other occupants of the waiting room. A kinky-haired bitch with a Lawn Guyland accent; a frat boy reading *Sports Illustrated*; a bovine black woman with bright yellow earrings and matching shoes, bulbous feet spilling out of them like yeasty loaves of pumpernickel. Humiliating that she would have to share a room with these bottom-feeders.

The frat boy gave her the once over, twice; his eyes meandered from the tips of her shiny Nine Wests, up the divine contour of her black-stockinged legs, held for far too long on her chest, and then found her glare.

"Hey baby," he grinned. "Come here often?"

Not a terrible line, under the circumstances, but its underlying truth, and the pathos to which it alluded, did not sit well with Taylor. And neither did the frat boy. "Save it," she said.

This did not deter him. "What's Pee-wee Herman's favorite baseball team?"

"Excuse me?"

"What's Pee-wee Herman's favorite baseball team?"

Paul Reubens had been fodder for the tabloids and the late-night talk shows lately, after his arrest in Sarasota, Florida, for exposing himself in an X-rated theater, ostensibly to masturbate. These were innocent days, remember: the browser, that entrée to the pornographic cornucopia that is the World Wide Web, had only just been conceived.

"The Yanks," she told him. "I heard that one already."

"That's his favorite *American* League team," the frat boy gallantly explained. "In the National League, he likes the Expos. Get it? Ex*pose*?" and he burst into hyenic laughter.

While Taylor Schmidt attracted admirers indiscriminately, sure as a magnetic field attracts every piece of iron in its range, her curse was that shitbirds like *this* were the only ones who invariably worked up the nerve to make a pass. And as I said before, she wasn't easy. She had standards. And to her undying credit, she didn't dig on frat boys. Bad boys were her cup of tea. Like this dude J.D., a bartender at Continental, the heavy metal bar on Third Avenue—number seventy-four on the list. He had spiky hair and tattoos and a pierced lip, and his fingernails were painted black, and he was already bitching that the upcoming Metallica release was a piece of shit, that "Enter Sandman" was a sellout song. If Taylor had a type, J.D. was it. The jerk-off frat boy in the Fraulein lobby stood no chance.

Before he could further embarrass himself, a receptionist summoned Taylor.

Her spirits soared—"Today's the day," she thought to herself—and were promptly deflated when she was told, "First, we'll have you take some tests."

Taylor followed the receptionist into a tiny room, in which sat six computers and five of her nemeses.

"Enter your data and the tests you'll be taking. WordPerfect, and of course Typing. See me when you're done." Then the bitch curled her lips into a Susan-Lucci-at-the-Daytime-Emmys demismile and was gone, leaving Taylor to fidget with the PC.

An electronic wizard appeared on the screen and waved his wand, magically compelling her to enter her name and Social Security number. After a few clicks of the mouse, she navigated the same word processing program in which she'd written all her college papers, to prove to the world that she did in fact know how to open, print, and save documents. The bliss ended with her typing as much of this:

> *The telephone is an important part of the service industry. Most of our contact with our clients is done over the telephone. Without the telephone, we would not be able to talk to our clients. Also, our clients would not be able to talk to us. When you answer the telephone, you should be friendly. A friendly voice goes a long way. Mark Twain once said he could go a whole week on one compliment. Of course, Mark Twain didn't spend much time on the telephone. . .*

as she could in five minutes, on a keyboard with a temperamental space bar and half the letter markings worn away.

As this was her ninth time taking the test, Taylor kicked ass. She could now type eighty-five words a minute and was completely proficient in mail merge, although she had never used that particular feature in real life. She could almost do the whole test with her eyes closed.

Finished, she delivered the printout to one of the receptionist-clones (impossible to say which one), who accepted the offering, scoffed at the many inventive spellings of *telephone*, and motioned for her to wait in the lobby. By then there was a new crop of losers for Taylor to obsess over, and another frat boy fuckwad to declare his intentions.

Eventually, one of the employment agents—or placement co-ordinators, or personnel consultants, or whatever they called themselves—emerged from behind the double doors, displaying a sharp-toothed smile that made her look like an actual headhunter. "Hi, I'm Debbie! Nice to *meet* you, Taylor!" The resultant handshake was borderline battery.

Taylor followed her into the warren of desks that comprised the office. The place was bustling with activity: headhunters racing to and fro, distributing xeroxes, blathering stridently into headsets, navigating the jobless through the maze of desks, shaking hands, offering chairs and coffee and jobs that weren't open. The office resembled a trading room floor—which in effect it was.

As Taylor walked by the first cluster of desks, one of the agents—a slick-looking guy who was kind of cute, in a Republican/golf/cigar bar kind of way—cried into the phone, "Full editor? HarperCollins?" pretended to notice her for the first time, winked, and continued, "Sixty-five thou a year? Sounds great. Yes, he'll take it!"

When they had journeyed far enough, the headhunter motioned for her to sit down on a cracked plastic chair reminiscent of those in her high school cafeteria. Taylor sat. Debbie also sat, although she was so manic she seemed to levitate an inch or two above the cracked plastic. "I have a lot of terr-*if*-ic positions to tell you about, Taylor! And a lot of people for you to meet!"

"Great."

"But first, why don't you tell me about yourself?"

Taylor crossed her legs, smoothed her skirt, and launched into the litany. "Well, I graduated this past May from Wycliffe College," gauging the interviewer's face for a reaction, getting none, "where I majored in English lit. I copyedited the campus weekly—I brought a copy with me, if you'd like to see it . . ."

"That won't be necessary." Blinklessly, Debbie stared at her. Waiting for her to sweat. To break.

"Oh. Okay." Taylor's steel-blue eyes drifted to a sign on the wall reminding her to MAINTAIN EYE CONTACT.

"So what brings you to Fraulein?"

"Your ad in the *Times* piqued my interest."

I still recall the ad—I'd clipped it for her two days earlier:

Writer/Editor, up-and-coming 20's-geared mag,
great env, great benefits, salary low 20s,
call Debbie at Fraulein

Debbie dismissed this with a wave of her skeletal hand. "Yes, well, I'm afraid they're looking for someone with a bit more experience."

If you're keeping count, this was now the ninth time one of these people had fed Taylor this line. The bait and switch was alive and well.

"But it was listed under 'Recent College Grad.'"

"Yes, *recent* college grad. As in, two or three years removed from school. Preferably grad school. I do have some great openings to discuss, though. Tell me, Taylor, what do you want to do?"

This was the Million Dollar Question. That she'd had eight previous cracks at an answer didn't make responding any easier. "Well, I was thinking publishing. Because I have editorial experience. But advertising, I'd be interested in that. Anything that's, like, creative."

Debbie nodded, her cobra-like incisors gleaming in the fluorescent light. "I'll see what we have." And she flipped through a stack of loose papers in front of her, her head slowly but very surely shaking back and forth.

Two desks away, another agent exclaimed into his headset, "Creative Programming Consultant? MTV? Eighty thou a year? She accepts."

"We don't have anything right now in publishing or advertising," Debbie said. "August is a slow month. I *do* have a terr-*if*-ic opening as an admin assistant at Arthur Andersen!"

"Who's that?"

"You don't know Arthur *An*dersen? It's Big Six!"

"Big . . . Six? Of what?"

"Accounting!"

Taylor noticed, Scotch-taped to the wall behind Debbie, a cluster of thank-you notes. Perhaps they were just props. "Oh. But I, um . . . I don't want accounting."

"But it's not accounting, it's an admin assistant position!"

This was the first actual job any of the agencies had produced, sorry though it was, and Taylor probably should have jumped at it. If she had, she might still be alive. But she let it go. It was beneath her, period. She was holding out for something better, she told me later; something with a future.

"That's . . . I mean, I'm not interested in that."

"I see." Now visibly annoyed, Debbie returned to the stack. "Well, the only other thing I have right now that you're qualified for is an underwriter training program at CryoHealth. It pays twenty-five a year!"

"Yeah?"

"It's located in Newark. But it's a growing *section* of Newark."

"Newark? No, that's . . . I can't work in Newark. I don't even know where that is."

Debbie was not pleased. "Well, that's all I have. I will of course give you a holler if anything comes in. And you feel free to call and check in with me." She handed her client an appropriately flimsy business card. "But first I'd like you to meet some people! I'm sure someone will have a terr-*if*-ic job for you!"

Taylor was then whisked from plastic chair to plastic chair. First Sherrie, then Terri, then Laurie, then Missy offered similarly lame jobs. Which she politely declined. Then she was introduced to a series of balding middle-aged men who were about as couth as the frat boy in the lobby. All of them handed her business cards, promised to call, encouraged her to check in. Taylor shook their hands, accepted their cards, was introduced to the next headhunter in line, and, when she had met everyone in the agency, was escorted out the double doors.

She knew the drill. Nine times now she'd been through the rigmarole, with nothing to show for it but a stack of business cards and more dry cleaning bills than she could afford. Sometimes the agents would call her a day or two later, only to offer her the same pathetic job she had previously declined, as if a few more days of poverty would change her mind about an exciting career in underwriting. But usually they not only neglected to call her, they didn't even recognize her name when *she* called *them*. Hopeless, was what it was—hopeless and humiliating.

On the way out, one of the agents—the golf/cigar bar chap who had winked at her when she first walked in—yelled into the headset, which she was sure wasn't plugged in, "Creative Director? Young & Rubicam? A hundred twenty thou a year? He'll take it!"

On the way home, Taylor stopped at the dry cleaners to fetch her other suit. After a detour to the TCBY, she headed to the architectural blight that was our apartment building.

Like the neighboring buildings on the downtown side of the street, it was five stories high. Unlike the neighboring buildings, it lacked the requisite integral support. All five stories listed to the left; this was noticeable if you tried to hang up framed pictures. If the building on either side ever came down, our piece of shit would tumble like a huffed-and-puffed-upon house of sticks.

The vestibule reeked of curried sweat. It was hot to begin with, and there was no ventilation in there, so the air was stagnant. She coughed, held her breath, collected her mail—three catalogues, a Have You Seen These Children postcard, her Visa bill, and a form letter from Wycliffe Alumni House soliciting donations. No letter from Kim Winter. No new issue of *Sassy* ("I know I'm too old for it, but I don't really care"). Nothing good.

Taylor raced up the three flights of stairs, unlocked the door, and beheld the glory that was our apartment. The cat emerged from a pile of dirty clothes, looking for love, and Taylor obliged with a hug. Then she hung her dry cleaning on the door knob, kicked off her shoes, threw her handbag on the floor, and peeled off her sweaty clothes. She grabbed a spoon from the sink, rubbed it on a dishtowel, and opened the quart of fro-yo. Then she repaired to her walk-in-closet-sized room, sprawled her half-naked body on her futon, and was about to enjoy a frosty bite when the phone rang.

Nowadays, caller ID has eliminated all suspense from the ringing phone. Not in 1991. Most people didn't have call waiting. Many didn't even have answering machines. Busy signals and ringing-off-the-hook were still commonplace—and so was the thrill of receiving a surprise telephone call. Long distance was still expensive, in those days; still a big deal.

Who could the caller be? Debbie from Fraulein, lining up an interview? J.D., the metalhead bartender, who'd been blowing her off since their last tryst two weeks ago? Yours Truly, checking in on her?

Taylor put the fro-yo on her nightstand (which I'd found in front of a townhouse on Eighteenth Street the week before), and on the third ring—you always waited for the third ring, so as not to seem desperate or overly eager—picked up the receiver.

"Hello?"

"Taylor, honey."

The flip side of the thrill of receiving a surprise telephone call, and the reason for the eventual hegemony of caller ID, was the agony of receiving a telephone call you *didn't* want.

"Oh. Hi, Mom."

Taylor's mother was not a drinker and not a born-again Christian. Those were the only two points in her favor, to the best of my knowledge. Darla Jenkins was vintage white trash, from the walrus-like heft of her bloated belly, to the cheap-tobacco reek of her thick feathered hair, to the missing front teeth, to the monthly state disability check that made up her income even though she was perfectly capable of working, to the fact that her daughter was twenty-three and she was just forty, to . . . but you get the idea. How Taylor emerged from the womb of such a monstrous creature is a mystery for the ages, and could well provide the incontrovertible proof Darwin apologists have long sought.

"I have some great news."

Taylor said nothing.

"Guess."

"You got a job?" Her voice oozed sarcasm, not that her mom could tell.

"No, no. Nothing like that."

"You won the lottery?"

"Sort of."

"I give up, Mom. Just tell me."

"I'm pregnant!"

Besides her eldest, Darla had two other daughters, aged ten and seven, courtesy of a drunk named Popeye, whereabouts unknown. She was currently shacked up with a slovenly gas station attendant named Billy Ray. Try as she might, Taylor could not fathom how the addition of another mouth to feed could possibly be considered good news.

"How far along are you?"

"Five weeks. Isn't it exciting? And at my advanced age! Billy Ray thinks it'll be a boy this time."

Taylor first thought was, *Good. Plenty of time for a miscarriage.* But she choked that down. "I'm sure he does."

"Well? Aren't you excited?"

She could say no, but then she'd have to explain *why* the news failed to elicit the requisite enthusiasm. That would be an exercise in futility—Darla never listened, and was too dense to comprehend whatever did sink in. Taylor could play nice and play along, but she wasn't in the mood to lie. Not at all. So she decided to be honest for a change and tell her mother exactly what she thought.

"You're an asshole."

And she slammed down the phone, so hard she cracked the plastic receiver cradle.

Before her mother could call back, Taylor placed a call of her own. After five rings a machine picked up. "Hey, this is J.D. I'm either not here right now, or I'm ignoring you. Leave a message, and if you're lucky, I'll call you back."

It beeped; she spoke: "Hey, it's Taylor. Haven't heard from you so I figured I'd give a call, you know, see what you were up to. Call me back. If you feel like it. Talk to you soon. Um . . . bye."

Immediately she regretted the move. But what could she do? Simple: unplug the phone and wolf down fro-yo. This made her feel better. TCBY always did. Her despair, her panic, her anger slowly washed away. She rolled onto her back, stared at the cracks in the ceiling, listened to our loud-as-fuck downstairs neighbor, who liked to play AC/DC at all hours on a sound system more bass-heavy than the one at Limelight. The cat, sensing a change of mood, made his way toward her. She scooped him up and cradled him in her arms. "Here, Bo." (I hadn't let the fact that he was male stop me from naming him for Bo Derek.) "Good boy. Good, good boy."

Bo purred, Taylor smiled, they shared a moment. Then Bo abruptly scrammed—he was that kind of cat—leaping from her warm belly to the cluttered desk, in the process knocking over a tower of newspapers, magazines, duplicate résumés, and old mail. Catalogs and low-APR credit card offers and unread complimentary issues of unwanted magazines tumbled to the floor, along with a old letter from Kim Winter chronicling a South Beach party at which she'd met MTV heartthrob Adam Curry. Out of the latest Victoria's Secret offering and onto the bed spilled a small envelope made of parchment paper that Taylor must have missed when she first went through the mail.

She picked up the envelope, turned it round in her fingers, and held it up to the light. Her name and address were printed in a hand that was elegant, feminine, and unfamiliar. Curiously, the stamp had not been canceled.

With a shrug, she tore through the envelope. Inside was an ornate card that resembled a wedding invitation, except for the 212 phone number at the bottom. In embossed letters it read:

JOBS TO KILL FOR

Had it with other agencies?
Try the best. QUID PRO QUO.

"Is this a joke?"

If the cat knew, he wasn't saying.

"Only one way to find out."

She dialed the number, all the while staring Bo down. On the second ring, someone picked up. A gravelly baritone said, "Quid Pro Quo. Asher Krug speaking."

"Oh . . . hi. I, um . . . well, I got your ad in the mail just now? And, well, I . . ."

"You've had it with the other agencies." Something in his voice suggested a prior intimacy, like they were both in on something, and put her instantly at ease.

"That's an understatement."

"What's your name?"

She told him.

"Yes, of course, you were recommended to us."

"By whom?"

But there was some sort of crossing of telephone lines just then, and not hearing her question, he did not reply. Instead he asked several of his own: How long had she been in New York? How many agencies had Taylor been to? In what sort of industry did she want to work? She answered all of Asher's questions, still not entirely convinced that this phone call was not the work of some prankster. Was someone putting her on?

"I'm giving an orientation tomorrow at eleven," he told her. "Would you be able to attend?"

"That'd be . . . that'd be great."

"Perfect. Just let me add your name to the list . . . Okay, so we'll look forward to seeing you tomorrow. Be well, Taylor."

"You, too."

Taylor waited for the click on the other end of the line before resting the receiver—which five minutes ago she'd hung up with enough force to crack hard plastic—in the cradle as if it were a sleeping baby.

The positive experience with this Asher Krug person (his last name rhymed with the first syllable of Google) inspired her. Not that she expected anything from his agency—why would it be different from the nine other agencies, whatever they claimed?—but at least Quid Pro Quo had taken her call.

"To hell with this," she told the cat, as she slipped into a well-worn *Pyromania* T-shirt and not-quite-stylish denim cutoffs. "I just need to work harder, send résumés to every job that looks even remotely promising, follow up every cover letter with a phone call."

This was when Taylor discovered that almost two-thirds of the ads in the *Times* employment section were placed by employment agencies. That it didn't matter if you were a recent college graduate, a dime novelist, or a New York Knick—you either found work through an agent, or you didn't find work.

This was also when she had a sort of nervous breakdown. It started, as nervous breakdowns will, with a loud scream, and quickly segued to her storming around the bedroom, hurling clothes to and fro, scaring the bejesus out of the cat, and kicking everything that could be kicked: the baseboard, the bed frame, the closet door. Inevitably she stubbed her toe. As the waves of pain rippled over her, Taylor collapsed onto the futon and burst into tears.

At that exact moment, like some silent film hero who appears in the nick of time, I came home. Immediately I sensed trouble; this was not the first time I'd found her crying on the futon; Prozac can only do so much. Without wasting valuable time knocking, I burst in, bearing a bottle of chardonnay and two glasses. I helped her up, I embraced her—O, the warmth generated by that radiant body! O, the wonder of her lavender-tinged scent!—and I successfully fought off my nascent erection.

Once Taylor calmed down sufficiently to speak, I asked her what was wrong this time, and she gave me the skinny.

"Don't worry," I told her. "This is just temporary. It won't last. It's just a rough patch; that's all."

"I know that. I mean, *intellectually*, I know that. But it seems totally fucking hopeless, you know?"

"I know all about hopelessness," I said, trying like hell to disguise my obvious lust. I could watch her for hours—she was better than television—and the tear-strewn face only added to her allure. "More than you know."

I poured wine.

"You know what you need? You need a back rub. Would you like a back rub?"

She considered the proposal. For a minute, I was afraid I had scared her off—my duties as pro bono personal assistant had not yet extended to massage therapy—but she quickly eased my mind. "If you don't mind."

I didn't mind. On the contrary, I savored any opportunity to touch her, however clinical. I sat on the futon, she on the floor, and I began to work out a knot in her shoulder the size of a tennis ball. We said nothing, just sat there, me caressing her shoulders (would that I could take her shirt off!), Taylor letting out the occasional pleasure-moan. Soon the silence became awkward, and to fill it,

I said, "So. Could it *be* any more obvious that Andrea is hot for Brandon, or what?"

This made her laugh—success! Awkward silence averted! As we rehashed the latest installment of *Beverly Hills 90210* (then in its second season), and as I poured every ounce of my being into massaging her shoulders, we methodically polished off the wine.

"You feel better now?"

"Yeah. Thanks, Todd."

I crackled my knuckles and shook out my tired fingers. "Hey—that's what I'm here for."

"I feel like we always talk about me," she said, turning to face me. "Let's talk about *you*. How was *your* day?"

"My day? It was pretty fucked up, actually."

"Do tell."

"Well, the features editor—features are stories that aren't breaking news stories . . ."

"I wrote for the school paper, Todd. I know what features are."

"Right. Sorry. Anyway, the features editor is this guy named Doug Schiffer. He's old—in his seventies I think—and he's got this big bulbous nose and lots of hair in his ears, and he's sort of out of touch. People like him well enough, he's a nice guy, but he's been working there *way* too long. People call him—this is funny—they call him Schiffer Brains."

"That *is* funny."

"I can't take credit—they've called him that for years. And he's so oblivious, he doesn't even realize it."

"So it's an appropriate nickname."

"Oh, yeah. Anyway, come to find out, over the weekend, he was—this is the not funny part—he was murdered."

"No shit."

"Yeah. Someone broke into his apartment—he lives on Riverside Drive, on the Upper West Side—someone broke into his apartment, tied him up, and shot him in the back of the head, like, execution-style. Like a Mob hit or something."

"Jesus."

"I know, right? Really grisly stuff. And no one has the foggiest idea why. I mean, he was a doddering old man, but he wasn't, like, a dick or anything. People are, like, totally baffled."

"Were there any witnesses or anything?"

"No. His wife died a few years ago. Lung cancer. Let me get that for you." Before Taylor could wave me off, I had the Zippo I kept on hand solely for this purpose (I didn't smoke) fired up and waiting at the tip of the cigarette she'd just installed between her well-ChapSticked lips.

"Thanks."

"No problem. And, like, whoever did it must've used a silencer, because none of the neighbors heard gunshots."

I finished off the last of my wine.

"I didn't know him that well," I said, "but it's weird, you know? I mean, someone I knew—someone I saw every day—was *murdered*."

We sat there a moment, pondering the last of Doug Schiffer and the last of the chardonnay. Finally Taylor took a long, slow drag on the smoke—would that she would kiss *me* with such desperation, such longing!—and said, "Look on the bright side. One more job opening, at least."

You probably think I made that up, but no: she really said it, she was really that disillusioned. And maybe it was because I was pretty loaded—I have the alcohol tolerance of a prepubescent ballerina—but I laughed my ass off.

CHAPTER 2

A piercing ring woke Taylor from a fitful, alcohol-induced slumber. Instinctively she swatted at the alarm. When that didn't stop the ringing, she picked up the telephone. In the process she knocked over the empty wine bottle from the nightstand.

Her voice was heavy with the husk of hangover: "Hello?"

"Is Taylor Schmidt there, please?"

"Speaking."

"Taylor, this is Debbie from Fraulein. I have an opening you may be interested in."

"Yeah?" This had the stimulant effect of three cups of coffee and a can of Jolt. Taylor's hangover evaporated like so much morning dew. "Where is it?"

"It's a publishing house—Braithwaite Ross. You'd be an editorial assistant. They pay sixteen-five. Are you interested?"

"Yes. Yes, of course."

"I know it's short notice, but could you come in for an interview this morning at eleven a.m.?"

Six interviewless weeks and now they wanted her two different places at the same time! Taylor socked the pillow. "Could we make it after lunch? This afternoon is better for me."

"I think so. How's three o'clock?"

"Perfect."

After giving her the low-down on Braithwaite Ross—it was a smallish publishing house that dealt in murder mysteries and political thrillers—Debbie reminded her to maintain eye contact, sit up straight, ask questions, and bring several copies of her résumé, as well as addresses and phone numbers of her professional references. Halfway through the briefing, the alarm clock went off.

Taylor completed her morning routine with more vim than usual. So what if J.D. never called back? She actually had an interview! There was reason to hope! She fixed herself French toast. Enjoyed a long, hot shower. Posed naked in the cheval glass I'd found for her in a thrift store on the Bowery. After restocking her cigarette case and packing her hardcover copy of *The Firm*—a review copy bought for her at the Strand by *moi*—she stepped into a beautiful summer day.

Sometimes I wonder, clichéd as it sounds, whether she would have bothered leaving the apartment that morning if she'd known then what the future held in store for her. Whether she would've even gotten out of bed, for that matter. What-If is a fun game to play when you have time to kill, like I do, but the bottom line is, things happen for a reason. All things: good, bad, and indifferent. So no, I don't think foreknowledge would have saved her. I think that if she had it to do again, she would have played it exactly the same way. Then again, what choice did she have? It's not like Taylor inhabited the world of *Terminator 2: Judgment Day*—the highest-grossing film of 1991—and could go back in time to alter the future.

Say what you want about free will; we are all Destiny's slaves.

* * *

Quid Pro Quo was headquartered in a dazzling high-rise on 520 Madison Avenue, a few blocks from Central Park—as distinct and separate from its rival employment agencies as Tiffany's is from the cut-rate jewelers on 47th Street. The lobby was breathtaking: all gilt and marble, with potted palms and plush carpets and a grand piano. Walking in, Taylor was awed, her eyes drawn to the gold, to the gaud, to the sinfully high ceiling. In Manhattan, nothing is as decadent as wasted space.

She was a few minutes early, so Taylor waited by the piano, listening to an arthritic old crone stumble through, appropriately enough, the *Pathétique* sonata. It was the biggest waste of a Baldwin since Alec did *The Marrying Man*. Then she stepped into the elevator, which boasted in addition to gilt and marble a cushioned bench and a live operator.

"Floor, please?" He looked just the way she expected an elevator operator to look—stately, respect-commanding, Anthony Hopkins–esque.

"Fifty-four."

"Yes, miss." A white-gloved finger depressed the requisite button, and the contraption made its upward climb. How different, this lift from the one at Fraulein! Taylor watched her reflection in the gold-plated doors until they opened to a foyer. The foyer terminated in a mammoth oak door. On the mammoth oak door was a bronze plaque that read THE QUID PRO QUO EMPLOYMENT AGENCY.

Taylor stepped into the foyer. She wondered if maybe she should tip the operator, but before she could open her handbag, he was gone, swallowed by the elevator's gilded jaws.

The Quid Pro Quo lobby looked like a Victorian aristocrat's study. Bookcases lined the far wall. Sconces peeked from mahogany paneling. Hand-carved end tables were crowned with vases of flowers. The most eye-catching objet d'art in a room full of them was a rough-hewn statue of a creepy-looking owl, twenty some-odd feet tall, that looked like it had been carved from a single giant stone.

"Who," Taylor whispered as she walked past.

On catty-cornered leather divans, faces buried in hardbound novels, four slackers lounged. A fifth was rotating an enormous globe. Behind an ornate rolltop desk sat a pale Asian girl, who rose as Taylor entered. She looked about fifteen, and was thin as a parenthesis.

"Good morning. You must be Taylor," she said, gliding across the Persian carpet and extending a dainty hand. "Welcome to Quid Pro Quo. I'm Mae-Yuan. "

"Nice to meet you," said Taylor, gesturing to the statue. "And nice owl."

"Yeah, it's quite the conversation piece." Mae-Yuan's black gown seemed more formal than the job required. "All I need from you is your résumé and a list of references."

Taylor handed her the two sheets of paper.

"References are personal rather than professional, yes? With addresses listed as well as telephone numbers?"

"It was tough," Taylor quipped, "but I managed to dig up three friends."

Mae-Yuan giggled.

The other occupants of the room checked out Taylor, and vice versa. The four men wore T-shirts and Levi's—the same clothes that are in style now, but in 1991, the jeans were tighter and bluer, the shirts baggier and boxier, and the high waist of the former and the long cut of the latter ensured the concealment of the ass-crack (it was not until our current decade that the peekaboo ass-crack became chic, for reasons I will never understand). All of them had longish, messy hair, and one had scraggly whiskers above his lip and below his chin that didn't quite connect. The lone woman was wearing Buddy Holly spectacles, a shiny labret, and an orange sundress that matched her Annie Lennox-circa-1983 hair.

To look cutting edge in 2009, all you have to do is shop at Urban Outfitters and stop combing your hair. In 1991, it took work. Back then, there was no such thing as "vintage inspired." You had to scour the thrift shops—Manic Panic, Screaming Mimi's, Andy's Chee-Pees, and the good ol' Salvation Army store—for hip threads. That way, if you found something cool, you knew damn well it was unique. And how, you might ask, did you know what was cool? If you spent enough time on St. Mark's Place, you figured it out through osmosis, just like you figured out how to walk with purpose, how to glare at cabbies, how to not say hello to anyone. Taylor was green, too new for all of that. She dressed fashionably for Warrensburg, Missouri, but so what? With her predilection for pink and her heart-shaped lockets and charm bracelets, she might as well be on a different planet. The hipsters in the Quid Pro Quo lobby, they *knew*.

Taylor sat down on one of the divans, as far away from the others as possible, took out her cigarette case, and, because she couldn't light up, tapped her fingers on the silver. The hipster at the globe—who was both the closest to her and the most attractive of the bunch, probably because of the facial hair—plopped down on the divan across from her. His bedroom eyes locked in on hers, which she liked; nothing worse than a shy suitor who broke off eye contact like she was Medusa.

"Dig that cigarette case," he said. "Flapper chic."

"Thanks," she said. "It sucks I have to keep it closed."

"We were born at the wrong time," he said. "In the fifties you could smoke in an elevator if you wanted to. I'm Bryan, by the way."

"I'm Taylor."

"Taylor. I like that." He nodded at the cigarette case. "You'll have to let me bum one off you when we're done."

"Sure."

"Hey, do you like Soundgarden, by any chance?"

"Is that, like, a club?"

"It's a grunge band. From Seattle. They're playing Irving Plaza this weekend. Maybe we could . . ."

Before Bryan could follow through on the invitation, Mae-Yuan announced that the presentation was about to begin and that everyone should follow her to the conference room. The hipsters followed their hostess down the hall, with Bryan and Taylor bringing up the rear.

The conference room contained what appeared to be the same table on which Michael Keaton and Kim Basinger dined in the first *Batman* movie, which is to say, it was big. The six job-seekers took their seats—there were plenty of chairs, but Bryan sat right next to Taylor—and Mae-Yuan passed around tall glasses of iced tea.

"Some room," Bryan whispered.

Taylor took a sip of tea and found herself a minute later unconsciously chewing on a piece of ice. This was an old habit of hers, which Kim Winter was forever telling her indicated sexual frustration. As if she needed pop psychology to explain something so painfully obvious. It had been almost two weeks since her last sexual encounter—which was, for the frisky Taylor Schmidt, a dry spell of Saharan proportions. But she was hopeful, because Bryan seemed interested, and while he wasn't exactly her type, he would do.

"Twice the size of my apartment," she said. "Literally."

The refreshments served, Mae-Yuan moved to the back of the room and dimmed the lights. When she turned them back on, Asher Krug entered. And when Asher Krug entered, he *entered*.

"Good morning. Welcome to Quid Pro Quo."

Asher was the sort of tall-dark-and-handsome, All-American hunk who crops up in aftershave commercials wearing only a towel, though this morning he was packaged in a dark suit of European cut that looked very expensive.

Taylor was expecting him to be good-looking. She was not expecting him to be *this* good-looking. Her heart was "Stairway to Heaven" when the drums kick in. The bustle in her hedgerow was alarming.

Asher Krug glanced at his Rolex, prompting Taylor to glance at her Swatch. It was exactly eleven o'clock. "What I'm hearing is, you guys are disillusioned with the job search right now. When you leave here, I promise you, you won't be any longer. Mae-Yuan, can I get some water?"

Mae-Yuan poured him a tall glass from a tray in the back of the room and brought it to him.

"Thanks," he said to her, and then continued: "This past May, you received a rolled-up piece of sheepskin that cost you about eighty thousand dollars. A week later, two solicitation letters turned up in your mailbox. One from the development office of your alma mater, the other from a glorified collection agency. The first note you could ignore, and did—but not the second. In December, you have to start repaying your student loans. Merry Christmas, and ho-ho-ho. They give you a six-month grace period, Sallie Mae, in the same way they give you fifty bucks and a new suit when you get out of jail."

Everyone reacted to the joke—even Mae-Yuan. Taylor caught herself laughing a bit too loud, and silenced herself before Asher could meet her glance.

"I know how you feel," Asher said. "It was just four years ago, I was right where you are now. Confused. Bitter. Frustrated. Desperate. I know exactly what you're going through."

Asher Krug's brooding eyes locked on Taylor's. She plopped a fresh piece of ice into her mouth and champed.

"You probably feel a little down on life right now," he continued. "Maybe even a bit suicidal, am I right? Before you put your head in the oven, remember: life is temporary, but Sallie Mae is forever. If you kill yourself—I'm not making this up—if you kill yourself, your student loans don't die with you; they just transfer to your parents, who cosigned your loan. Think about that: if you were to jump off the Empire State Building, the government would hit up your *parents* for the balance of your student loans. Mob tactics, if you ask me. Uncle Sam is just Don Corleone with a goatee and a red-white-and-blue hat."

Taylor had heard all about Kim Winter's brushes with hot celebrities in Miami: River Phoenix, Peter Horton, Rob Lowe, Ian Ziering, Johnny Depp. None of them, Taylor was sure, could compare with Asher Krug. Taylor was never one to drool, but her breathing was actually getting heavier just watching this guy. She'd only felt this way once before, at age fourteen, in the sixth row at a Duran Duran concert, when John Taylor's eyes met her own. She champed on the ice, which hurt her hypersensitive teeth—and didn't stem the sexual frustration, either.

"So Sallie Mae is going to send Rocco and Vito to your house, and your parents don't understand why you don't have a job yet, and you've been to every employment agency in town, and *no one will hire you*. That's because—and it's very simple—you don't have any experience. It's a catch-22: to get hired, you need experience, but to gain experience, you need to get hired. All you have going for you right now is your college degree. And if an employer doesn't see Ivy or the Seven Sisters on your CV, in this job market, it goes right in the circular file."

Taylor glanced at the orange-haired chick across the table, who seemed more interested in the speech than the speaker. At any rate, *her* ice was still in the glass.

"I know, I know, you went to some private liberal arts college that *Peterson's* and *Barron's* and *U.S. News and World Report* claim is 'most competitive.' You know how many liberal arts majors graduated from 'most competitive' colleges? All of them. They get people from Bucknell, Haverford, Middlebury, Amherst, Wesleyan, Oberlin, Williams, Swarthmore, Wycliffe, Kenyon . . . Kenyon has a terrific English department. Think most people know that? Think most people have even *heard* of Kenyon? Please. You'd be better off going to Kent State—at least the baby boomers who do the hiring have all heard of Kent State.

"The employers, see, they don't give a damn if you know your Shakespeare, or if you can play the piano, or if you copyedited your campus weekly. The first thing they do, when you go to an interview at a publishing house, is give you a typing test. A typing test! Four years of hard work, intensive study, and massive debt, all so you can take the same typing test they give some ex-con with a GED. It's insulting. It's an insult to your intelligence."

Asher Krug paused dramatically, and dramatically took a sip of water. Everything he did was dramatic. She couldn't keep her eyes off the guy. He was in the wrong line of work, Taylor thought. The guy was a movie star, pure and simple.

"Now," he continued, "let's give you a hypothetical situation. Let's say that you wangle an interview at a publishing house, and they really like you. They narrow it down to two candidates: you and some freak from Harvard—everybody at Harvard is either a freak, a legacy, or both—and they choose you because you didn't pick your nose during the interview. You know how much they pay entry-level hires, starting salary? Eighteen grand a year. Eighteen grand! Try living in New York on eighteen grand. Let me break it down for you. After taxes, you're taking home a thousand bucks a month. Your rent is eight hundred, your loans are a buck-fifty, your transportation is another fifty—those tokens add up. That's already your entire salary and you haven't even eaten yet, let alone developed a social life. *I* think—and this is my own philosophy—that your starting salary coming out of a top-drawer university should be more than what it costs to attend that university for one year. Eighteen grand! A year at Bennington costs almost twice that."

Asher began to wander around the room, Jesus among the lepers. As he drew near, Taylor felt flushed, short of breath. Her teeth actually chattered. And it wasn't because of the ice.

"I'm not saying it's impossible to find a job," he said. "It's not. But it requires a hell of a lot of energy, a hell of a lot of patience, and more than a hell of a lot of luck. And it can be a humbling experience. An ego can only be trampled on so many times."

"You can say that again," the orange-haired chick exclaimed. The others gave empathic laughs. Remembering the losers in the Fraulein lobby, Taylor nodded in agreement.

"Quid Pro Quo," Asher resumed his post at the head of the table, "is not like the other agencies. We operate differently. You pick from our list of jobs, and *you* interview *them*. If you like what you see, the job is yours. Sound too good to be true?" Again his eyes found Taylor's. He winked in such a way that no one else in the room was aware that his eyelid had moved. She just about swooned.

"Maybe it is. Maybe it is. If you're interested, give me a call this week. It's been a pleasure meeting you." This last sentiment he delivered right to Taylor. Who almost choked on the piece of ice sliding down her throat.

"I hope to hear from you soon." And Asher Krug's exit was just as imperial as his entrance.

Taylor stared at the door for a good thirty seconds, as if he'd left trails of smoke in his wake. Yes, she'd been predisposed to liking him, as he'd been so kind on the phone, but this was something she'd never experienced before. This was Love at First Sight. She was so fixated on Asher that she actually started when she heard a voice say, "Hey, we can go have that smoke now."

She had completely forgotten Bryan was there.

CHAPTER 3

Power corrupts, but power also attracts. Wealth, celebrity, and talent all enhance a man's sex appeal—in 1991, for example, fifty-five-year-old Woody Allen was shooting nude photographs of Soon-Yi Previn, who was just old enough to legally drink; it's a safe bet that the latter was not attracted to the former's matinee-idol looks—but nothing sets a woman's heart aflutter like power. JFK was wealthy, famous, talented, and handsome besides, but the primary reason he got laid so much was because he was the Leader of the Free World.

Asher Krug was as good-looking as straight men get, he dressed like he had money, and he had a way with words. None of this is what titillated Taylor. She was drawn to the sense of command that he radiated. The dude oozed power, and she soaked it up. I said before that her tastes ran to bad boys; that was because bad boys seemed powerful. That's why she liked J.D.

Although his job as a bartender at a heavy metal club was not that important in the scheme of the universe, it required him to exercise power. In the realm of the Continental, J.D. was Master and Commander. But his kingdom was one small club that Taylor didn't even like because it was so fucking loud. Asher, by contrast, was real-world powerful. He took power to a whole new dimension. And she had never met anyone like that before. *Of course* she was attracted to the guy. How could she not be?

Taylor leaned against the side of the building, enjoying the cigarette—she had blown off Bryan—and the image of Asher Krug that was still fresh in her mind. Kim Winter's Adam Curry sighting didn't seem so impressive all of the sudden. She checked her watch—it was quarter to twelve, so she had plenty of time to kill before her Braithwaite Ross interview.

Quarter to twelve, she discovered, is when the City That Never Sleeps sleeps. The bars and restaurants are deserted, the cinemas are still closed, the TKTS line is only ten or twelve deep. Even Herald Square is dead. So how to while away the afternoon? There was no way to stretch lunch for more than an hour and a half, even if she read all three daily papers and a gratis copy of the *Voice*. She wasn't in the mood to shop and didn't have any money to spend even if she were. And her Coliseum Books threshold was ninety minutes, tops. Where to go with no money? How you gonna make some time, when all you got is one thin dime?

Passing a gallery, Taylor remembered that the Museum of Modern Art was only a few blocks from her current location. So she headed downtown, thinking it was ironic that tourists come from half a world away to visit the museums and she would never even consider going to one unless the only other option was a four-hour lunch at a subterranean Sbarro.

The MOMA was as dead as the rest of the city. A handful of SVA students, some aging trophy wives, a gaggle of geeks from some church in Minnesota—that was it. This pleased Taylor; she had little patience for crowds.

In the ticket line, she remembered that she didn't have that much money. A gander at the list of admission prices: adults, $9; students, $6; senior citizens, $4; children, $4; members, free. All of them but the last were more than she could afford, if she wanted to eat lunch.

The kid behind the ticket counter couldn't have been more than sixteen. Nephew of one of the donors, probably, padding his résumé. He sported a houndstooth jacket and one of those then-stylish skate-rat haircuts that made his head look like a circumcised penis. Sheepishly Taylor handed him three crumpled dollar bills. "Sorry," she said. "I'll pay more next time."

"*Next* time?" He examined the offering with disgust, the penis haircut bobbing. "What *next* time? Nine dollars, please."

"Nine dollars?"

"That's what the sign says, doesn't it?" For her benefit, he pointed to it.

"I thought those were, you know, *suggested* admission prices."

"Well, they're not. Nine dollars, please."

"Doesn't the Met have suggested rates?"

The force of his sigh almost blew her backward. "This isn't the *Met*, miss."

This threw Taylor for a loop. It was her recollection that you paid whatever you wanted, so long as you paid something. "You're saying there's no reduced rate, that to get in I have to give you six dollars?"

"*Nine* dollars," the kid corrected. "Please, miss. There's a lot of customers want to get in this afternoon."

Taylor checked behind her. A few people, but by no means the waiting-for-your-freshman-advisor-to-sign-your-course-schedule line. Whirling back to face him: "But I'm a student."

He looked her up and down. Grinned snidely. Crossed his arms.

Taylor remembered that she was dressed up. "Just because I'm wearing a suit doesn't mean I'm not a student."

"Yes. Of course. Well, I don't see an ID. If you were a student, you'd have an ID. I need either an ID and six dollars, or nine dollars."

Taylor opened her handbag. Eight bucks and change. Which she needed for lunch. And no Wycliffe ID.

"Look," she pleaded, "can't you . . ."

"Nine dollars."

"Oh, just pay it, for God sake," cried the woman behind her.

Taylor turned around to face the speaker: a middle-aged bitch with eggplant-purple hair, taut face, retroussé nose, drawn-in eyebrows and lips—a triumph of knives and plastic.

"I don't have it," Taylor roared. "I'm not being cheap, I'm . . ."

"Hurry up, would you."

"*Please* step aside." The kid tossed the crumpled bills at her like so much used toilet paper. "I suggest you browse in the gift shop. They have *postcards* of the exhibits you can peruse." He then turned his attention to the offended lady, whereupon both of them ignored her.

That Taylor did not have enough money did not break the proverbial straw. Neither did the snide tone of the kid with the cut-cock haircut, or the taunting tone of the plastic-faced bitch. But to be completely ignored by both of them, as if she were a ghost, as if she didn't even exist—this snapped the camel's spine. Tears welled up in her eyes. The assorted stresses of the last few weeks undammed.

"I hope you fucking die," she shouted. "Both of you. I hope you drop dead."

Which, in retrospect, was not a particularly clever thing to say, as both of them certainly would, someday. The Minnesotans and the SVA students, however, were amused enough to stop and stare. With a grunt of disgust Taylor stormed out, vowing never to return, and marched uptown. By the time she hit Central Park, her blood pressure was back to normal.

"What a day this is turning out to be," she muttered to a passing businessman, who did not slacken his barbarian-at-the-gate pace to comment, talking to yourself being in New York what whistling is anywhere else.

After some searching, Taylor found a bench unoccupied by derelicts and unspoiled by bird shit. She sat, lunched on falafel and Tab, read *The Firm*, watched the people mill around. At two-thirty she packed up her things and headed to the Braithwaite Ross offices.

Just as Asher Krug had predicted, the interview began with a typing test. And then a spelling test. And then a proofreading test. Which would have driven Taylor bat-shit, except that her scores impressed the interviewer, an affable editor named Angela Del Giudice.

Despite her tall-thin-and-flat-chested body, Angie was quite ungainly. Her natural stance resembled Carlton Fisk's in the batter's box: her heels almost touching, her toes ninety degrees apart. She wore her chestnut hair in braids, faded blue jeans, and a ribbed, formfitting, black tank top. Her face was pretty if you could ignore her left eye, which was not quite aligned with the right, and the Dukakisian eyebrows.

From the get-go Angie did most of the talking, complimenting Taylor's "impressive" résumé, her suit, her imitation-leather handbag, detailing the duties of the job, and apologizing for Braithwaite Ross. "I realize the space is cramped," she would say, or "We're getting new computers soon," or "The AC is on the fritz." As if any of these deficiencies would compel Taylor to snub an offer.

The office was not so much cramped as cozy. The décor consisted of framed blowups of various BR book covers (*Memoirs of a Headhunter, The Stockholm Détente, Murders in Alphabet City, The Kindergarten Killers*) plus a gigantic poster of Humphrey Bogart and Lauren Bacall in *The Big Sleep*. The only principals over the age of thirty-five, Taylor learned, were the publisher and the editorial director. The age factor was a big selling point, in her mind; Jason Hanson and I were her only friends in the city, if we could even be called that. Taylor was depending on her job to jump-start her social life.

Turned out Angie's girlfriend from high school had gone to Wycliffe, so at least she didn't confuse it with Wesleyan. And she was also from the Midwest—Ohio, in her case. The kicker, though, was a mutual fondness for true-crime books. Taylor loved that stuff. Even before *Silence of the Lambs*, she was big into serial killers. She knew more about the Black Dahlia than James Ellroy.

"I have a positive feeling about this, Taylor," Angela said. "I think this went well. I don't have the final say, of course, but you're definitely the best candidate I've seen. By far, actually."

"Thank you. I'm just as impressed with Braithwaite Ross. This seems like a great place to work." Taylor wondered if and when she should broach the subject of salary, benefits, vacation time, that sort of thing. She was curious, of course, but she didn't want to come off as presumptuous. And for some reason Angie didn't seem the right person to ask.

"We'd like you to meet with our editorial director. Do you have plans right now? I know it's after four, but it'll speed things along if you could see him today. He has to meet with all the candidates, and we'd like to make a decision as soon as possible."

"No, that'd be great." A surge of adrenaline washed over Taylor. Which lasted two whole minutes, until she was introduced to said editorial director.

Walter Bledsoe looked like he stepped out of an ad for Grecian Formula. His hair was the color of shoe polish, and didn't quite match his bushy eyebrows. He reeked of tobacco and Aqua Velva and wore a glove-tight three-piece suit, gold cuff links, and the pained facial expression of a chronic hemorrhoid sufferer. He reminded Taylor of her high school guidance counselor. The one who got his suits secondhand from the funeral parlor.

"Good afternoon, Miss Schmidt. Please sit." Bledsoe beamed, extending his paw. His teeth and fingertips both had the same yellowish tint.

Bledsoe took Taylor's hand, holding it a few seconds longer than she would have liked. Both sat.

"Generally speaking," he began, "we only look at Ivy Leaguers. Braithwaite Ross has a reputation to maintain, and Princeton and Yale haven't steered us wrong yet."

Taylor struggled to maintain eye contact but found it impossible, as her interviewer was staring at her C-cups.

"Wycliffe does enjoy a sterling reputation, to be sure, but let's be candid. There's a big difference between Wycliffe and Yale."

Taylor wanted to shoot back, *About a hundred miles of I-91*, but didn't have the nerve. "Yeah. So I've read, anyway."

Interesting that Bledsoe had picked Yale. Taylor had, during the application process, set her heart on Yale, but Yale did not reciprocate her ardor. The rejection had haunted her ever since.

Bledsoe laughed the same way the kid at MOMA had at her three dollars. Which meant something was going to get thrown back in her face. Her résumé, most likely.

"So, tell me, Miss Schmidt—the book industry is moribund. Why publishing?"

Somehow she was able to check her vexation enough to answer the question, supplying the usual reasons: she had a degree in English, she liked to read, she liked to write, she had a critical mind, she wanted to work with other creative people. Throughout, Bledsoe's lecherous eyes did not stray from her chest.

"And the salary doesn't daunt you?"

"I'd rather it be six figures, sure. But if I have to pay my dues, I have no objection to paying my dues."

By now, the old man had stopped blinking. There was no pretense; he was hypnotized by her heaving bosom (not that I can blame him). She crossed her arms. He raised a bushy eyebrow.

"Good, good. So, tell me. What is the most important thing you learned in your undergraduate career at Wesleyan?"

"Wycliffe."

"Sorry. At Wycliffe."

"The most important thing I learned . . ."

At first, she could only think of joke responses: *Fake an ID. Mix a mean martini. Get through a full day on two hours' sleep with a raging hangover. Give head without gagging.* All of which were more important in the context of everyday life than the answer she finally arrived at: "Well . . . that's hard to say. I learned a lot at Wycliffe, met a lot of great people, took some great classes. I'd have to say . . . how to, like, put my ideas into words. How to, you know, express myself. Eloquence. I learned eloquence."

Bledsoe inspected his yellowed fingernails. "Well, Miss Schmidt, there's not much I can do for you at this time, I'm sorry to say." He stood and walked around the desk. "There are few openings to begin with, and most of them have to go to the *minorities*, the blacks and the Chicanos and these Orientals. Perhaps . . ."

"But I'm a woman," Taylor protested. "Doesn't that count for anything?"

"Miss Schmidt," shaking his head, "half the people in the world are women. More than half. I'd hardly call that a minority. If you were black, or Chippewa or something, then I could help you. But you're as lily-white as I am."

Now he was perched in front of the desk, his crotch three feet away from her face and bulging perceptibly.

"But . . ."

"What can I do? My hands are tied. These damned quota laws and so forth. Believe you me, if I had my druthers I'd hire you over any of the candidates I've seen." His eyes darted up and down her body. "With legs like yours, I'd hire you just to walk to the watercooler and back. But it's a small house, and we have a reputation to maintain."

Taylor abruptly stood up, shifting so that the chair was between them, lion-tamer-style. "Thanks for your time, Mr. Bledsoe. It was really *swell* meeting you."

"Please," he said, inching closer, "call me Walter."

* * *

Guys hit on Taylor a lot. Maybe it was the way she dressed. Maybe it was the way she looked at them. Maybe it was her body language. Maybe it was because, on some subconscious and involuntary level, she wanted them to hit on her. What *was* the key to her sexual magnetism? Taylor couldn't say for sure. But to be hit on by a tattooed bartender at Continental, or a frat boy in the lobby of an employment agency, was not the same as being hit on by an older man, an Ivy League–educated man, a *married* man, during a job interview. That was more than just a harmless nuisance. That was a violation. That was. . .

"Sexual harassment," Taylor told the mailbox, in front of which she was now standing. She opened it, looked inside, found nothing, shook her head, closed the box, and headed up the stairs.

On the first landing Taylor bumped into one of the last people she wanted to see just then: our downstairs neighbor, Trey Parrish. Trey Parrish was a nominee, along with Kirk Gibson, Rock Hudson, Rhett Butler, Conrad Hilton, and Charles "The Hammer" Martel, for Coolest Man's Name of All Time, but his name, alas, was the only cool thing about him—although nobody ever broke the news to Trey. He sported a Steve Miller Band T-shirt tucked into madras-print J. Crew shorts (the lone brick-and-mortar store where they were available had opened two years before at South Street Seaport), a black weave belt, Polo Sport cologne, Bass docksiders, and, on his ankle, a tattoo of some or other fraternity. Wisps of blond hair peaked out from the sides of his white Delaware Lacrosse cap.

"Well, well," he said. "Look what the cat dragged in."

Trey worked for a financial consulting firm, whose name was a series of desultory capital letters, as either a consultant or analyst; Taylor wasn't sure which. The only reason she knew that much was because he accosted her every time he heard her on the steps (which was often, as he was in the habit of leaving his door slightly ajar for just that reason) and initiated a conversation. Although *conversa-*

tion implies that Taylor also spoke—*soliloquy* is a more accurate word. Trey was under the delusion that the mundane events of each day were some sort of chain letter that he had to meticulously share with as many people as possible. He was also under the delusion that these events were of considerable interest to the members of his audience, whom he regarded as biographers.

"How's it hangin', Schmitty?"

Plus he called everyone by nicknames. Even people who didn't have nicknames.

"Uh . . . hi, Trey."

"What's up?"

"Not much." Taylor wondered what would have to be up for her not to answer the question by rote. "How are you?"

"Pretty good, actually. Pretty good." Trey's head bobbed as he spoke. "Had a great weekend. Went down to Manasquan. Friends of mine have a place down there for the summer. You should come sometime."

Trey interpreted Taylor's polite nod as a green light to detail his entire weekend—the traffic on the Parkway, the "babes" on the beach, the level of sunscreen used, the number of beers consumed, and how *fun* Manasquan, New Jersey, was (as if places were inherently fun) because "the Hoboken crowd" summered there. Taylor groaned inwardly. It was a hell of a response to a perfunctory question, the answer to which interested her not in the least.

"How goes the job search?" Trey wanted to know. Or maybe he was just asking to be nice.

"It's still going," she said. "So not so good, I guess."

"I bet you have a job offer by the end of the week." There was a twinkle in his eye. "I'm serious. You wanna bet?"

"Not really."

"Doesn't have to be for money. I'm flexible. Sexual favors work for me just as well. Better, actually."

"Really, it's okay."

"Suit yourself." Trey was holding on to the doorknob, half inside, half outside, affording a view of the pizza boxes, beer cans, and dirty clothes that passed as decorations in his dorm-like studio apartment. Other than the spunk-stained futon mattress that served as a bed, the only other furnishings in the room were a poster of Pamela Anderson, three clothes baskets, an old stereo, and an older TV set which, to the best of her knowledge, had never been shut off. Trey was watching a ballgame, Pirates at Mets. "So . . . are you and Todd, like, an item?"

"Todd?" Taylor smiled at the ridiculousness of the concept. "No. We're just friends."

O, my wounded heart! The kiss of death!

"Friends. That's cool, that's cool. He's a good man, Hot Toddie."

"He is."

"Not! Just kidding."

Taylor flashed the duplicitous smile best supporting actress nominees give one another—the same one desirable women unleash on undesirable male neighbors—and moved to go upstairs.

But Trey wouldn't let her escape that easily. "Yeah, work's going well for me, too. They're sending me down to Orlando next month. Big conference. Been working like sixteen, eighteen hour days. It's nuts."

If he could read the disinterest in her eyes—and Taylor was trying her best to write it in flashing neon letters—Trey ignored it. Instead, he spun an Algeresque tale of how The Orlando Conference (it practically demanded capital letters) would make his career. Every time he paused to take a breath Taylor would climb one step higher, but then he would begin another chapter, and she would have to stop. Finally, the sound of a crowd cheering from the TV set diverted his attention. One of the Pirates had hit a home run. Trey glanced at the television, scowled, and turned back around— only to find her gone.

Taylor could hear him call her name (or rather, his nickname for her), but she didn't stop running until she was safely in her apartment. Once the door was bolted she fixed herself a rum-and-

Coke, pounded it, then fixed herself another. A wave of nausea came over her; she clutched her stomach and groaned.

The more removed Taylor was from the Walter Bledsoe incident, the more violated she felt. In need of venting, she called me, her resident shoulder-to-cry-on, but I was in a fucking *staff meeting* at that precise moment, and thus unable to take the call. Had I called in sick that day—I was so hungover when I woke up that I'd seriously entertained the idea—I would have been there to comfort her. I could have taken her to dinner, or to the movies—*Barton Fink* was playing at the Angelica, or we could have opted for *Boyz N the Hood*, *Point Break*, *Thelma and Louise*—hell, even *Bill and Ted's Bogus Journey* would have done the trick. Maybe we would have just stayed home, cooked some mac and cheese, watched TV. Whatever. The point is, if I'd burned a sick day, Taylor might still be alive right now.

But no—I had to be at the staff meeting, and Taylor had to talk to someone about Walter Bledsoe, had to vent, and *now*, or she would throw up. Already she could feel a gurgling in the gullet. Who else to talk to, if Todd Lander wasn't available? Her mother? Trey Parrish? J.D. wasn't answering his phone. And Kim Winter, assuming she could be tracked down, would just insist that Taylor do something: file a complaint, sue, get the asshole fired. Which Taylor didn't want to do. There was enough grief in her life without filing a sexual harassment claim. Who else to call?

Taylor's steel-blue eyes strayed to the embossed card taped to the wall above her desk. Completely on impulse, as if on autopilot, and without any idea of what she might say, she rang the Quid Pro Quo offices.

Asher Krug was in, and sounded genuinely delighted to hear from her. He picked up on her discomfiture almost immediately. He was a master at reading people, especially women. "You sound upset. Is something wrong?"

"I had a terrible interview today."

"Yeah?"

"Yeah." And she unloaded on him, told him the whole story,

right down to the bulge in the guy's crotch. "What a slimebag. You should have *seen* the look he gave me. He did this thing with his tongue—he looked like Jabba the Hut."

"Despicable. Truly despicable. I'm so sorry you had to go through that."

Suddenly Taylor realized she'd been babbling for ten minutes—she was more tipsy than she'd thought—and was awash in self-consciousness. "I'm sorry, Asher. I didn't mean to . . . I mean, you must be busy."

"No, no, please. That's what I'm here for."

That's what I'm here for—the lousy prick even appropriated my line!

"I knew you'd understand." Taylor took a sip of her rum-and-Coke and vented on. "I mean, it's just, Angie was so cool, you know? I mean, she really liked me. And it's not like you have much contact with the editorial director, not on a day-to-day basis." Slamming the glass on the nightstand, she said, "What really gets me is, I couldn't even tell him off, because he could, like, blacklist me or something."

"It's a conspiracy, is what it is," Asher said. "Nobody takes us seriously. Not just you and me. Our whole generation. They treat us like children. Like *infants*."

"I don't think it has anything to do with when you're born, what *generation* you belong to or whatever." Taylor rolled onto her back. "People are all the same. They're all assholes."

He laughed. It was the first time she'd heard his laugh. Most people, when they laugh, they sound silly. Not Asher Krug. Oh, no. Even his laugh was seductive.

"You need to come in here," he said. "What's the soonest you can come in here?"

"I don't know. Tomorrow morning?"

"Why not right now?"

Why *not* right now. Why not indeed.

"I'm all the way downtown. I wouldn't be able to get there before five."

"I'll wait."

"I don't want to put you out."

"It's nothing. Really. I usually don't leave till six or seven. Beat the traffic."

"Are you sure?"

"Don't give it another thought. I have paperwork to catch up on anyway. Take your time, don't rush, get here when you can—but get here."

I beat myself up over it still—can you blame me?—but the truth is, even if I had called in sick, even if we had watched Bill and Ted beat the Grim Reaper, or Thelma and Louise drive off the cliff, it would have only delayed the inevitable. Taylor would have met with Asher Krug eventually. He was irresistible, and besides—it was meant to be.

CHAPTER 4

As she hurried from the tumult of rush-hour Madison Avenue, with its too-narrow sidewalks, to the spacious lobby of 520, Taylor was greeted by the most dazzling live piano music she'd ever heard. Clearly it was not the same old biddy at the keys. A crowd had gathered around the big black Baldwin, blocking the performer from view. Taylor stood in the back and struggled to see. Only when a couple in the front moved did she realize that the virtuoso at the keys was a pimply-faced kid who couldn't be out of high school. In jeans and a ripped Megadeth T-shirt, no less.

"Wow," she remarked to a young woman of the dress-suit-and-white-Reebok set to her left. "He's really something."

"What's even more surprising," the woman said, "is that he's only filling in because the regular pianist is ill."

"Who is he?"

"No idea. I heard he got the job through that agency up-stairs."

Taylor did not stay for the rest of the performance; Asher Krug was waiting for her, after all. And with a glance at her watch—it was half past five—she headed for the offices of That Agency Up-stairs.

The Quid Pro Quo lobby was empty and startlingly quiet, giving it the serene and unused look of an *Architectural Digest* spread. Then Mae-Yuan emerged from a back room, speaking in soft tones to three impeccably-dressed businessmen, one NBA tall, the others short and squat, all three with long black beards and turbans. Arabs, probably. Who else wore turbans?

There was a hush as they noticed her. Taylor felt like she'd walked in on her mother and Billy Ray having sex.

When Mae-Yuan saw her, however, she only smiled. Standing next to the three men—not to mention the towering stone owl—the receptionist was no more than a shadow, a wisp of smoke. "Hello again, Taylor. Asher is expecting you. Please have a seat; I'll be right with you."

The tall Arab, who had a beatific charisma, fixed his endlessly dark, almost womanly eyes on hers. "Such great beauty, you see? This is why women should wear veils."

The others laughed, and with stately bows, the threesome took its leave.

"Sorry about that," said Mae-Yuan once they had gone. "Important clients."

At the end of a long hall was an oak door similar to the one that marked the agency entrance. Taylor followed her hostess that way. "Through the big door?"

"No. That's the Director's office." The capital D was evident in the intonation.

"Who's the Director?"

"The Director is not in." Mae-Yuan halted in front of the great door, barring entrance, and gestured with her left arm to the only-slightly-less majestic entryway to Taylor's right. "This way, please."

Thanking Mae-Yuan, Taylor stepped into a side office that was as swanky as the rest of Quid Pro Quo headquarters: antique desk and file cabinets, leather chairs, a velvet chaise lounge, oak paneling. Magnificent view of Central Park. Two paintings: a Modigliani and a Mondrian. Martini stand. And Asher Krug, eyes aglow, hair perfect, and wearing a different but equally *GQ*-worthy suit.

"Thanks so much for waiting. It's really nice of you."

"Don't mention it." He rose to greet her as she entered; they clasped hands. He had a firm, Teddy Roosevelt handshake. "Well worth the wait, to see you again."

This caused the hair on Taylor's neck to stand on end, but she played it cool. She gestured to the window. "Nice view."

"Yeah. I should probably spend more time enjoying it. I would have killed for a little sunlight the last place I worked."

"Where was that?"

"I was a trader at Drexel Burnham, if you can believe it. It's kind of embarrassing, actually."

"Embarrassing?"

Taylor Schmidt knew nothing of junk bonds, the Keating Five, Michael Milken, the S&L scandal from which the country was still fighting to recover. Even if she had, she could not imagine Asher Krug being ashamed of anything.

Asher, in any case, did not hear her. He was back behind his desk, rustling through some papers. "Have a seat. You want a drink? Coffee? Tea?" Noticing perhaps the weary look in her eye: "Scotch?"

He was wearing cologne. The scent had the same effect on her body that Selsun Blue is alleged to have on a psoriatic's scalp: it made her tingle.

"What are you having?"

"Scotch."

"Scotch, then."

"Excellent choice." He strode to the martini stand, poured two fingers of scotch, and handed her the drink. "Cheers."

"Cheers." They clinked glasses, sipped, and then took their seats.

"I'm sorry your interview was a washout."

"He kept staring at my chest."

Asher seized the opportunity to do the same, but unlike Walter Bledsoe he very artfully kept his eyes moving. "I'm not surprised. Men of that generation, they rarely know how to behave around women smarter than they are." He shook his head as if to say *tsk tsk*. "What did he say during the interview segment? Or *was* there an interview segment?"

"No, there was. But he was such a jerk. He told me my college wasn't impressive enough. Because it wasn't *Yale*. Fucking Yale. You didn't go to Yale, did you?"

Asher smiled in such a way—the guy had an incredible ability to convey complex emotions with a slight curl of his lip—that indicated that while he had gone to Yale, he took no umbrage at her comment.

"Figures." She took another sip of scotch.

"It's the lay of the land right now. There's a glut of college graduates, so employees can afford to be choosy."

"Why *is* that?"

Taylor was not expecting a response, but Asher Krug's espresso-brown eyes twinkled like he was Cecil Fielder locking in on a hanging curve. (The portly Detroit Tiger had hit fifty-one dingers the previous year, a big deal pre-steroids.)

"Because the baby boomers fucked it up," he said. "See, back in the fifties and early sixties, not everyone went to college. It wasn't the foregone conclusion it is today. Most people, they graduated high school and went directly into the workforce. You only pursued a higher education if you were an intellectual, or if you wanted to be a doctor or a lawyer—something that required an advanced degree. Universities were different back then; the students were there because they chose to be, not because society made it compulsory. A college campus was a center for intellectual development, for academic rigor, for personal growth—not a four-year extension of high school, like it is now."

One of Taylor's more formidable weapons of seduction, as I mentioned earlier, was her ability to gaze at men with Miranda-like awe. Her eyes would grow so wide, so reverential, that it was impossible to tell whether or not she was sincere. Those bewitching eyes were now cast on Asher Krug. "So what happened?"

"Vietnam happened, the war. And the baby boom generation," he said, his voice so thick with derision she could almost taste it, "shirked its civic responsibility to serve. They said, 'We don't agree with what's going on over there, so we're not gonna fight.' *I* say, if you want to live in this country, you have to take the good with the bad. *You* elected the president. *You* elected the Congress. If *they* say fight, you gotta fight. But the baby boomers didn't see things that way. When the going got tough, they dodged the draft. They got doctor's notes, they claimed religious opposition, they feigned homosexuality, they intentionally caught venereal diseases, they fled to Canada. But most of them just went to college—not because they wanted to go to college; because they wanted to avoid combat. Because they were cowards."

While Taylor was not particularly interested in what Asher was saying—she had no use for historical context; she inhabited the moment—she was very interested in how he was saying it. The conviction, the ardor in his voice, the fire burning in his dark eyes, the clenching of his strong hands into stronger fists. His passions had been excited; hers, too.

"Then what? The war ended, and the veterans, these brave and selfless men who risked their lives for us, came home looking for work. But they could't *find* any work, because the draft dodgers all had *college* degrees, and were therefore more quote-unquote qualified. So the college kids got the jobs, and the vets got the shaft. All because these fucking *poltroons* went and got BAs in health or some other bullshit while their less fortunate and more patriotic classmates were getting shot at by gooks. Now, thanks to these draft-dodging baby boom crybabies, *everyone* has to get a college degree, just to keep up. The baby boomers fucked it up, like they fuck up everything they touch. That's why they must be stopped."

A look of what appeared to be panic flashed suddenly across Asher's face. His eyes darted to the door. Only when he saw that no one was there did he revert to normal.

"Stopped?" Taylor asked, noticing the change in his expression. "What do you mean, stopped?"

He ignored her question. "Not that the so-called Greatest Generation has been so great, either. The AARP's lobby makes the tobacco companies' look Third World. They got all the tax laws changed, to help the retirees. A young family with one child earning thirty grand a year pays *five times* as much in federal taxes as a retired couple with the same income. Five times! And where is that money going? To pay off a Treasury debt incurred by the baby boomers, with all their ridiculous spending on bullshit social programs. Basically, *we* are paying off our parents' credit card bills—at a *Merchant of Venice* interest rate. And Social Security? Fuck. There won't *be* any Social Security when we retire. It used to be that parents and grandparents *provided* for their young, tried to make the world a better place for them. Not anymore."

Asher's eyes drifted toward Madison Avenue, where strolled middle-aged men in blue suits who were the focus of his rage. When he looked back at Taylor, his gaze was so intent that for a fleeting moment she was frightened. He looked like he could kill somebody with his bare hands.

"Think they're interested in their children? Look at the abortion rate since 1970. Look at the divorce rate since 1970. If my 401(k) climbed that high that fast I could retire at thirty. The baby boomers are too selfish to even *have* children, let alone raise them properly. They only care about themselves."

Asher's Adam's apple quivered as he spoke. So did Taylor.

"I never really thought about it like that before," Taylor told him. "It's a fascinating take."

"No reason you should. The baby boomers control the media.

They make it seem like what they did was *honorable*, for the good of *humanity*. They're not about to criticize *themselves*, certainly. And there's no way they'd allow someone *our* age to do it."

Beads of sweat had formed on Asher's forehead. "This is the generation that brought us chemical dependency and the budget deficit and the health insurance crisis. This is the generation that brought us AIDS and prenuptial agreements and Blockbuster Video. This . . ."

Asher stopped his polemic then—suddenly, as if some cosmic puppeteer had yanked him backward. He unclenched his fists, found a handkerchief, mopped his brow. "Sorry. I get carried away sometimes."

He took another long belt of scotch, wiped his mouth with the handkerchief, and was back to business as usual. "Okay. Let's get down to brass tacks, shall we? This is how we operate. You pick a job from our master list. You interview, and if you like the job, it's yours. In two weeks, you come see me. If you're not satisfied with your placement, we find you a new job. If you are satisfied—and almost everyone is—we discuss reimbursement. Sound fair?"

Did it sound fair? Sure, it sounded fair. It also sounded—as Asher himself put it at the orientation—too good to be true. How were they able to offer jobs at other companies so easily? How could she be in control of a job interview? Why did she need to wait two weeks to find out the cost of such an enterprise? There was something fishy about all this, maybe even something dangerous. Taylor could sense it. She was intuitive in that way. Or maybe it was just that the Grisham book she was reading had gotten to her.

"Reimbursement? You didn't mention reimbursement at the orientation."

"It's not a big deal."

"Then can't we discuss it now?"

Asher handed Taylor a fat three-ring binder. "Here's the list. Publishing is the third tab in."

As she flipped through the pages, her heart pounded, the pulse of a bad poker player with a straight flush. The list was astounding. The jobs were all for associate editors, with starting salaries in the high twenties (for the sake of comparison, Mitch McDeere is blown away by an offer of eighty thousand dollars from the eponymous firm in Grisham's bestseller). Starting as an associate editor at a publishing house is like starting as a lieutenant in the army. And the wages were a decent take for a full editor, never mind a recent college grad with no meaningful work experience beyond Planet Hollywood.

"Is this for real? How is it possible?" she wanted to know. "There's an opening at Braithwaite Ross for an associate editor at twenty-seven thousand dollars. Walter Bledsoe wouldn't hire me as an editorial assistant for sixteen-five. How . . ."

"Our reputation helps open doors," Asher said. "That's why we're the best. Is that the job that interests you the most?"

"I really love their catalog. And the people there are really cool. But I don't think I could work for that guy."

"Who, Bledsoe? I wouldn't worry about him. You said it yourself: How much interaction do you have with the editorial director? Besides, if it doesn't work out, you can get a new job in two weeks. Think of it as a lease with an option to buy."

"I guess." Taylor took another sip of the scotch, which, while imported from Scotland and beyond pricy, was not as tasty, in her mind, as a Bacardi and Coke. "Twist my arm. I'll take it."

"Excellent. You start in two weeks, but you get paid right away."

"Really?"

"Really."

"That's all I have to do?"

"Not quite." Asher opened a Filofax, picked up a fountain pen. "We have to schedule your follow-up. Let's see . . . how about first of October? That's a Tuesday. At noon, shall we say?"

"Won't I be at work?"

"Oh, they'll let you out for this. You'll be meeting with the Director." He indicated with his thumb the larger office next door. "How does that sound?"

"That sounds . . . great. Unbelievably great. Thank you *so much*, Asher. I don't think I could handle another day like today. You can only be disappointed so many times, you know? Really— you're a lifesaver."

Asher Krug laughed at this, more heartily than the comment deserved.

In April of her senior year in high school, Taylor was notified of her admission to Wycliffe by Madame Gaudrault, her favorite teacher, who had been sniffing around the guidance department. Taylor jumped up and down and hugged everyone and then raced home to await an acceptance notification that did not come. That day, or the next. The letter would have made it official, cemented what she already knew, but she didn't have the document, just hollow assurances from a French teacher. Doubts formed. Yes, guidance departments are alerted of acceptances and rejections, but what if Madame Gaudrault had been wrong? The guidance counselors at her high school—at any high school, let's be honest—were not exactly paragons of competence. What if she had to tell her mother and Billy Ray and her half sisters and all her friends that in fact Wycliffe had rejected her, just as Yale had? What little sleep she got during those three days of limbo was plagued by nightmares of the all-of-the-sudden-my-clothes-are-gone variety. When the letter (which wasn't as thick as acceptance letters were purported to be) finally came, Taylor locked herself in the bathroom, fearing the worst. Madame Gaudrault did wind up being right, but still. . .

"It was such a letdown, you know? I mean, I should have been riding high, but instead I was so relieved that the guidance department hadn't fucked up that it spoiled everything."

We were at Phoebe's, a hole-in-the-wall on Cooper Square that had good burgers and even better beer specials (four bucks for a pitcher of Rolling Rock; the good ol' days), celebrating, on my dime, Taylor's attainment of gainful employment. Like the Yankees on the TV behind the bar, we were on our second pitcher.

"What would it take," I mused, more for my benefit than hers, "to make you happy?"

Because Taylor was not, had never been, a particularly happy person. Studies have shown, again and again, that prettier people are generally happier than us normal-looking folk. The reason money can't buy happiness is, money can't buy good looks. Plastic surgeons can only do so much. If this were true, why was Taylor so downcast most of the time? Why did she have such crippling nightmares almost every night? Why did she drink so much? She was young, and smart, and beautiful. The world was her proverbial oyster. Why, then, the perpetual blues?

At the time, of course, I didn't know that she'd stopped taking her Prozac. Nor would I have cared had I known. I was focused on the prize—which meant figuring out how *I* could capitalize on her doom-and-gloom.

"Don't get me wrong. I *really* want this job. But it's like, if they had made me an offer . . . if that Walter guy told me, 'You're the best person for this job, congratulations,' instead of being a total shithead . . . I'd feel more, I don't know, *appreciated*, you know? Like I really deserved it. This almost feels like cheating." She took a long drag on her Parliament. "Why must everything in life be so disappointing? Why can't anything be as emotionally fulfilling as I want it to be?"

"You're a dope," I told her. "So *what* if you're not as thrilled as you should be? You're making almost twice what they were originally going to pay you. Two weeks from now, you'll appreciate *that* a lot more, believe me."

"Yeah, I know. It's just that there's something, I don't know, *anticlimactic* about finding out you have a job through a third party."

"If you're going to be a writer," I said, "you better learn to trust your agent."

"I guess." Taylor snuffed out the cigarette in an already-over-flowing ashtray. Remember ashtrays? You never see them anymore. "The other thing is, I can't figure out this whole Quid Pro Quo thing. How can it be that *they* can offer me this job? Even if I wind up paying them, it doesn't make any sense. The office is, like, totally plush. They obviously have money. Where does it come from? How does it work?"

"Well, let's break it down. What do we know? We know that regular employment agencies get about fifteen percent of the starting salary for placing a hire. So if they found you a job at twenty grand, say, they'd make, what, three thousand bucks? The reason it costs so much is, it's expensive for companies to do their own recruiting, to go through résumés and post jobs and stuff. And it's expensive to train new employees. Maybe Quid Pro Quo is just better at screening its candidates."

"But they didn't screen me at all. I didn't take the tests or anything."

"Yeah, but who cares about the tests? You can learn Word in a few days, no big deal. People are either competent or they're not. And you're competent."

"But how do they *know* that?"

"I don't know. How did they find you?"

"I got their card in the mail."

"Well, they must have gotten your name from someplace. And they obviously were not misinformed."

"You flatter me. More beer?"

"Please."

She filled our steins, emptying the second pitcher.

"All I'm saying is," I told her, "they must have some kind of system in place—a better business model than their competitors'."

"But *what*?"

I couldn't have cared less about her employment agency. All I wanted to do at that point was finish the beer so we could go home. There was a good chance that she'd let me give her a back rub—she usually did if she was sufficiently drunk—and sooner or later, the back rub might lead to more intimate activities. Or so I hoped.

"Maybe they're like, did you see that *SNL* sketch about the bank that makes change?" I said. "How do they make their money? One word: volume. Maybe it works like that."

"Ha ha. I know this—what is this?"

A new song had replaced "Things That Make You Go Hmmmm .·. ." on the jukebox.

" 'When I Think About You, I Touch Myself,' " I told her. Not only was that the title of the song—Divinyls, we hardly knew ye!—it also happened to be true.

CHAPTER 5

Taylor's first day of work was wrought with the same mixture of hope, nervousness, and bathos that marked her first day of hostessing at Planet Hollywood, her first day of college, her first day of high school—most first days of anything she could recall. Throughout what would become her morning routine, she wondered where she would be sitting, if she would have her own letterhead and business cards, which of her coworkers she would befriend, if there were any cute guys she had overlooked during the interview, whether Walter Bledsoe would make any more passes at her, if she was over- or underdressed (she was wearing a black suit, a recent purchase at the Limited, that looked more Price Waterhouse than Braithwaite Ross), why they had hired her without an interview, if she could handle the job, where she would go for lunch, and a million other details—trivial and otherwise—people fret about on their first day of work. During her commute, she paid attention to places of interest she passed: book stores, record stores, Japanese restaurants. The route took her directly through the Theatre District. In her diary, she mused on how long it would take for the thrill of Times Square to grow old. (Answer: about a week. And that was back when there were still peep shows and prostitutes, before Benito Giuliani turned it into Disney World North. Taylor had a short attention span.)

Despite the fact that there was no dress code, it turned out that Taylor was not too formally attired. The entire BR staff was dressed to the nines, the men in too-thin ties and ill-fitting starched shirts, the women in suits that had been in the closet longer than Liberace and were therefore several sizes too small. Angie met her at the front desk, looking ill-at-ease in a fuscia number that was not in style during the heyday of *Miami Vice* and was certainly not hip in 1991.

Taylor asked about the threads.

"The publisher is stopping by today, so . . ." Angie's eyes shifted back and forth, as eyes do in spy movies. "Let me show you your office."

They walked down a long hallway—briskly, to avoid making introductions—and stepped into a small, windowless room with a stained imitation-wood desk, a few wood-and-vinyl chairs, a bookcase teeming with BR fare, and the computer St. Paul used to write his letters to the Thessalonians. It made the Commodore 64 look like HAL.

"This is you." Angie flipped on the lights, closed the door. "You picked a hell of a day to start. You'll probably quit, you'll think we're so nuts." She collapsed into one of the chairs, her legs spread in a most unladylike manner. The fuscia was even brighter under the fluorescents that buzzed overhead.

"We *had* to dress up today. As you can tell, we're not used to it. I can't even remember the last time I wore this thing."

Taylor said nothing. The first-day-of-work smile she slapped on with her new suit was taking a coffee break.

"Mr. Ross," Angie said, "*Averell* Ross, owns the company. He's based in Washington, so he's not around much. I've been here six years and I've only seen him twice. Compared to his other business interests, this place is small fry. As long as we're in the black, which we always are—barely, but always—he leaves us alone. He and Paul went to Yale together, so . . ."

Yale again.

"Paul?"

"Paul Walldorf. He's the publisher. Or, he *was* the publisher. Until this morning."

"Ah." On this particular morning, Taylor was more concerned with the social than the political; she hadn't been on board long enough to establish ties, and therefore had little reason to fear a new regime. Aimlessly, she flipped on the computer.

"Averell fired him—no one knows why—and replaced him with his son. Nathan."

"Nepotism rears its ugly head."

"I didn't say that." Angie held up her hand in the stop formation. She didn't want to go there. "Nathan's stopping by today to look the place over. That's why everyone's dressed up. And nervous."

The computer was louder than most Boeing products. It bitched and moaned and filled the gaps in conversation. "What's he like, Nathan?"

"No one knows. He has his MFA from Columbia, so he can probably write a little, but he's got zippo experience. I mean, nada."

"What'd he do before?"

"Nothing. He just graduated. He's twenty-four years old."

"That's pretty gnarly."

"Like I said," Angie shrugged, "you picked a hell of a day to start. The chatter in this place is straight out of one of our thrillers."

"It's just office politics," Taylor said. "Everything will work out fine. Besides, you can't have a thriller without at least one dead body."

"At the rate we're going . . ." Angie shook her head and rose to her feet. "You want some coffee? The coffee here sucks, but it's free."

After a detour to the break room—the coffee was even worse than Taylor'd expected—Angie gave her the tour and introduced her to her new colleagues, almost all of whom were around her age. (There were more women than men, but curiously, Taylor never mentioned any of the women.)

Mike moonlighted as a stand-up comic. He was a few years removed from NYU, where he was involved in writing *The Plague*, a satirical student publication that did things like run photographs of homeless people with the Gap logo in the corner, as if they were print ads. It was damn funny stuff. Mike looked sort of like Ron Darling.

Brady organized elaborate scavenger hunts around lower Manhattan. Last time there were two hundred people involved, and the *Village Voice* did a feature about it, which he had laminated and tacked to his cubicle wall. (Headline: *Midnight Madness in Manhattan*, a reference to an obscure Michael J. Fox movie.) Brady was a dead ringer for the kid from *Witness*.

Charles was an obsessive Elvis Costello fan. He produced his own Elvis newsletter—*The Silly Champion*—and was in the process of establishing an Elvis listserv, whatever that meant. Elvis rarities and B-sides were forever playing on his tape deck. Charles could have passed for MTV's Alan Hunter.

And then there was Chris, a *Dungeons & Dragons* enthusiast and SCA member who wore a ponytail and dressed like Blackbeard. Despite these obvious shortcomings, Chris managed to be the cutest of the bunch, probably because of his feline eyes—he was like a piratical River Phoenix.

"It's a good group," Angie said. "We go out a lot."

There was still a knot in Taylor's stomach that didn't abate, even when she noticed that Walter Bledsoe's office was dark.

"Where is Mr. Bledsoe?"

"He's not in today. He has, like, six weeks of vacation, he's been here so long. But he doesn't come in on Wednesdays regardless."

Angie deposited the newest BR employee in her office and went back to work. Her belly full of bad coffee, Taylor stared alternately at the slew of tax and benefit forms on her desk and the clock on the wall (whose ticking was only slightly less loud than the computer's whir). Most of her questions had been answered. By lunchtime, the only mystery left was in the plots of the slush-pile manuscripts.

At two o'clock, Angie announced that Nathan Ross would not be in for another two weeks; some sort of delay involving a closing on a Georgetown townhouse. The entire staff seemed to exhale in unison. Ties were doffed, heels kicked off, radios switched on, witticisms bandied about.

All of the guys in the office wandered by at some point to say hello. Taylor wound up giving her number to Chris the Pirate, who offered to take her to Medieval Times, which had opened in February of the previous year near the Meadowlands. Were it not for her fascination with a certain employment agent, she probably would have gone out with Chris, and almost certainly slept with him—and I definitely wouldn't be writing this. As it was, she only gave out her number to get rid of him; her heart already belonged to Asher Krug.

CHAPTER 6

The task of writing Taylor's story has fallen to me because her own voice—unusually high in register, it was, and breathy, like she'd just sucked on a helium balloon—has been permanently silenced. This is her story, not mine, and it would dishonor her memory to tarry on my own recollections, however pleasant the trip down Memory Lane might be.

That said, I think it best to interpose, before we get too far along, and make one thing crystal clear: while she was my roommate and friend—and, as I said before, the nightly muse of my masturbatory fantasies—there was more to my life in the summer of 1991 than Taylor Schmidt. I'd been living in the East Village, the hippest place on earth, for four years. I had more going for me than some Show Me State sexpot taking over Laura's half of the lease. A lot more.

There was the acting, of course, which vocation

brought me to New York in the first place. I was taking classes, I was studying with some of the best teachers out there, I was auditioning for nonequity jobs. I appeared in a slew of student films. None of them panned out in the long run, but not because of any deficiencies in my abilities. I was a pretty good actor, truth be told. The leading-man looks I lacked, yes—I was no Harrison Ford, no Mel Gibson—but I had *a* look. I was six-two and somewhat gawky in gait (though thankfully I've filled out since), with a wild mop of curly hair, and a wide, crooked nose, courtesy of a barroom brawl my junior year of college (some drunk asshole whacked me with a beer stein). I was twenty-six but could play older. In the student films, I was cast as stooges, stoolies, henchmen, yokels. One time I played a sexually repressed used car salesman, and damn if I didn't *inhabit* that role.

This is not to say I could have made a living as a character actor, had the chips fallen differently—even with the Julia Robertses and Kevin Costners of the world factored in, actors made on the average about six hundred dollars a year in 1991—but I certainly showed promise. Plus I had connections. Tenuous connections, but connections. That spring, for example, I participated in a read-through of an early draft of *Clerks*—I played Dante Hicks, the lead role—and I got along swimmingly with Kevin Smith. Unfortunately, it took three years for him to secure financing; by the time he was ready to shoot, my acting career was effectively kaput. And it's not like Brian O'Halloran, my replacement, has had much of a career. Would I have succeeded where Brian failed?

Probably not.

In *Us Magazine's 1991 Entertainment Yearbook*, eight rising stars, virtual unknowns in 1990, were cited as being Ones to Watch. They were, in order: Brad Pitt, John Corbett, C&C Music Factory, John Singleton, Julie Warner, Andrew Strong, Trisha Yearwood, and Chris Rock. If some of *them* couldn't even hold serve, with fortune smiling upon them—Andrew Strong never made another movie after *The Commitments*—how far would I have gone, with my crooked nose and reckless hair? Still, I can't help but believe

that there is an alternate reality in which I *am* a successful character actor; someone limited, someone with a bag of tricks, but someone whose face you recognize—"Oh, *him*! He's been in a *million*
things!"—if not his name. Would that I could click my heels and
change places with the Todd Lander in *that* reality, my starfucking
doppelgänger!

I almost forgot about the screenplay I was writing at the time—I
used to work in the back room at Yaffa Café on St. Mark's, with its
rococo-bordello décor—whose working title was *The Rat*. The plot
revolved around a bank robbery gone bad, told from the point of
view of the bank robbers, one of whom had turned snitch. Blood,
guns, testosterone, and a messy Shakespearean ending where everybody dies these hideous, violent deaths. By no means was *The
Rat* a world-changer, but it was a tight little story, and would have
been a fun little movie. Eric Roberts would have been a perfect lead
bank robber. Could it have been made? Well, independent film was
about to go supernova. And I knew people who knew people who
were producers. If *Clerks* could fly, with its continuity errors and
blow-job jokes, why not *The Rat*?

Okay, enough about me. No one gives a rolling doughnut about
my doomed acting career, even Kevin Smith himself, and really, no
one should. All I'm saying is, Taylor Schmidt was not my raison
d'être. Not now, and certainly not then. She was just my roommate, my newest friend, and a chick I was working. That's all.

It was on her first day of work that I discovered Taylor's diary.

On the way home from my own job—I'd left after lunch for a
dental appointment—I picked up our laundry at the East Village
Launderette (we sent our clothes out together, in one big bag, like
a married couple; I paid, natch, but it was worth every penny to
have my tattered polka-dot boxer shorts pressed up against her silk
panties). I'd just unpacked the bag, and was transferring her items
to her futon—I'd put everything away for her until she confessed
to being "creeped out" by me accessing her underwear drawer; as

if I were sniffing her panties or something—when I noticed the notebook peeking out from under her pillow.

There was nothing inherently special about it; your basic black-marble-covered composition book, wide-ruled, with a series of light blue horizontal lines and one dark pink one running perpendicular down the left margin. But I knew at once it was a diary.

I realized it was wrong to snoop, but I was *curious*, maddeningly so, and it's not like she didn't trust me—I was handling her undergarments, wasn't I? Plus, my spying had a specific purpose. What I wanted to know was what Taylor thought of Yours Truly. Did she have any sexual feelings at all for Todd Lander? Was she intrigued by my heroic restraint? Was my plan working? I had to know. My ego demanded it.

I opened that composition book without hesitation.

The first thing I noticed was her handwriting, all flowery and dainty, in flourish-filled cursive, with the occasional heart dotting the *i*. A child's hand, a little girl's. And what grown-up person uses pink ink? My second observation was that this was a relatively new journal—which meant that, in all likelihood, more black-marbled composition books were stowed somewhere in her room. No way she'd left them in Missouri with Darla and her hick half sisters.

To my disappointment, I found precious little. I was only mentioned a few times, and then in passing: "Todd and I went to Phoebe's," "Todd lent me $20," "Todd and I drank two bottles of wine," that kind of thing. Just the facts, the straight dope. Nothing nay, but nothing yea either. Nothing subjective at all.

Maybe that was Taylor's style. Maybe she just wrote what happened, and nothing more. Maybe. . .

But no. Because she managed to fill *three fucking pages* on Asher Krug: how he was such a bohunk, how he helped her out of such a precarious situation, how she wanted his body (those were her exact words: "I want his body"). So much paper, so much pink ink, for a guy Taylor didn't know existed forty-eight hours ago. He got three pages, and I got "Todd lent me $20." Who said life was fair?

The Asher lovefest was followed by her musings on the Quid Pro Quo operation. Boring stuff, of no interest to me at the time. I skipped that part and jumped to the next mention of my name:

> *Been seventeen days since last X. What to do, what to do. Must take action. Will go gaga soon. Might have to resort to Todd—my in-case-of-emergency-break-glass guy, ha ha ha.*

Ouch!

Most guys would read that and figure all hope was lost. What she was saying, after all, was that she'd only fuck me as a last resort, if every other man on the face of the earth spontaneously combusted at the stroke of midnight. But I'm a glass-half-full type of guy, or I was in September of 1991. What I took from this was that she would *consider* sleeping with me—that the notion, however unpalatable, had crossed her mind. And this was good news. This was Gospel. Because one day, or so my logic went, there *would* be an emergency, and one day she *would* break the glass. (And, as it happened, I was right.)

I found the rest of her journals in a box in her closet, under a pile of clothes, shoes, and old magazines. There were nineteen of them. I took them out of the box, and buried it back under the junk. She'd never miss them. Then I locked myself in my room and spent the rest of the afternoon reading.

Taylor's earliest childhood memory was of her mother screaming. She was two at the time—maybe even younger; she might not have been walking yet—but she remembered her mother screaming, and her father flying into a rage, brutal fists silencing the screams. A bottle of generic whiskey falling off the kitchen table, shattering on the linoleum floor. Cigarette butts everywhere. Her mother's eye black and blue, swollen shut. Why were they fighting? Was *she* the source of their discontent? Yes, to the best of her recollection;

from that moment on, in any event, Taylor was aware that the circumstances of her birth were accidental. She was an unwanted child, abortion was not yet an option, and Darla wasn't giving up her baby regardless. She'd use the baby, like she used everything else at her disposal, to ensnare her man.

The plan worked. Tommy Schmidt stuck around, for a few years at least. He was in and out of the clink—petty crimes, drunk-and-disorderlies, bar fights—but he stuck around. He had tattoos, and this was back when only sailors and truckers had tattoos. He smoked Luckies, no filter, and his teeth were the color of deli mustard. He routinely spanked Taylor, and worse, for a variety of infractions. He died when she was nine—single-car accident, enough alcohol in his system to KO Mickey Mantle—and no one exactly mourned his passing. He haunted her dreams ever afterwards, this brick shithouse of a man, fists flailing, chasing her down darkling streets in some Warrensburg from Hell. . .

When Taylor was ten, her mother was hit by a Greyhound bus. She broke her hip, was in traction for months. That bus was the best thing that ever happened to Darla Jenkins. The state disability checks liberated her from a lifetime of minimum-wage jobs. It freed her from the shackles of work. Now she could buzz around the local bars, offering her wares to whatever men were sufficiently drunk and/or desperate. Eventually she fell in love with a forty-five-year-old lush who went by Popeye. Everyone called him that; Taylor didn't even know his real name. Popeye moved into their prefab house, fathered Taylor's two half sisters, collected unemployment, carved his initials into the kitchen table, shot his pistol at possum. It was a happy, healthy household.

By then, Taylor was thirteen. She'd been an ungainly child, but now, as if by magic, some gift of the gods, awestriking hotness was bestowed upon her. Suddenly all the boys wanted her number, wanted to skate her round the roller rink. Suddenly all the girls didn't like her anymore. Not that they liked her much to begin with; of all the white trash at her school, she was the trashiest, and no one let her forget it. Her sixth grade teacher, the wonderfully named Mrs. Mount, made a point of lecturing her on personal hygiene. "You have to shower, Taylor . . . every day, okay?" When she left the classroom, Taylor overheard Mrs. Mount telling one of the other teachers, "Not much hope for that one. The acorn doesn't fall far from the tree."

Was this the moment when she vowed not to wind up like her mother, to renounce her white trash roots, to succeed where everyone expected her to fail? Only in the movies is motivation so contrived, but Mrs. Mount's aside certainly added fuel to the proverbial fire.

One afternoon, Darla took the two girls out for ice cream, leaving Taylor alone with Popeye (you can already see where this is heading, I'm sure, and it ain't pretty). Popeye had a greasy NASCAR moustache and a limp. A real looker. This grown man named for a children's cartoon accosted our young heroine in the kitchen.

"You've bloomed into quite the young lady," he said, his mouth full of Skoal.

"Thanks."

"Pretty soon the boys will be lining up to have a crack at you."

Taylor didn't say anything—they were already lining up, not that it was any of his business—just kept doing the dishes.

"Maybe they already have. Have they?" He came right up behind her. "You still a virgin, Taylor?"

She knew this was inappropriate, but Popeye was the only father figure she had, and she wanted to please him. "Yes," she said.

"That's good. That's a good girl. These boys, they're no good. They're no good for you." His fingers found her bare shoulders, caressed them gently, as gently as Popeye knew how. "What you need is a man, a good man, to show you the ropes."

One of the dishes slipped out of Taylor's soapy hand, landed with a thwack on the bottom of the sink, but did not shatter.

"When you're ready to have sex, Taylor, you come to Popeye. You hear?"

With his hips he pinned her against the sink, and Taylor felt the stirring against her tush. Her rude introduction to the male anatomy in its excited state.

"You hear?"

"Yeah, I hear."

"That's my girl."

After spitting tobacco juice on the floor, he kissed her on the nape of her neck, a wet, saurian kiss that at once creeped her out and turned her on. Indeed, as he withdrew, she was plagued by these conflicting emotions. Popeye was gross, and way too old, and her mother's live-in boyfriend, but he was also a man, and attracted to her, and had made her feel special. None of the boys at school were like him.

She did not, thank the gods, take Popeye up on his chivalrous offer, and one day, not long after, he vanished. Really vanished. The police were called, missing persons reports filed, the whole nine yards. The guy was history, a poof. They never did find him. You might think Taylor'd be relieved when this happened, but no—she was broken up. That was the start of her battle with depression. The Popeye Era had, if nothing else, afforded some modicum of stability to the household. Now it was back to chaos . . . until Billy Ray rode in with his unemployment check to save the day.

While the seminal male figures of Tommy Schmidt and Popeye are worth noting, most of Taylor's early journals, the ones from before her sexual awakening, dealt almost exclusively with her selfish and abusive mother, who was constantly exposing her to unsafe situations—evictions from lousy apartments, sketchy tenants subletting spare rooms, secondhand cigarette smoke, lack of supervision and attention. The ink poor Taylor expended on that heinous witch! The tears shed!

But her mother did teach Taylor something, though more as a case study or an object lesson than a role model. *I don't want to grow up like my mother* was a favorite refrain. Make no mistake, the fecund seeds of her ambition were irrigated by Darla Jenkins.

I mention Taylor's childhood here because it is essential to understanding her alacrity in accepting her fate. At the time, however,

I didn't give a hoot about Taylor's unhappy upbringing. I was after the good stuff, the Skinemax stuff. And boy, did I hit the mother lode.

After the loss of her virginity—at the age of fifteen, to a sophomore Deadhead named Matt Harris—Taylor wrote voluminously about sex. Her tone was journalistic, almost clinical. She described every last detail about what happened, but without passion, like she was observing rather than participating in the activities. She must have been, when she worked at the school paper, a dynamite reporter.

As for the activities, they were mostly drunken rolls in the hay—nothing to write home about, as the saying goes. But there were exceptions. And when there were exceptions, the exceptions were exceptional. I'll relate one story, although there were plenty— such as the time she gave a hand job to a flabbergasted freshman in the men's room of a dive bar for a dollar—that were of the same variety:

Her junior year of college, when Kim Winter was studying in Prague, Taylor shared an off-campus apartment with a clueless coed named Jody, who was dating this Army ROTC guy, Brad. Jody and Brad were pretty serious; at twenty years old they were already engaged.

One night, Brad and his friend Scott, another lughead, came to call on his girlfriend. Jody was at the library studying for her ethics final, but Taylor, who was halfway through *Othello* and therefore bored, let them in anyway. The three of them polished off a bottle of Southern Comfort, and then Brad started getting friendly. Rather than reject his prurient advances, she instead offered herself to both. "I've never had two guys at the same time before."

The ROTC guys had no qualms about sharing. They were used to showering and defecating in each other's presence, because that's what ROTC guys do, and had been through enough homoerotic ritual hazing not to mind seeing each other's bony peckers. Once decided, the threesome set about realizing the full potential of a ménage à trois. At one point Taylor was fucking Brad and sucking Scott simultaneously, like a porn star, while the two lugheads slapped hands like they'd scored the winning touchdown at the Rose Bowl.

Brad, her roommate's fiancé.

I don't, unfortunately, have access to Taylor's diaries any longer—they are as lost to me as Michael Jackson's original nose— or I would transcribe a snippet, just to convey the blasé tone. The nonchalant play-by-play of this dalliance was devoid of color commentary. Taylor described the proceedings as if it were a late-September doubleheader between two cellar-dwelling ball clubs, or a way to make brownies. If she felt guilty, she did not say so. If she felt the weight of the betrayal, there was no mention of it. It may well have been that she wasn't even aware that what she was doing was, at best, sleazy.

Wherefore this nostalgie de la boue? Clearly *something*, something more powerful than her own force of will, lured her into the muck, time and again. Was she looking for love? Attention? Was she legitimately turned on? Or could it be that Taylor, after a childhood spent flailing around like a willow tree in a hurricane, at the mercy of the elements, was grasping for power in the only way she knew how?

CHAPTER 7

To celebrate her first day of work, I took Taylor to dinner at Dojo, a hole-in-the-wall Japanese place on St. Mark's, where a halfway decent meal cost about as much as two subway tokens. I would have rather taken her someplace where you didn't need a key to open the bathroom door—and where the key in question was not chained to a sawed-off plunger handle—but my credit card was maxed out. Plus, Taylor dug the carrot dressing.

The tables out front, clustered on the sidewalk beneath the green and black awning, were all taken, so we sat in the main dining room, which had all the aesthetic splendor of a soup kitchen. Over plates of salmon and brown rice (me) and soy burger and salad (her), we discussed her new job—she was already given a book to edit, a historical thriller by a first-time author named Roger Gale—my current job, and the topic du jour: her crush and my archenemy, Asher Krug.

"I think maybe he likes me."

I would have rather heard my own diagnosis of syphilis than Taylor's diagnosis of Asher's affections. But arguing would've only made me look pathetic. Check that—*more* pathetic. I had no choice but to stick to my passive-aggressive plan, and that meant playing along.

"Well of *course* he likes you, dummy. What's not to like?"

"You're just saying that." She bit into her soy burger. "Hey look, it's Oxana."

Out on the street, an old Ukrainian lady was walking a three-legged dog. Her stout body was layered with sweaters and coats and scarves. A red babushka adorned her substantial head. She was a throwback to another era, a proud remnant of what was here before the hipster invasion, when what Realtors fairly recently dubbed the East Village was just the Ukrainian section of the Lower East Side. The two of them, the old lady and her dog—a Toto-like creature, but with matted hair and a missing hind leg—were a neighborhood fixture, as integral to the East Village as the Holiday Cocktail Lounge and Tower Records. Her real name wasn't Oxana; we called her that as a joke—there was something ox-like about her gait.

"She's got the red babushka going today," I said.

"Second day in a row."

"Maybe she has more than one."

"Nah. How old you think that dog is?"

"Old," I said. "Maybe it was Peter Stuyvesant's dog. He was missing a leg, too." I picked a fish bone out of my mouth, a hazard of the Dojo salmon-dinner special. "But back to the matter at hand. Here's what you do about Asher. You ask him out."

"I don't know," said Taylor, after a long sigh. She was still watching Oxana through the plate-glass window. "I'm, like, old-fashioned when it comes to that kind of stuff. I like when the guy makes the first move."

"Don't tell me you've never initiated anything with a guy before."

"Usually they tip their hand, and I just kind of, like, go with the flow."

"That makes sense," I stammered, although it didn't. This revelation did not bode well for my passive-aggressive seduction plan, but never mind. "I'd like to think we've moved beyond that, as a society. Traditional gender roles, I mean. I'd like to think it's okay for a woman to make the first move."

"It's okay," she said, "but it's not my style."

"It's not your style. I concede the point. But how the hell is he supposed to make a move when he never sees you?"

"Oh, shit," she said. A large dollop of carrot dressing had dropped on her pink sweater. While she dabbed her napkin in her glass of water and cleaned it up, I drank in the view of her chest. "I'll see him in two weeks. At my follow-up."

"Two weeks? That's an eternity. You'll *totally* kill the momentum. And if he's everything you say, he might be off the market in two weeks."

"There is that, yes. Holy shit." She pointed to a baseboard on the wall behind me. "I just saw a mouse run into the kitchen."

Rodents were part of the ambience. She hadn't lived in New York long enough to appreciate that. "Mice gotta eat, too. If I could take you to Le Cirque, believe me, I would." Outside, Oxana had moved on. In her place were four punkers with spiked mohawks and torn outfits, smoking. "Men like to be pursued. *People* like to be pursued. It makes them feel wanted. As long as you don't go overboard, I don't think you'll turn him off."

"So I should pursue him, but at the same time play hard-to-get?"

"Well put."

"And how do you propose I do that?"

I felt like Jesus being forced to make his own cross. But I had to answer. My only hope now was that she'd tire of Asher and return to me.

"That's the easy part," I said. "He helped you find a job, right? He deserves a formal acknowledgment of his efforts on your behalf.

It's the Emily Post move. So what you do is, you tell him that you'd like to thank him by taking him to lunch."

"You think that'll work?"

"Look, you got the vibe from him, right? That means he wants to see you again, so he'll accept the invitation. And if he doesn't, hey, it's just lunch. People take people to lunch all the time, and most of the time, there's no romantic pretense. He won't really know if you're asking because you're interested or because you're just being polite. So even if he turns you down, you save face." I poured the remains of my brown rice into the bowl of soy sauce and stirred them together. "But I don't think he'll turn you down."

"I don't know, Todd."

If I pressured her to pursue him, I risked losing her forever, if Asher Krug was even half as wonderful as her diary suggested. But if Taylor didn't take action, she'd just daydream about him—and the Dream Asher *would* be perfect.

"Trust me. I do." I took a bite of soy-sauce-sodden rice. "And if you're worrying about hurt pride or something, forget it. No one knows about Asher Krug except you and me."

Taylor considered this a moment. "Okay. Lunch it is."

That raised another problem: *how* to ask. Calling him on the telephone seemed too forward. Plus there was no way she could handle a verbal rejection. She might contrive to bump into him "accidentally" on the street, like in *Hannah and Her Sisters*, but how could she accomplish that? She didn't even know where he lived. What was she supposed to do, hang around the Quid Pro Quo lobby at all hours?

The best course of action, of course, would be to send him an e-mail—more casual than a letter, less intrusive than a phone call. Unfortunately for Taylor, this was 1991; years away from ubiquity, e-mail was the exclusive province of professors at technological universities, government operatives, and Rush fans.

The only other recourse, we decided over coffee, was to write a thank-you note. It was good etiquette anyway—Asher *did* help her land a job—and he'd get it the next day. The New York postal service was, and remains, a paragon of reliability.

So that's what Taylor did. She spent her entire lunch hour the next day in a Hallmark store, agonizing over which card to buy, and finally decided, reluctantly, on a blank one with the Doisneau kiss on the front. When she returned to her office, she sat at the whirring computer and set about writing her note:

> Hi, Asher,
> I'd like to thank you again for helping me land such a swell job. And I'd like to thank you in person, by taking you to lunch. If you're free in the next week or two, please give me a call.
>
> > Talk to you soon,
> > Taylor

It took just two hours to compose. Drafting three sentences should not be such a laborious activity, but laborious it was—it felt as though each word had been pushed through the birth canal. Should it be *Dear Asher* or the more congenial *Hi, Asher*? Should she allow him to pointedly reject her (*Would you like to have lunch?*), or deny him that chance (*Are you free this week?*)? And which hackneyed sign-off to employ? *Sincerely? Regards? Till then? Yours? Yours* was the most intimate, and therefore to be avoided.

At the exact moment she finally got it right, Angela appeared at her door and went into a lengthy lecture about Roger Gale, the author whose manuscript she was slated to edit. Taylor had to hit ALT-TAB fast, filling her screen with a rejection letter in WordPerfect. When she was left alone, she transposed the copy from computer screen to blank card, addressed it, stamped it, and brought it to the post office, so he'd get it as quickly as possible.

Approximately twenty-four hours later, Asher phoned her at work.

"Thanks so much for the note," he said. "It's a generous offer, but I'm afraid I have to decline. I have a strict policy never to lunch with clients."

"I see." Stomach acid began to eat away her insides. This was Worst Case Scenario. Why had she listened to her idiot roommate? Why hadn't she followed her gut instinct?

"What I'd like to do instead," he went on, "is take *you* to *dinner*. Are you by any chance free on Saturday?"

There was an experimental play at P.S. 122 that Saturday, written by a chick I knew from acting class, that we had planned to attend. Two naked lesbians shining flashlights on their pudenda and chanting the c-word at the top of their lungs, all to protest of Hollywood's exploitation of women. Or was it women's exploitation of Hollywood? No matter. Performance art was no match for Asher Krug.

"I'd love to."

CHAPTER 8

Our apartment opened on a narrow hallway, the walls pockmarked and badly spackled, the paint an unappealing canary yellow. On your left as you walked down the hall was the door to what used to be Laura's home office but was now Taylor's room. Past that door was a row of cheap appliances the real estate broker ridiculously called a European-style kitchen. The hallway terminated in the cramped living room, with just enough space for a table, two chairs, a torn red vinyl sofa, a footlocker with a tablecloth on top, and the TV. Above the sofa was my Jim Morrison poster—the one where he's wearing the necklace and you can see his nips. On your left was the bathroom, all rust-colored tub water and leaky fixtures; straight ahead, my room.

Taylor's lone window overlooked the brick wall of the adjacent apartment building. As long as there was no traffic in the stairwell—never a given, even late at night—her room was quieter than mine. My two windows looked down on always-raucous East Ninth Street. Veselka, the twenty-four-hour Ukrainian eatery and Village landmark, was half a block away. My dreams were haunted by the sounds of screeching tires, beeping horns, shrieking car alarms, and the serenading of sentimental drunks.

On the flip side, I had access to the fire escape, which I was pleased to call "the terrace." On balmy nights I sat out there, reading *Spy* magazine, nursing a Rolling Rock, watching the crazies pass by. It was from this cozy perch that I caught my first glimpse of Asher Krug. He pulled up a few minutes before eight in a '92 Jaguar XJ12 convertible—cream with tan leather interior—top down, music pouring from his state-of-the-art sound system. Passersby stopped to check him out as he parked in front of the fire hydrant out front and strode up our stoop. A guy like that *had* to be famous, right?

"Bye, Todd," Taylor called from the hallway. "Wish me luck!"

"Have fun," I told her, as if not having fun on a date with this guy was in the realm of the possible.

I watched Asher lead her to the car, his left hand on the small of her back. He was a *GQ* insert: blue linen suit, formfitting V-neck dress-tee, loafers, no socks. She had on a cotton dress with a floral print, which clung to the contours of her body the way that XJ12 clung to the contours of the road, and cork-soled sandals. The two of them together, in his spiffy car, embodied the yin and yang of manliness and muliebrity.

Once the Jaguar powered round the corner and the awestruck crowd dispersed, I left the terrace, thoroughly depressed, and helped myself to more old diaries.

"That's your car? Whoa."

"Yeah, that's us. Not the most practical thing, I guess, but sometimes you've got to indulge a little, right?"

Asher led Taylor around to the passenger side, opened the door,

and helped her into the car. This was the sort of gesture the lesbians at P.S. 122 were protesting (or so my actress friend claimed; I
never did make it to the show), but "old-fashioned" Taylor found
it charming.

She slid into the leather bucket seat and inhaled the intoxicating
fragrance that is New Car Smell. She watched her date get in, fire
up the ignition, and hit the gas pedal a few times, for show. The
sound system kicked in—I was still buying cassettes, but Asher
had a six-CD changer in the trunk—to a song already in progress,
a song Taylor knew well.

' "The Reflex!' I haven't heard this in years!"

"You approve?"

This was a loaded question. Although it's now clear that 1991
was the beginning of a new and distinct decade, at the time it seemed
like the death throes of its lamentable predecessor. And the eighties, as conventional wisdom had it, sucked. Everything about the
decade sucked—the music, the clothes, Ronald Reagan, cocaine,
AIDS, Donald Trump. Not enough time had passed for us to evalu-
ate the era objectively. We were still years away from the eighties
retro movement: the VH1 *I Love the Eighties* specials; *The Surreal
Life*, with its washed-up eighties celebrities; comebacks by eighties
icons like Cyndi Lauper, Boy George, Rob Lowe, Matt Dillon, and
Robert Downey, Jr.; the renascence of the Lacoste alligator and the
word *awesome*. To admit that she liked *Duran Duran* of all things,
in the summer of '91, would be the quintessence of uncool.

Taylor hedged: "Is this on the radio?"

"No, it's the CD. *Decade*, the greatest hits album. It has the
radio edit of 'Save a Prayer,' which is disappointing, but the single
versions of this and 'View to a Kill,' so it's a must-have."

Once she learned that Asher owned the CD, Taylor decided to
fess up. "I used to be *obsessed* with Duran Duran," she said (I later
confirmed this, in one of her oldest diaries). "I used to clip their
pictures out of the teenybopper magazines and tape them all over
my wall. My mom would get all pissed because I totally ruined the
paint. When Simon got married, I didn't eat for three days."

The thought of a teenaged Taylor, Aqua Net in her hair and Madonna bracelets on her wrists, ululating over a tearstained issue of *Tiger Beat* made Asher chuckle. "They're one of my all-time favorites," he said, "cheesy as that may sound. Listen to the bass, man. That guy can play."

Indeed he could. And still can.

"So you're a fan of the Duran," he said. "What's your favorite song?"

"I don't know. 'Save a Prayer' is up there. 'The Seventh Stranger' is totally rad. But my favorite? Probably 'The Chauffeur'. You know that one? On *Rio*?"

"Of course. Great song. The keyboard is hauntingly beautiful."

"What's yours?"

"This."

He pushed a button on the console, and a woman giggling, an electric guitar, and then Simon LeBon's voice came through the eight speakers.

Dark in the city, night is a wire. . .

" 'Hungry Like the Wolf.' I might have known."

Asher Krug flashed a decidedly wolfish smile. "I wasn't too forward, was I? Asking you to dinner? I've never gone out with one of our clients before, and . . ."

Woman you want me, give me a sign. . .

"No, no. Not at all."

"Good. I was concerned." But he didn't appear concerned. He appeared the epitome of chill, with his perfect teeth and luminous hair, manicured fingers drumming on the stained-wood steering wheel. "I've been asked to lunch before, but lunch, it can mean a lot of different things. Especially a thank-you lunch. Some of my clients, they come up with creative ways to express their gratitude. I've had people send me all kinds of things. One guy—Japanese cat named Takeshi—actually sent a call girl to the office."

"Really?"

"I kid you not."

"What did you do?"

"Well, it was awkward, being at work and everything, but what could I do, look a gift horse in the mouth?"

"You didn't."

"I did. It would have been rude to refuse."

Taylor didn't know quite how to respond until he smiled and winked, and then she laughed and so did he.

"One of the drawbacks of my line of work is that you achieve success vicariously. You meet these great people, you get to know them, you help them, and then, if you're good at your job—and I'm good at my job—you never see them again. And I wanted to see you again. I really wanted to see you again."

I'm on the hunt, I'm after you.

"I deliberated," she said. "But then I figured, what the hell. Worse thing was you'd turn me down, right?"

"Has anyone ever turned you down?"

Asher sounded like he wasn't expecting an answer, so she gave him one: "Plenty of times. Plenty of times."

"I bet."

They had gone a block south on Second Avenue, banged a left on St. Marks and another on First, and were heading uptown. At Fourteenth Street they stopped at the light. Taylor saw Oxana at the L-train stop, again in her red babushka, and layers of clothes despite the heat, walking her three-legged mutt. She waved, but the old lady was busy inspecting bodega apples and didn't see her.

The light changed, and Asher hit the gas. Fourteenth Street was the frontier, the outer edge of the East Village. Beyond was a marshland of hospitals and power plants and medical buildings, where there were fewer pedestrians and it was easier to catch a cab. Then the Jaguar passed the creepy ivy-lined brick walls of Bellevue, which looked exactly like the insane asylum it was. In the distance, the gleaming blue glass of the United Nations building winked at them. Diplomats lived around the UN, in ritzy neighborhoods like Turtle Bay and Beekman Place—enclaves of wealth that Taylor had never heard of. In fact, this was the first time she had driven up First Avenue. She rarely took cabs, and no one in New York has a car—not in my circle, anyway.

"Where are we going?"

"Chez Molineaux. The steak house. Near Rock Center."

"Steak house?"

"Yeah. Why, are you a vegetarian or something?"

"I don't usually eat meat."

"Really?" He seemed stunned than anyone would forego such sybaritic pleasure. "We can go someplace else, if you like. It's tricky without a reservation, but I know a great Japanese place across town."

"No, no, it's fine."

"You'll love it," he said, over the stereo blare—now it was "Union of the Snake" playing. "I promise."

Chez Molineaux was on West Fifty-second Street, and distinguishable from the rest of the high-towered block by a black awning, a red carpet, and potted plants flanking the door. Asher pulled the Jag right up front, alit, and tossed the keys to a muscle-bound dreadlocked guy.

"Keep it close, Kareem."

"Yes sir, Mr. Krug."

Before Taylor could open the door herself, Asher did it for her. He helped her out, offered his arm, which she took, and led her into the restaurant. The inside was old New Orleans splendor: damask wallpaper, oil paintings, candlelight, and more silverware on the starched white tablecloth than she knew what to do with.

The hostess, a dim-looking woman with eyes too close together, greeted Asher by name as they walked in. They followed her into the labyrinth of the dining room and to a table tucked away in the dimly lit corner. Ever the gentleman, Asher held her chair, pushing it in as she sat down. Then he took his own seat, the one facing the restaurant proper.

"Is this where you take all your dates?"

"I eat here a lot," he said, "but with clients. I haven't been on a date in a long time, to tell you the truth." His voice got faraway. "A long time."

She doubted this, but decided not to press. "It's pretty swanky, Asher. And certainly an improvement over Burger Heaven. That's where I would have taken you for lunch."

"But you don't eat meat. Isn't Burger Heaven vegetarian hell?"

Taylor grinned at his joke. "Their veggie burgers totally rock, in fact."

"Truly," he said. "I love that place."

She doubted that, too. Not that Burger Heaven was a dump or anything, but she simply couldn't imagine the dashing Asher Krug being rushed in and out of the upstairs dining room, with its giant clock on the far wall.

"I always order the same thing," he said, "so you should look over the menu."

"I'll have whatever you have."

"You sure?"

"I trust you."

The waitress appeared, a busty brunette with a Southern accent. More likely an aspiring actress from White Plains getting set to workshop *Streetcar* than a bona fide Biloxi belle. Whoever she was, she deposited a basket of bread on the table.

"Can I get y'all something to drink?"

"We'd like the La Dominique, '82."

"That *what*?"

Coolly Asher indicated his choice on the wine list.

"Oh. Let me fetch the sommelier, honey. Be right back."

Taylor had never heard of a sommelier (and neither had I; her diary was my first encounter with the term), but deduced soon enough that this was the gentleman in charge of the restaurant's extensive wine cellar. He was lithe and dancerly, with a moustache and a monocle, and she could tell from clear across the room that he was gay.

"Mr. Krug," he said as he drew near. "I might have known."

"Hello, Marcel. This is Taylor Schmidt."

Marcel bowed gallantly. "My dear."

Asher repeated his request.

"Excellent choice. Coming right up, sir."

Marcel pirouetted about, vanished.

"Are you, like, a connoisseur?"

"Hardly. All I know is, if it isn't French, it's turpentine."

In a flash, Marcel returned. With a somber bow, he presented the bottle of wine with the pomp and circumstance usually reserved for visiting heads of state. With one deft movement he removed the cork and gave it to Asher to sniff. Then he splashed a finger of the stuff into a glass he'd brought just for that purpose.

Asher slid it across the table. "Taste."

Taylor took a careful sip, swished it around her mouth like it was Listerine, and swallowed. However much it cost, La Dominique '82, to her untutored lips, tasted like grape juice. Good grape juice, but still. She shrugged.

Asher took the glass, swished the wine around, and held it up to the candle on the table—examining the legs, I believe this is called. He took a small sip, then a larger one, and made a face like he just got wind of a particularly unaromatic fart.

"Something wrong?" the sommelier wanted to know.

"It's turned," Asher told him. "How long has that been down there?"

"Let me see." Marcel took a sip from what appeared to be an oversized coke spoon hanging around his neck. "You're right, Mr. Krug. My sincerest apologies."

"Don't mention it, Marcel. Just bring the Pauillac '84."

"I'm sorry about that," said Asher once the sommelier had left. "I don't like sending back wine, but for what they charge for the stuff, we'd better enjoy it." He picked up a piece of bread, buttered it. "I love your hair."

"Oh," said Taylor, flipping a stray strand behind her ear. "Thanks."

"You look amazing."

Taylor was used to such blandishments, but it was still nice to hear, especially from Asher.

Marcel returned, abashed that one of his prized bottles had gone sour, and lavished them with the new choice. This time Asher approved, and after filling the glasses, the sommelier flounced off.

"To life," said Asher. "May we live it to the fullest."

"Amen to that."

They clinked glasses and drank.

"Holy shit," she said, surprised. "Wow. This wine is delicious. I'm not a big fan of red, usually, but this . . . oh my. Asher, you've ruined me."

He said nothing, just smiled that debonair smile and squinted his predatory eyes ever so slightly, like James Bond when introducing himself to the villain's voluptuous and invariably fickle girlfriend.

The waitress returned. Asher ordered for both of them—strip steak, rare, with garlic mashed potatoes, and to start, portobello mushrooms.

"So this guy you're living with . . . Tom."

"Todd."

"Are you two . . . you know . . . ?"

"Who, Todd? Oh, no. He's a sweet guy, but more of the brotherly type. Although I've only known him for a few months. Friend of a friend."

"I see."

He shot her a look that she construed as disapproving.

"Does it bother you, that I live with a guy?"

"Bother is a strong word. It's just *unusual*, that's all. I'm traditional, when it comes to cohabitation."

Taylor knew going in that there must be some flaw with Asher Krug. Gentlemen of his apparent quality were simply not single unless they were damaged goods—not in New York, anyway. Could he be—gasp—a virgin? Her heart sank. "Traditional as in waiting for marriage?"

"Not that traditional."

Taylor tried not to make her exhalation too obvious. "So you live alone?"

"I have a place at the Dakota."

The snazzy address meant nothing to the Missourian.

"It's on Central Park West," he explained, visibly annoyed that she was not sufficiently wowed. "Did you see *Rosemary's Baby*? You know, that baby boomer dreck about how babies of our generation are the devil's spawn? They filmed it there. That's why I chose the Dakota, actually. I get pleasure out of knowing that I live in an apartment some baby boom asshole covets."

A little light went off in the recesses of Taylor's brain. "Wait . . . wasn't the Dakota where John Lennon lived?"

"Yoko still does. I see her and Sean in the elevator sometimes. She's nice as can be. Hell of an artist. Unfortunately her husband and his nasty heroin habit sort of curtailed her career. She was avantgarde, a rare talent. Why she fell for that guy I have no idea."

Before Taylor could reply, the appetizers arrived.

Asher was about to change the subject, but Taylor, intrigued, cut him off. "Wait a minute. Did you just say that Yoko Ono was good and John Lennon was bad?"

"No. I said she was a true artist, and he was a fraud."

"That puts you in a very small minority." Taylor took a bite of the portabellos. "Just you and Yoko, I think."

"I hate the fucking Beatles."

"The Beatles? How can you hate the Beatles?"

"Talentless hacks, the lot of them." Asher plopped a piece of mushroom into his mouth, chewed, and swallowed, as she hung on his every word. "It's the baby boomers, turned them into gods. The apotheosis of John, Paul, George, and Ringo. *They* bought all their albums, *they* packed all the stadiums, *they* were the target audience—and they still are. Them—not us. Not you and me. Our music gets marginalized. Duran Duran, they suck. The Smiths, they suck. Guns N' Roses, they suck. But the Beatles, they shit ice cream. You like the portabellos?"

Taylor wasn't a big fan of mushrooms particularly, but she lied and said she did.

"Good." He wolfed down the rest of his as he spoke. "The Beatles embody everything I despise about the baby boomer generation. They went from ripping off Buddy Holly and Chuck Berry to recording these self-indulgent druggie anthems without producing a single song I actually enjoy listening to. And I'm so sick of hearing what a *poet* John Lennon was, what a wordsmith. 'There's nothing you can do that can't be done, there's nothing you can sing that can't be sung.' I'm no Harold Bloom, although I did take his class at Yale, but come *on*. That's not exactly *Paradise Lost*, is it? In a perfect world, Chapman would have killed John Lennon twenty years earlier and spared us all the national embarrassment that was Beatlemania."

The vitriol, the bile that Asher spewed forth, surprised her, even through the wine-induced haze. At Wycliffe, Taylor'd heard many a suitor's kill-'em-all polemic against any number of people—Bill Gates, the Ayatollah Khomeini, Michael Eisner, George Steinbrenner—but *John Lennon*? Asher must be joking. Lennon was in a stratum with Jesus, Gandhi, and Abe Lincoln. He was unassailable. Also, the Walrus was born in 1940, which is to say during the war, so technically he wasn't a baby boomer. But no matter.

"Forgive me," Asher said, wiping his chin with his napkin. "I didn't mean to sound so callous."

"Whatever, it's fine."

Suddenly, the nauseating aroma of charred beef overcame her; the main course had arrived. As the plates were set in front of them, Taylor fought valiantly against her gag reflex. The last time she'd had beef was in college, in the dining hall, when the shepherd's pie didn't mix with her hangover.

"Boy that looks good." Asher set upon his strip of beef with fork and knife, inspected the bleeding raw cow flesh at the center. "Blood red. Perfect."

Taylor eyed at her dish hopelessly. She watched Asher polish off a few bites.

"God, I love this place." A trickle of juice at the corner of his mouth gave Asher the look of a vampire, or perhaps a cannibal—he was a headhunter, after all. "Oh, you've *got* to try this."

The initial wave of nausea had worn off, but Taylor was afraid that, no matter how choice the cut of beef, it would make her ill. The last thing she wanted was to decorate the tan leather interior of his Jaguar XJ12 with chunks of meaty spew. But Asher was waiting. And buying. And she wanted to make him happy. With tremulous hand she forked a small piece into her mouth.

"Well?"

It was delicious. A little too rare, perhaps, but intensely flavorful. She told him so.

"Oh, good," he said, looking genuinely relieved. "I'd hate for you not to like it. I'll have to tell Roland next time I see him."

"Who's Roland?"

"The . . ."

The head chef and owner. And there he was, Roland Molineaux, in white apron and cap, looking, despite the French surname, every bit like Dom DeLuise's long-lost brother. He extended a plump hand, which Asher shook without standing up.

"How's everything tonight, Mr. Krug?"

"Excellent as usual. Roland, this is Taylor Schmidt."

"*Enchanté.*"

Drawing on all her powers of French 101, Taylor replied, "*Enchanté.*"

"Bon appétit." He gave Asher a hearty pat on the shoulder and waddled off.

"Nice guy, Roland. Makes a hell of a steak."

Taylor only managed to consume half her New York strip. Asher inhaled the rest, along with his own entrée and two helpings of the buttery garlic mashed, with the voracity of a half-starved Bowery bum. As he ate, his jaws clenched and unclenched in an almost animal way. Watching him chew, she understood why the teeth used for ripping into meat were called canines.

When the entrées were finished, they downshifted into small

talk—books, bands, movies. His cinematic favorites—*La Femme Nikita* and *The Ipcress File*—she'd never heard of. (Hers were *Pretty Woman* and *Steel Magnolias*, as I well knew—she owned them both on VHS and often forced me to watch them.)

While the busboy cleared the plates, Asher asked how her job was going.

"So far, so good. I have my first author, which is way cool. Roger Gale is his name. Lives up in New Paltz. I think you'll really like his book, actually."

"I'm always up for a good read. What's it about?"

Set in 1909 Russia, *The Lap of Uxory* is the story of Natasha, a sexually repressed housewife who contrives to murder her abusive and impotent husband. Boris, a disabled foot soldier in the czar's army, spends the first few chapters subjecting his vivacious young helpmate to drunken fits, verbal and physical abuse, and the be-heading of her beloved kitten, Koko. The drinking, cussing, and beating Natasha can endure. But when she finds Koko's severed head in the butter churn, swarming with flies, she vows revenge.

After several attempts at poisoning go awry, she seeks out one Madame Popova, a pioneer in the field of marriage counseling. For a modest fee, Popova & Co. will eliminate conjugal strife—by eliminating the husband. Natasha contracts with Popova & Co. to finish the deed. She purloins the purse of the passed-out Boris, forks over the rubles, and five pages later her hubby's body is found by a dashing young constable in a dark alley behind the second-largest brothel in Russia.

Once free from the bonds of matrimony, Natasha indulges her inchoate saturnalian desires, shacking up with, among others, the aforementioned constable, the local apothecary, and Zydrunas, her sister's husband. She also gets it on with Katya, the Popova & Co. assassin who whacked Boris. A malevolent minx peculiar to the novels of Sacher-Masoch and the screenplays of Joe Ezsterhas, Katya is a proponent of androcide. "All men deserve to be murdered—not just abusive husbands," she remarks to Natasha, between delirious sessions of *soixante-neuf.* "But we've got to begin somewhere."

Seduced by her lover's rhetoric (to say nothing of her shapely body), Natasha agrees to help Katya murder her next victim, who turns out to be—bet you didn't see this coming—her sister's husband, Zydrunas. Predictably, the plan to slit his throat while he is asleep backfires. Natasha trips over a broomstick, Zydrunas wakes up, and in the ensuing melee, Katya is knocked unconscious. It is up to the heroine to finish him off. Which Natasha does, driving a knife into the heart of her hapless brother-in-law.

This is followed by an introspective chapter in which Natasha is overcome with guilt, which she demonstrates by—wait for it—compulsively washing her hands. Afterwards she pays a visit to her friend the constable, to whom (after a fellatio sequence more superfluous than the one in *The Brown Bunny*) she confesses all. Popova & Co. is raided by police, Katya is hanged in the public square, and Natasha commits suicide by jumping in front of a locomotive, Anna Karenina–style. The constable, carrying her limp body off the tracks, gives a speech in the tradition of Fortinbras or Albany, and thus ends *The Lap of Uxory*.

(This tripe actually got published, believe it or not; it's long out of print, but you can still find it in used bookstores.)

Though overwritten and tragically flawed, the manuscript held Taylor's interest. The ending she wasn't crazy about. And the Natasha character proved as three-dimensional as a Mercator projection. But the whole business of Popova & Co., an organization devoted to the killing of husbands—that made for an intriguing hook.

"Industrious, don't you think, to start a business like that? Of course it's only fiction."

"Actually," Asher said, "Madame Popova was real. I'm sure the story *itself* is bullshit, but she really did run a husband-killing service. For almost thirty years, if memory serves. It was famous for its discretion and its low rates."

"No way."

"It's not *that* hard to believe, is it? Why *not* a husband-killing service, back before fingerprints and databases and video surveillance, when the life expectancy was so short? All she had to do was bribe the cops and the coroner—easy enough to do, with all those undersexed widows at her beck and call."

"You've really thought this through."

"I read about an article about it once." Asher tapped his temple. "Steel trap. You want coffee?"

Without waiting for a reply, he flagged down the waitress and ordered. Taylor drew a Parliament from her silver cigarette case and lit up. His eyes squinted, like he was taking aim. Judgment was about to be passed; she could feel it.

"How long have you been smoking?"

"Sophomore year of high school."

"Ever thought about quitting?"

"I don't want to quit."

"Those things'll kill you, you know."

"Yeah. It says so on the package. That's why I throw it away."

"There are better ways to be rebellious."

"I don't smoke to be rebellious. Maybe I did back in high school, but not anymore. I smoke to relax. I enjoy a nice cigarette after dinner."

He didn't say anything, just studied her with an intimidating intensity. Was her dirty little habit going to spoil her chances? Well, tough shit. Taylor wasn't going to quit smoking just because a guy asked her to—even if the guy was Asher Krug.

"I was thinking we'd have a nightcap," he said, letting the matter drop. "They have fantastic bartenders at the Rainbow Room. Real pros. Have you been?"

"To the Rainbow Room? Oh, sure. I go there all the time. Me and Todd, we like to cut a rug. No, of *course* not."

"We should go."

The Rainbow Room was—and is, although now under new and more corporate management—on the sixty-fifth floor of the GE building. It was, and is, something of a tourist trap, where real New Yorkers rarely deign to set foot, but unlike, say, the World Trade Center (I mourn its loss, like everyone else, but let's not kid ourselves: Windows on the World sucked), the Rainbow Room had much to recommend it. Because it was not the Twin Towers or the Empire State Building, you could *see* the Twin Towers and the Empire State Building from its vantage point. The orange juice in the screwdrivers was fresh-squeezed. Plus, it had cachet. Even Billy Ray and Darla had heard of the Rainbow Room.

It was three piddly blocks on foot, but Asher, oblivious to and unaffected by the recession that had crippled even some of the big spenders on Wall Street, and looking to show off, insisted on taking a cab. "Too hot," he told her. Taylor didn't argue.

Ever try to find a cab in the Theatre District on Saturday night? It's nigh impossible, for us mortals. But no sooner did that smooth sonuvabitch raised his arm then a taxi magically appeared.

Once nestled in the cool backseat, Asher put that same magical limb around her, and Taylor rested her hand on his thigh. Just as they were comfortable—she could have stayed in that cab all night, truth be told—there they were. He took her hand from his leg and, after overtipping the cabbie, led her into the dark and deserted lobby of the GE Building.

Once in the elevator he suddenly, and with an almost nervous urgency, kissed her. If Taylor was unprepared for this turn of events, it didn't show; she went from zero to sixty faster than the Millennium Falcon. Her left and right hands found the nape of his neck and the small of his back, respectively, and urged him closer. Asher tilted her head one way and his the other, sucked the whole of her lower lip into his mouth, and bit down hard. Before Taylor could retaliate, the doors opened, and they had to separate.

There was a long line out front, but Asher—if his truck with maîtres d' was supposed to impress her, it was working—said two words to the right person and the next thing she knew they were sitting at a cozy, candlelit table in the bar area. Taylor had been to the top of the Empire State Building once, when she first came to town—her mother insisted she send pictures—but the view from the Rainbow Room was far superior. But then, Asher Krug was better company than the herd of bewildered tourists on the observation deck. For one thing, he knew the names of all the buildings. Not that she cared about the skyline just then. All of her being was focused on him, and what she wanted to do with him as soon as possible.

Asher, meanwhile, was admiring a different view. His eyes were trained on her like twin gun barrels. Taylor found it difficult to stand his gaze, she wanted to continue the elevator hanky-panky so badly, so she feasted her eyes on his fingers instead. Ten strong digits resting on the table, interwoven with her own. On his right middle finger, he wore a thick silver band, engraved with some sort of hieroglyphics.

"I like your ring," she said.

He held his hand out and examined the band. "Thanks."

"Is there some significance to it?"

"It's a fraternity ring," he told her.

"What were you, like, in Skull and Bones?"

"If I were," he winked, "I wouldn't be able to tell you. You know how secret societies are."

"I heard Averell Ross was in Skull and Bones. Same year as President Bush. Nathan, too."

"Is that a fact."

An effete waiter came and took their drink orders. When he sashayed off, there was a lull in the conversation—a long, pleasant lull—during which Taylor and Asher fondled each other's fingers, in that ardent way lovers fondle fingers when circumstances prohibit fondling more.

"Do you take all your girlfriends here?" Taylor asked. This was a calculated move—an open-ended question, as they called it in her journalism classes, designed to get him to reveal more about himself. She was possessed, as I've mentioned, of great journalistic instincts.

"I wish. The last woman I dated worked with me at Drexel. That was five years ago."

"What happened?"

"You want the long story or the short story?"

"Both."

"The short story is, she dumped me. The long story is, I drove her away. I got the job at Quid Pro Quo, and I started working all these crazy hours. Eventually she got sick of it. She left me for a bass player in a jazz fusion band. His lifestyle was more stable, she said."

"Well," said Taylor, "it's her loss."

"You're too kind." He caressed her fingers. "What about you? You have a special guy back in Missouri or something?"

"No." Taylor laughed off the suggestion. "I've *never* had a special guy. I always seem to date creeps, for some reason. I'm a creep magnet. Like flies on shit. You're not a creep, are you?"

Asher took longer to answer the question than she would have liked, as if he first had to work it out. This made Taylor wonder what his inevitable flaw might be, and when it would reveal itself.

"No," he said finally. "Some might allege otherwise, but I'm not a creep."

"Modesty doesn't become you."

"I'm just being honest. I have intense relationships with people, but for a brief period of time. I've always been that way. The candle that burns at both ends. And my job just makes it worse."

"So why don't you quit? I'm sure it'd be easy to find another gig, being a headhunter and all, no?"

Asher looked at her like she'd grown a third breast. "I have the best job in the world. I'd be insane to give it up."

Taylor imagined being a headhunter, what it must be like, meeting with new hopefuls every day, scouring résumés, maintaining relationships with ill-tempered employers. Even if the pay was good—and it clearly was, if the Jaguar and the Dakota were any indication—it didn't seem particularly fulfilling.

"What exactly do you *do* at Quid Pro Quo that, like, makes it so great?"

This caught him off guard. Asher shuffled in his seat, and she felt his palms begin to sweat. "What do you mean?"

"I've met a lot of headhunters. They're all the same—but you're nothing like them."

"A backhanded compliment, but I'll take it." Asher withdrew his hands, wiping them on the tablecloth. "I'm an executive. I do what all executives do. I execute."

"Ha ha ha."

He signaled for the check. "You want to get out of here?"

"I thought you'd never ask."

If Asher was past the legal limit—and he must have been, given the liquor he'd consumed—it wasn't evident in his driving. Which was even more remarkable, when you consider that the Jag was a stick shift and his right hand was on her knee most of the time. Whenever they hit a red light they were all over each other. Somewhere in Chelsea, Taylor's updo collapsed. He spent the rest of the ride running his greedy fingers through her Rapunzeled hair.

Finally they reached Ninth Street. Asher parked in front of the fire hydrant, and they fell upon each other. (From my perch on the terrace, I could see the car rocking back and forth and the windows fogging up.)

Wine-primed and sex-starved though she was, Taylor was unsure what her next move should be. On the one hand, she wanted very badly to add Asher's name to her list. It was now twenty-eight days since she last had sex, her longest-ever dry spell (not counting the two months in high school when she was laid up with mono). On the other hand, she didn't want to come off as easy. She'd been on too many dates just as promising as this one, only to sleep with the guy and never hear from him again. J.D. was but the latest example.

Asher was different. Asher was a keeper.

Then again, it wouldn't hurt to invite him up for a nightcap, would it? Her roommate was home; how out of hand could things get?

"Would you like to come up?"

"I'd love to," he said. "But it's getting late. I should go home."

Suddenly, Taylor felt insecure. She disentangled from him,

grasping at the door handle, and studied him closely—impossibly handsome, meticulously groomed, perfectly dressed, practically unavailable, somehow single. Of course!

"You're not gay, are you?"

This made Asher laugh. "No, I'm not gay, thank you very much. I'm just . . . old-fashioned." He gazed into her eyes until the idea of him being gay melted away. "This isn't the greatest timing, I'm afraid. I'm leaving tomorrow for a business trip."

"When will you be back?"

"Not for two weeks. I'm gone until the end of the month. It sucks, I know, but what can I do? I have to work. Can I take you for drinks when I get back?"

A guy who liked her but *wasn't* in a hurry to get in her pants? What a novelty! "You weren't kidding about the crazy hours."

"Don't I know it."

"Whatever, that's fine. Where are you going?"

"Nowhere exciting."

They kissed again—this time gently, tenderly—and she stepped out of the car and into the still-stifling heat.

As Taylor stood there, quite literally hot and bothered, watching the Jaguar speed off, she had no idea that I was out on the terrace, nursing my fifth Rolling Rock of the evening, watching her with the same lustful longing she trained on the departed Asher Krug.

Given that her date did not accompany her up the three flights of stairs and into her little room—given that she came home at all, as I hadn't expected her until the following afternoon, glowing from what was certain to be a satisfying fuck followed by a satisfying breakfast—I knew that it was possible that tonight, the night Asher Krug revved her engines for hours only to leave her motor running, could very well be the night when Taylor decided to break the emergency glass.

But it was not to be. By the time I climbed back through the window and reached the hallway, Taylor had already barricaded herself in her room. A Whitesnake album was playing on her—on *my*—tape deck (she loved Duran Duran to death, but her heart belonged to eighties hair metal bands—Iron Maiden, Poison, Def Leppard, etc.). Pressing my ear to the door, I heard, over the tin-eared strains of "Here I Go Again" and her own soft grunts, the whir of what I believe they call a pocket rocket.

So much for broken glass.

Following Taylor's example, I retreated to my room, where the Lubriderm and Puffs awaited. As I lay on my bed in the pathetic afterglow, I thought of that Hadesian Greek who can never quench his thirst, even though he's standing in a pool of potable water. What was his name? It hovered tantalizingly on the tip of my tongue, but I could not give it voice.

CHAPTER 9

In the summer of 1991, I was working as a librarian at the long-since-defunct photo archive at API—the latest, and what would be the penultimate, in a series of McJobs I'd tenuously held since my graduation from Trenton State in 1986. I was a glorified file clerk. Customers, usually magazines, would call up with special requests—photographs related to the JFK assassination were big that summer, thanks to Oliver Stone; Lee Oswald, J. D. Tippett, stills from the Zapruder film—and I would fetch the negatives. Then . . . I'd put them back. The only requirement was a working knowledge of the (English) alphabet, although you could sing the song if you were too hungover to remember if *R* or *S* came first. The job was beneath my talents, for sure, but it was decent enough: easy, vaguely interesting, and never more than forty hours a week per collectively bargained rule. I'd been there nine ho-hum months.

The main drawback was my boss, a hulkingly obese woman named Donna Green, who, for some reason, did not like me. Not that I much cared for her, either—especially her habit of bursting into song at the drop of a hat. Her voice was loud and, if you're into Whitney Houston, pretty good. But I'm not into Whitney Houston, and even if I were, I wouldn't like the way Donna riffed her way through "Happy Birthday" every time we had cake for one of the admins. It was a photo library, not *Star Search*.

The Monday after Taylor's date with Asher, I was pulling a photo of Defense Secretary Dick Cheney, when who should stroll into the library but my unbeknowing Cupid, Jason Hanson. After the usual pleasantries—Jason and I met for beers at 119 Bar every once in a while, so we were pretty tight—he asked how it was going with Taylor.

"Dude," I told him, "you should have warned me."

"Is it that bad?"

"Um, *yeah*."

"You said you were desperate."

"I know, but *dude*. You should have given me a heads-up."

"Oh, shit. I'm sorry, man. I haven't seen her in ages. I figured she'd have calmed down by now."

"Calmed down?"

"Yeah." He gave me the same nonplussed look I was giving him. "Isn't that what you meant?"

"Isn't *what* what I meant?"

"*You* know." He drew close and mumbled under his breath. "That she's a friggin' *nympho*, man."

What I meant, in actuality, was that Taylor was clockstoppingly hot. But I played it cool. "Oh, yeah. I mean, she's a total superfreak."

"The kind you don't bring home to mother. You know what I heard?" Jason put his arm around me, leaned in conspiratorially. "I heard she turns tricks."

"Turns tricks?"

"Yeah. That's how she paid her way through college, is what I heard. It's not like her old lady has a pot to piss in."

I remembered the hundred-dollar bills crumpled in her mini-skirt the day she arrived; five crinkly pieces of evidence that seemed to corroborate Jason's claim. Then again, there was no mention of prostitution in Taylor's diary. Moreover, I didn't *want* to believe it. So I decided to discard what was most likely the truth, in the same way that creationists ignore science.

"I don't know if I believe that," I said. "She doesn't seem the type."

"She still keep the list?"

"The list?"

"Of her sexual partners. Should be like a fucking telephone book by now."

"Not that I know of."

"Don't tell me you *like* her, dude."

"Well, I . . ."

"Whatever you do, Todd, *don't* go there."

"Why shouldn't I go there?"

Before he could reply, Donna Green lumbered in, with all the grace of the Juggernaut in the old *Fantastic Four* comics, hollering at me to hurry along. Jason never did answer the question. Taylor a nympho? This was a new twist. Her diaries suggested a laissez-faire attitude toward sex, certainly, but symptoms of this complaint had yet to manifest themselves in the time I'd known her. Diddling after her date with the clit-teasing Asher Krug hardly qualifies—a Carmelite nun would have done the same thing. Then again, if Jason Hanson was right—and he had more knowledge of the subject than I did—it could only bode well for her in-case-of-emergency-break-glass roommate.

I went home immediately—I told Donna I had a follow-up dental appointment—and searched Taylor's room. The two-page list was folded neatly and tucked into the pages of the King James Bible she kept, for purposes of irony, on her nightstand. The first name therein, Matt Harris, was dated September 30, 1983. Jason Hanson checked in at number sixteen, June 8, 1986. J.D. (no other name supplied), the most recent entry, dated August 22, 1991, was number seventy-four.

Seventy-four different men in seven and a half years! I did the math: that's almost ten new partners every year, roughly one every six weeks. Not exactly Wilt Chamberlain territory, but for a twenty-three-year-old from Warrensburg, Missouri, either impressive or notorious, depending on your view of promiscuity.

And, of course, it made me want her all the more.

Across town, the object of my lust sat in the Braithwaite Ross cafeteria with her new colleagues. It was an awkward lunch. You could have cut the tension with a proverbial knife . . . or maybe even a real one. Why the long faces? The new publisher was expected any minute.

Taylor was characteristically blasé about the whole thing. Why should she give a shit? A new publisher would probably update Walter Bledsoe as editorial director (whom she had yet to see in the offices, although she'd been there almost two weeks), and she was fine with that. Plus, she was still buzzing about her date with Asher.

But everyone else—Charles and Brady, Mike and Chris, and Angie, who was sitting next to Taylor—looked like someone had died.

Suddenly, the door opened and a short, handsome, and fastidiously groomed fellow strode into the room. He wore black jeans, a black turtleneck, and a black blazer. Black eyes peered through black Calvin Klein spectacles. The man in black stood at the head of the room, surveyed the assembly, arched one eyebrow, and spoke.

"Good afternoon. I'm Nathan Ross." He sounded so much like Jack Nicholson that Taylor thought he must be putting it on. "I had intended to come here today to meet with you and ease any concerns that I'm sure you have. I had intended to talk to each and every one of you, to see what you like about the company, what you don't like about the company, what you suggest I can do to make this a better place to work. I wanted to wheel in trays of hors d'oeuvre and glasses of champagne and toast the success of Braith-

waite Ross. I wanted you all to think that even though my old man
owns the company, I'm not unapproachable, nor am I inept."

His eyes fell to the floor. "All that, unfortunately, will have to
wait. I'm afraid that my first order of business as publisher is to be
the bearer of bad tidings."

This unexpected twist had a pronounced affect on the stomachs
of those in attendance, Taylor included.

"Walter Bledsoe is dead."

Judging from their reaction to this news, the rest of the company liked Walter Bledsoe as much as Taylor did. There were cries
of surprise, but none of genuine grief.

"Late Sunday afternoon, he had a heart attack. By the time the
ambulance arrived, it was too late to revive him."

Somebody—one of the many female employees Taylor failed to
mention in her diary—gasped.

"I'm sorry to have to be the one to tell you this, I really am. I
was really looking forward to this day, and this is not the way I en-
visioned starting off." Nathan Ross took off his glasses and wiped
his eyes, although he was not crying. "Walter Bledsoe meant a lot
to this company. More than I can possibly convey. We'll have that
celebration in a few weeks. At that time, I will announce Walter's
successor as editorial director." A smile crossed the new boss man's
baby-smooth face. "And if you're dressing up on my account, you
can stop. There's no reason for an editor to wear a coat and tie."

And Nathan Ross strode slickly out of the room.

"You called it," Angie whispered to Taylor.

"Called what?"

"You said we couldn't have a thriller without a dead man. Now
we have a dead man."

Other than adding a few more weeks to Taylor's dry spell—and,
needless to say, a few more to my own—Asher's fortnight away
passed uneventfully. She concentrated her energies, in the daytime
and nighttime respectively, on Roger Gale's witless manuscript and

her pocket rocket. I continued to harbor the delusion, optimist that I still was, that my hour would soon arrive, that Taylor would have to break glass. But she held out. Like a Mother Abbess, she held out. And it was a torture, lurking by her locked door every night, like some unloved puppy left out in the rain, my dick heavy as a slab of granite, listening to the whir of the piece of plastic whose company she preferred to my own. But all I could do was wait my turn.

I tried to keep busy. I went on some auditions. I saw the Violent Femmes at Irving Plaza and Soft Parade, the Doors cover band, at the Red Lion. I read *The Stand*. I took Syd Field's seminar at the Learning Annex. I bumped into Laura and her new boyfriend, Chet, near the fountain in Central Park. They were walking their bichon. They were living on the Upper East Side. They were engaged.

Bored, I called up Jason Hanson and met him for beers at our usual watering hole, 119 Bar, off Union Square. He was a big music guy, so I wanted his take on *Use Your Illusion*, which had just come out—there were two albums, and Jason would know if I needed to buy both of them. But it wasn't all ulterior, meeting him—I liked the dude. He did a hilarious impression of Donna Green riffing on "Greatest Love of All." Plus he was an upbeat guy, and I needed more upbeat in my life.

But it was a somber Jason Hanson I found at the bar, already on his second beer.

"Dude," he said, over the Ramones blaring on the PA, "I'm worried about my job."

"Why? Did you fuck something up?"

"All this shit with the Mirror Group."

The goateed bartender came over, and I ordered a Guinness.

"I have no idea what you're talking about," I said.

"The guy who owns API, Robert Maxwell? He's in serious shit, man. There's some sort of big pension scheme or something. He's in trouble with the regulators over in England. If the company goes under, dude, I'm fucked."

This was news to me. I knew API was owned by the Mirror Group, but I had never heard of Robert Maxwell. Not that it mattered; API was the largest company of its kind in the world—too big, and too important, to fail. The bartender brought me my pint—a perfect pour, down to the shamrock in the foam.

"Where did you hear this?" I asked.

"I read it in the *Post*," Jason said, chugging the last of his beer.

"The *Washington Post*?"

"The *New York Post*."

"Dude." I chortled, and foam from the Guinness stuck to my nose. "That's like one step removed from the *National Enquirer*. They do stories about UFOs and shit. Next thing, you'll tell me Elvis is alive and working the copy desk. Fuck API, man, and give me the skinny on the new GNR. I hear there's a song where Axl tells Vince Neil to fuck off."

"And Andy Secher at *Hit Parader*." Jason brightened up a bit. " 'Get in the Ring,' it's called. Great track. But the highlight is the cover of 'Live and Let Die.' That's, like, totally killer."

CHAPTER 10

Nathan Ross, in a different but still completely black outfit, summoned the BR staff to the conference room, where they found a case of Korbel and enough appetizers to feed the Ethiopians, who in '91 were still starving. When everyone had downed a few glasses, and spirits were sufficiently high, Nathan announced the changes he'd planned for Braithwaite Ross.

"From now on, we're working a flexible schedule. You all work more than forty hours a week anyway; as long as the work gets done, what difference does it make if you're working here or from home? You're required to attend the weekly ed meetings, but that's all. Second, it was brought to my attention that the vacation policy was lacking. I agree. Starting in '92, you'll all have four weeks of paid vacation. I already covered the dress code. What else? Oh, the best part. On those days when you do find yourself at the office, for purposes of encouraging camaraderie, I ordered a pool table, an air hockey table, a jukebox, a soda fountain, and some arcade games for the break room."

"Which arcade games?" asked Chris, after the shouts of joy had dissipated.

"*Frogger*, *Donkey Kong*, and *Spy Hunter*."

"Awesome."

"Did I mention the new computers?"

"No."

"You'll all be getting new computers." Nathan held up a glass. "Last but not least, I have an announcement to make. My fellow publishers complain that young people don't read anymore—that they've lost the eighteen-to-thirty-five demographic—and then they refuse to listen to their editors in that age group. How is that good business sense? If the rest of the industry is trending older, I say, let's be contrarian. Let's do the opposite. Let's find ourselves new authors, young authors, edgy authors, authors we believe in. Let's find them, let's develop them, and let's help them make Braithwaite Ross the best publishing house in the world. To that end, I'm pleased to announce that Angela Del Giudice will be our new editorial director."

Nathan's speech was met with a thunderous ovation.

Taylor drank in the moment. She felt blessed to be in such a position, a few months removed from college, especially in such a dismal financial climate. Her job involved working creatively, with creative people, when she felt like working. It was fun, it was intellectually stimulating, the benefits were great, the people were cool. She felt the buzz in the air, and was, for a change, happy.

But her happiness, alas, would prove short-lived.

Pravda, in chic Soho, was one of those hot spots that was hip for about two weeks, until they started selling T-shirts and baseball caps, thereby guaranteeing that no discerning New Yorker would ever set foot there again. In 1991, it was still undiscovered, and, therefore, cool.

Taylor arrived a few minutes after nine for her drinks date.
Asher Krug was nowhere to be found, but when she dropped his
name to the Christy Turlington look-alike hostess, she was immediately shown a private table. She slouched into the chair, ordered
a Bellini, and scoped the place. The waitresses were all cast in the
supermodel mold. The waiters were similarly beautiful—too beautiful to be straight. As for the patrons, they could have been an
alternate cast of *90210*—she was pretty sure she spotted Sherilyn
Fenn, and, nuzzling in a corner booth, Judd Nelson and Justine
Bateman. Pravda was where the Beautiful People lounged, and
Taylor Schmidt, although she didn't feel like it inwardly, was unde-
niably one of their number.

Her waitress, a dead ringer for Naomi Campbell, arrived with
her $12 Bellini.

"Can I run a tab?"

Naomi stared at her blankly. Taylor handed over her Visa.
Naomi looked at the piece of plastic like it was a *Star Trek* trading
card.

"Never mind. Here." Holding up a twenty: "Bring me change,
please."

The wisp of a waitress walked off. Taylor took a sip of her drink
and a deep breath, and snuck a casual glance at her watch. Nine-
thirty; Asher'd said nine sharp. In New York, even punctual people
are late from time to time. Subways stall, buses break down, cabs
collide. But half an hour. . .

More time passed. Taylor tried to nurse the drink but wound up
finishing it. She flagged down Naomi, who looked annoyed.

"How much is a beer?"

Taylor might as well have asked the half-life of strontium 90.

"Never mind. Just bring me a Bass."

Ten o'clock came and went. Lost Baldwin brothers detoured by
Taylor's table and offered to buy her a drink. She declined. Where
was Asher? Had he really stood her up?

At ten-thirty she called him from the pay phone (no cell phones yet, remember; life was still a joy). No answer. She tried the office. Straight to voice mail.

"One more drink," she decided. It was her fourth, and she nursed it, made it last. She could feel judgmental eyes cutting into her. Eleven o'clock on the nose, two full hours late, and Asher Krug was MIA. She left Naomi a tip and started out.

As she passed by their table, Taylor could have sworn Judd and Justine were laughing at her.

"Take me to the Dakota. On Central Park West," she slurringly told the cabbie, having no idea where exactly the building was but hoping he would know. Luckily, he did—on the corner of West Seventy-second Street.

The Dakota was, and is, one of the poshest residences in a city full of them. When it was built in the 1880s, the Upper West Side was as remote as the recently settled Dakota Territory; hence the name. I saw a circa 1890 picture of it at the Museum of the City of New York; so little surrounds its ten mighty stories, it might as well have been built on the surface of Mars. The building itself— a magnificent piece of North German Renaissance architecure, beige in color, with soaring gables and ornate balustrades—is like a keep. Flanked by two gas-lamp sconces taller than me, a pair of wrought-iron gates, each weighing as much as a school bus, enclose a porte cochère, through which you can glimpse a quiet Parisian-style courtyard complete with fountain. Imposing without being garish, the Dakota is like a mini Buckingham Palace off Central Park West. The contrast between it and our apartment building is too stark to adequately describe. We might as well have been living in an igloo.

A stately doorman popped out of a gold-plated, telephone-booth-sized guardhouse and informed Taylor that Mr. Krug was not in. Because it was late, he allowed her to wait underneath the spandrel in the porte cochère, between the two gates.

She slumped against the terracotta wall and waited.

It was half past one when he showed his face. His hair was

mussed, his suit wrinkled, and there was a stain on his collar that she assumed was lipstick.

"Where have you been?"

"I'm sorry . . . Jesus Christ, I . . ."

"You could of at least called."

"I couldn't . . . I . . ."

"Why the fuck not?"

"I . . . can't tell you."

"I want to know. I *need* to know."

"Tomorrow. I can tell you tomorrow."

"I want to know *now*."

Asher seized her, powerful hands digging into her shoulder muscles, holding her fast. His eyes were devoid of the usual slyness. "Taylor, I like you. I like you very much . . . you have no idea how much. And as God is my witness, where I was tonight has nothing to do with us. I swear. I know you were waiting for me, and it kills me to make you wait. Kills me. But please. Please trust me. I'll tell you why I was late. But you have to wait till tomorrow."

"Tomorrow? Why tomorrow? What's so fucking special about tomorrow?"

As he held her close and tight, Taylor had two realizations almost simultaneously. The first was that tomorrow was her follow-up meeting with Quid Pro Quo's Director, whose name Asher had never mentioned, on the subject of reimbursement.

The second was that what she'd thought was lipstick on his collar was, in fact, blood.

CHAPTER 11

Taylor stepped into an office that was the size of our entire apartment, closets, bathroom, and all. The décor was minimalist and sparse—everything was black, white, or gray. The floors were a disorienting checkerboard tile. There was a modernist couch that looked cool but was not the sort of thing you could relax on without throwing out your back. In front of the couch was a glass coffee table. There was a sleek black chair behind a sleeker glass-topped desk—it was like Wonder Woman's invisible jet; you could barely see it—and two more chairs up front. Two of the walls were floor-to-ceiling windows, no blinds, no drapes. The other two were bright white, the only decorations a series of framed black-and-white photographs, four along the far wall, one directly behind the Director's desk. On the desk, a telephone, an ink blotter, a fountain pen. Nothing else. Between the sunlight and the

floor tiles and the white walls, the room had the feel of a hospital. You could perform surgery in that office.

Taylor took a seat and studied the poster-sized photograph behind the desk. It was a giant female eye—the left eye—wide open, looking up and off left. Said eye was lined with fake lashes thick with mascara. Beneath it, one on each side, were two spherical glass tears.

"Do you like it?" asked a voice from behind her—a voice husky from too many cigarettes, a voice possessed of a vaguely European accent, a voice that danced the line between low alto and high tenor but was, unmistakably, female.

"It's a nice photograph," Taylor said, rising. "If you're into eyes."

The owner of the voice wore a plain black kimono, white silk pants, and a medallion. Its design matched the one on Asher's ring. Her thinning hair, so blond it was almost white, was cut in a rigid bob. The crow's feet about her eyes and the wrinkles in her brow and neck, starkly visible in the naked light, exposed her as a woman of middle age—a member of the very generation Asher so vehemently despised. Her middle-agedness was the second surprise (her gender was the first) in a meeting that would be full of them.

"Not the loftiest praise, but I'm sure Man Ray wouldn't object. Good morning, Taylor. Lydia Murtomaki." Lydia extended a gaunt and well-braceleted hand, which Taylor shook. "Please. Sit."

"Murtomaki. What sort of a name is that?" Taylor asked. "I hope you don't mind my asking."

"Finnish, and I don't." Lydia settled beneath the giant eye, her posture almost inhumanly perfect. "People usually assume it's Japanese—until they see me. Don't let the kimono fool you." She opened an onyx cigarette case, produced a cigarette, and twisted it into an onyx cigarette holder. When the assembly was complete, she placed the mouthpiece between sharp, pointy teeth and lit up.

"You may smoke, if you wish."

A smoke was, at the moment, exactly what Taylor craved. She rummaged in her handbag until she found her silver case. There was only one cigarette left, which she promptly dropped on the floor. As she bent over to retrieve it, Taylor fumbled the matches, too. *Why am I so nervous?* she wondered.

Then she remembered the blood on Asher's collar.

When she finally had the smoke in her mouth and a match in her hand, the damn thing wouldn't light. The strip had worn away. Lydia Murtomaki rose, leaned across the desk, and presented her onyx lighter. Cigarette at the ready, Taylor stood and leaned forward, and the Parliament caught fire. "Thanks."

"Asher doesn't approve of cigarettes," Lydia said. "He says they cause cancer. He says it's a nasty habit. I figure they'll ban them sooner or later. They do so love banning activities in which people take pleasure. In certain parts of California, they don't let you smoke in restaurants. Can you imagine? Ghastly place, California."

"That would never fly in New York," said Taylor, taking a long drag. She wondered about this careful dropping of Asher's name—was the Director aware of their budding romance?

"Nathan Ross was a good hire," Lydia said. "I hear he's made some long-overdue changes."

"He's great. Braithwaite Ross is wonderful. I've been really impressed with everything."

"That, my darling, is exactly what we like to hear. At Quid Pro Quo, we don't want to just find you a job; we want to find you a *perfect* job, a job you really enjoy. A job you'd kill for."

"Mission accomplished, then," Taylor said. "I honestly don't think I could have a better gig."

"Lovely. Then let us proceed." The Director smiled, flashing again her fang-like teeth. "If you should ever have a complaint about your job, come to us. If you should become dissatisfied and desire a new position, come to us. Any time you have need of us, Quid Pro Quo will be here for you. Are we understood?"

"Yes, Ms. Murtomaki."

"Then we can proceed to the matter at hand: reimbursement." Lydia took the remnants of the cigarette from the holder and crushed it into the ashtray. If this was designed to intimidate Taylor, it was a success. "We would prefer not to exact a fee for our services, but our overhead, for a variety of reasons, is considerably greater than that of our rivals. It costs a lot of money to maintain appearances, you must understand, and the rent in this building is usurious. So we must have our . . . pound of flesh, so to speak."

"How much?"

"Twenty percent of your salary."

"Twenty percent! I can't afford twenty percent!"

The Director's voice was sharp, impatient without being impolite. "Asher mentioned during orientation that our services would not be expensive, and they are not. Right now, you are paying twenty-seven percent of your salary to federal and state governments, correct?"

"Something like that."

"Instead of paying the government twenty-seven percent, you will be paying us twenty percent. Not to mention that your base salary is markedly higher than it would be if you got the same job through one of our competitors."

"Wait a minute. I'm confused. How can I pay you instead of the government?"

"You can either write us a check every month, or we can collect through payroll deductions. Most people opt for payroll deductions."

"No, I mean, isn't it, you know, illegal? Won't the IRS have something to say about this?"

Lydia Murtomaki laughed—a most disturbing occurrence. With all the tar in her lungs, it sounded like a death rattle. "We adhere to all existing IRS regulations. Under the provisions of the Consolidated Omnibus Budget Reconciliation Act of 1985, the . . . well, I shall spare you the technical details, but essentially, non-profit employment agencies can apply their fees to federal income tax. Most employment agencies are for-profit, so they don't qualify. We do."

"I've never heard of that before."

"Unless you spend your free time analyzing arcane pieces of

legislation, there's no reason you would have. You look like the kind of girl who has better things to do than that."

All through the discussion, Taylor couldn't stop looking at the giant eye. Who hangs a photograph of an eye in her office? "That's true."

"As long as you keep working a Quid Pro Quo job, your income tax is remitted to our agency. That, my darling, is our sole source of revenue."

There was an implied finality in Lydia's tone, so Taylor started to rise from the chair. A crisp shake of the Director's head prompted her to stay put.

"We're not done just yet. There is a second component to reimbursement that must be discussed. You must perform a task. It might take a day, it might take two."

This unnerved her. Taylor knew that the other shoe was bound to drop, and she dreaded where it would land. She tried to convince herself that her fear was irrational, and eventually she succeeded. Unfortunately, knowing her fear was irrational didn't make her any less afraid.

"Before I get into the specifics," said Lydia, "you need to understand why it has been so difficult for you, and others like you, to find gainful employment in the current climate. Bright, talented graduates of top-flight colleges, thousands of you every year, enter the workforce. But what are you doing? Killing time. Waiting. Working low-paying jobs that are not intellectually satisfying, or assuming major debt by earning superfluous graduate degrees."

Out came the lighter. Taylor saw the reflection of the flame in the iris of the giant eye.

"Take you, by way of example. Smart, creative, articulate, attractive. Very attractive. And you are not alone. Thousands of bright, talented graduates like yourself, with limitless potential—none of them can find work. Why?"

Taylor, assuming this a rhetorical question, did not respond. When she realized that it was not, she said, "We're not qualified, is what everyone says."

"That's the stock answer, but it is patently untrue. As you well know. You're *qualified* to do just about anything. You're *over*qualified for the job you have now. No, it has nothing to do with qualifications."

"Then what?"

"Simply put: there are no jobs available." Smoke billowed from her draconian nostrils. Maybe it was the cigarette smoke that made the giant eye tear. "Now. Why would this be?"

"Because the economy is stagnant?"

"Yes and no. Certainly the federal budget deficit, the trend toward corporate downsizing, the bulging Lorenz curve, and other economic factors do play a part. But there is a far simpler reason."

Taylor's freshly manicured fingernails dug into the armrests. The sword of Damocles was about to drop on her Nine Wests.

"Prince Charles is forty-two years old," Lydia continued, "and he is *still* the Prince of Wales. Who ever heard of a forty-two-year-old prince? Princes are supposed to be *boys,* not gray-haired men with bad prostates. Most British monarchs were in their early thirties when they were coronated. George III was twenty-two. Henry VIII, Defender of the Faith, was just eighteen. The few who ascended to the throne late in life made no lasting mark on the pages of history. They could not; their best years were behind them. Poor Prince Charles is one of these, fated to fade into oblivion. He has wasted his life waiting. Waiting, and waiting, and waiting for his immortal mother to gasp her last breath, so the crown can at last be his. From the looks of things, that will not happen anytime soon."

(Lydia Murtomaki was spot-on about that; eighteen years later, the Queen is still alive and well, and Prince Charles is not getting any younger.)

"Your generation, my dear, plays the same waiting game Prince Charles plays, on a much larger scale. Your parents and grandparents—my generation—hold the jobs you desire, the jobs that by all rights should be yours. And we are quite reluctant to pass along the torch. It's not that you cannot find the good jobs. It's that there are no good jobs to find—they're all taken."

Lydia Murtomaki let that hang in the air with the cigarette smoke, until both drifted away. "Do you realize that in my day, college graduates were uniformly hopeful and idealistic? Cynicism, sarcasm, and bitterness are unique to your generation."

"I . . . I didn't know that." Taylor wanted to smoke another cigarette, but she didn't have one. And her hands were trembling too much, anyway.

"Now. These jobs that my contemporaries hold . . . what is the simplest way to make them available to you?"

Taylor did not, could not, speak. By now, she'd figured out what was coming. She was a twisted enough cookie to get it. She didn't want to believe it, but she knew.

"What would Prince Charles do? If he were tired of waiting, and wanted to be king tomorrow?"

"He'd lose that crazy wife of his, for one thing."

Charles and Diana were not separated until 1992, and did not divorce until four years later. In 1991, however, the apotheosis of Diana that her tragic death inspired was years away; the public perception of her was more crazed bitch-on-wheels than better-coifed Mother Teresa.

But Lydia Murtomaki was not amused. "What would he *do*, Taylor?"

"He would . . . you know . . . depose his mother."

"Yes. He would kill the Queen. And with your generation, as I said, it is no different, it is just on a larger scale. The simplest way—the *only* way—to make the baby boomers surrender their jobs is . . ."

Both of them completed the sentence silently. Then Taylor completed it out loud: "To kill them?"

"We call it 'give them the pink slip.' It's much more pleasant, don't you think?"

In ninth grade, while climbing the rope in gym class, Taylor had had an accident. She was almost to the beam on which the rope was suspended, some twenty-five feet above the parquet floor, when the metal bolt snapped. Suddenly and without warning, she found herself falling, backward, toward the hardwood. She experienced the same sensation now, in the Director's office—the lump in her throat seemed to fall, suddenly and without warning, dropping like a stone through her esophagus, her stomach, her intestines, down down down. So great was the sensation that she lost her balance, and almost fell backward in the chair.

"Pink . . . slip?" Taylor's heartbeat was as loud as the computer in her office, her fingernails imbedded in the armrests. Her voice came from far away, as if she were listening to someone else speak. "You're talking about murder. C'mon, you can't be serious."

Taylor waited for Lydia to crack a smile. For Asher to step out of the shadows in the corner of the office with Allen Funt and say she was on a remake of *Candid Camera*. For the fire alarm to go off. For the phone to ring, even. Anything to break the tense silence. But nothing did.

Finally, Lydia Murtomaki spoke. "That's absolutely what I'm talking about. Don't be afraid, darling. We'll take care of you. Asher will assist you in the operation."

The blood on his collar . . . could Asher have come from helping another recent college grad—Bryan, maybe—pull the trigger?

"And I'm supposed to just smile and nod and play along?"

"What interesting phraseology," Lydia said. "Yes, my darling, you will smile and nod and play along—because you don't have a choice."

"Sure I do. I could march to the police and tell them everything."

"Oh, I don't think that's a smart play. For one thing, they'd never believe you. For another, Asher would then kill you, your mother, your two half sisters, and the three people you've listed as references. I don't think he'd enjoy that very much at all."

Personal rather than professional references. With names and addresses. What had she told Mae-Yuan? *It was tough, but I managed to dig up three friends.* The three friends being Kim Winter, Jason Hanson, and—gulp—me. Taylor imagined our corpses laid out in the hospital light of the Director's office, under the grim watch of Man Ray's crying eye. Meeting Lydia's merciless gaze, it was not difficult to imagine.

Taylor saw then that the giant eye was wide open because its owner had been surprised. Maybe it was an appropriate photograph, after all. Then she had another realization: in order for her job at Braithwaite Ross to have been listed—in order for her job to have been available—someone at BR must have contracted with Quid Pro Quo. And if so, someone had to be removed from the BR payroll to make room for Taylor. Which meant. . .

"Oh my God," Taylor said, putting two and two together. "You guys killed Walter Bledsoe!"

"We didn't kill him." Lydia flicked her cigarette into a glass ashtray. "But the guy who did has one hell of a plum job, for a twenty-four-year-old."

"Holy shit. Holy . . . *shit*."

"Come on, Taylor. You think Walter Bledsoe deserved to make eighty grand a year, working three days a week, making passes at every cute girl who walked into his office? You really think so? The staff is happy, Nathan Ross is happy, Averell Ross is happy . . . and best of all, your pal Angie is the new editorial director. Who are we to deny the happiness of so many?"

But Taylor missed most of Lydia's speech. Fight-or-flight had kicked in, and she found herself, quite involuntarily, making a break for it. When she opened the heavy oak door, however, she found her escape route blocked by Asher Krug. Unable to get by him—he was seven or eight inches taller—she pounded her fists against his chiseled chest and began wailing uncontrollably, like a toddler denied a favorite toy.

"Asher," Lydia said over the sounds of her screams, "please escort Ms. Schmidt home."

Although the fall from the gym-class rope had been sudden and unexpected, Taylor was quick to accept her fate. Falling, she reasoned later, was a metaphor for her childhood. She was used to not being in control, and she knew from experience that it was better to surrender to the flow of things than to fight back. In the case of the fall from the rope, that acquiescence paid off. Somehow, she managed to land most of her body on a three-feet-thick gymnastics mat. The wind was knocked out of her, but that was all. She fell, but she picked herself up and kept going.

Taylor was a survivor. She survived in high school, and she would survive now. She wouldn't let a pesky little thing like morality get in the way.

Whisking her into the Jaguar, Asher spoke in a kind, gentle voice that lacked its usual hubris—a phony, praticed voice. His business voice. Who knows how many Quid Pro Quo clients he'd spoken to in exactly the same tone? As they negotiated the traffic on the FDR (both hands on the wheel this time, no hanky-panky, no hint that they had hooked up two weeks ago), he explained the rationale behind making "civilians," as he called them, do the pink slips—their complicity was necessary to ensure their silence. Who would dare blow the whistle on Quid Pro Quo with blood on his hands? Not that there would be blood, necessarily. He went over that, too, as he loosened and then tightened the knot on his Armani necktie. The hit would be as painless as possible, for assassin and victim. A traumatized client, he explained while passing a cab on Second Avenue, would be more likely to spill the beans. At most, she'd have to inject someone with something. Lethal injections were popular, because certain poisons caused heart attacks, and were undetectable even with an autopsy. The victims, he added, were the Walter Bledsoes of the world—assholes who were better off dead. As for the police, she had nothing to worry about. Taylor would not be caught—guaranteed. Quid Pro Quo operated under the auspices of the DIA. Whatever that was.

"How are you?" he asked as they pulled in front of the apartment—where a parking space magically awaited them, as usual. "I know it's a lot to process."

Taylor, who had not said a word since they left the offices, replied with a shrug. It *was* a lot to process, and she hadn't even begun. Nothing had really sunk in. The whole thing was so absurd it was funny. Kill someone to get a job? It was a plotline from a old noir movie, *D.O.A.* or *Double Indemnity*. And Asher? That was the funniest part of all. Since the day she met him, she'd been waiting for his fatal flaw to be exposed. And here it was. He didn't live with his mother. He wasn't a divorcé. He didn't have hygiene problems. He wasn't gay, wasn't impotent, wasn't HIV positive. No—the problem with him was that *he was a professional hit man!* That was *absurd*. It was beyond absurd. It was the sort of cruel twist of fate that could only happen to Taylor Schmidt (or so she wrote in her diary; I know firsthand that cruel twists of fate happen to other people, too). And so, in the passenger seat of Asher's Jaguar outside our apartment, she had a laughing fit the likes of which she had never before experienced. It was like her body had been taken over by some cacodemonic hyena. She laughed and laughed and laughed, unable to stop herself, like a battery-powered toy on the blink.

"Is something funny?" Asher asked. He seemed confused—he'd obviously never seen that kind of reaction before.

"You are," she said, as the peals of laughter finally died down.

And when they did, all thought of Quid Pro Quo and Lydia Murtomaki and pink slips vanished from her mind. It was like the laughter had cleansed her system. All she cared about afterwards, with Asher so deliciously close and so predisposed to making her happy—it was practically in his *job description* to fuck her, if it meant getting her to do the pink slip—was that she was in a terrible dry spell, and Asher Krug was like a cold front blowing in. Let it rain, baby! This was her MO, always had been. When things got out of control, Taylor defaulted to sex.

"If you say so."

"Whatever." She wanted the full Asher Krug treatment. The hard sell. And she smelled opportunity in his Drakkar Noir. "Just take me inside."

* * *

Asher, unaware that Taylor had moved past the pink slip business, kept up the chatter. "It's right there in the Bible: thou shalt not kill. Exodus 20:13. It's the Sixth Fucking Commandment, etched in stone, no ifs-ands-or-buts about it."

They were in the living room/kitchen of our apartment now. Asher leaned against the sink, twirling his car keys around his index finger. He looked out of place there, like a hippopotamus would have; he filled the space too completely.

"You know what else it says in the Bible? That women who wear men's clothes—and vice versa—should be stoned to death. Now, if Lady Bunny were strolling through Williamsburg, would the Hasidim be throwing rocks? Of course not. No one believes in the cross-dressing law anymore; it's outdated."

He opened the refrigerator and grabbed a bottle of Rolling Rock. Of *my* Rolling Rock. In all likelihood, the first domestic beer he'd ever tasted.

"You mind?"

Without waiting for a reply, he popped the top, took a big gulp, made a face, and went on.

"The Bible also says thou shalt not commit adultery. And by adultery, they don't mean a married man boffing his secretary, or a married woman boffing hers. According to Exodus, *any* sexual contact prior to marriage is adultery. You could hook up with a guy, go on to marry him, and it'd *still* be adultery."

Taylor thought of her list, and the seventy-plus men it contained, and, in spite of herself, suppressed a smile. Old-fashioned Asher would have been aghast if he knew how experienced she was. I sometimes wonder if he ever found out.

"According to the Bible," he went on, "it's the same crime—adultery—punishable by death. And yet, no one is demanding your life because you gave your high school sweetheart a hand job. How come? The definition of adultery has changed, and along with it, the punishment. The Biblical version is outmoded."

As Asher took a few steps toward Taylor, the cat darted across the floor and hid under the sofa. He watched Bo run, wrinkled his brow, shook his head, and rested his beer on the table. "It also says in the Bible—and it says this right at the beginning, so it must be important—that women are inferior to men and are put on earth to serve them. Come on, now. Even macho guys don't believe that anymore. They might like the idea, but they don't *believe* a word of it. The concept of male superiority is outmoded."

Asher pulled out the other chair and sat across from Taylor.

"It's the same thing with murder, with thou shalt not kill. The concept has run its course. It's just that people have a harder time violating that rule, because we've been conditioned to believe that killing someone is immoral. And it's a question of morality, really—of personal morality. Because Quid Pro Quo operates above the law. The question is, what do *you* believe? Talk to inmates doing time for murder; they'll tell you. They don't feel guilty about doing the crime. They feel regret about doing the time. About getting caught. Big difference. Guilt is a conditioned response, a way we're taught to react to quote-unquote bad behavior. It's the province of the unenlightened. The meek. Who, the Bible also tells us, shall inherit the earth. Yeah, right."

Not to interrupt Asher's argument, but personally, I'm down with the Sixth Commandment—but I'm in the minority. Killing is an expression of raw power, and raw power, ugly through it may be, is of primary societal value. In classical literature, mighty warriors win laurels and, thus, girls. Achilles had no problems getting laid. In these so-called enlightened times, the act of killing is subtler, more sublimated—metaphorical, sometimes—but killing just the same. Who are the most esteemed men nowadays? Athletes, who excel in games that simulate killing, and actors, who star in movies that glamorize killing. In 1991, the three biggest box office stars were Arnold Schwarzenegger, Sylvester Stallone, and Bruce Willis—action heroes all, tough guys brandishing heavy weapons. Clearly killing resonates with people.

But athletes and actors are just symbols. Asher traded in *real* power. What act is more powerful than taking someone's life? At that moment, Taylor's attraction to Asher Krug was at its peak. She saw him as power personified. He was like Zeus, revealing himself to Semele. And like Semele, Taylor burned for him.

Her eyes drifted from his to the beer, which she raised to her lips and chugged. Then she stood up and walked in the direction the cat had gone. "So it's a matter of refining my definition of morality?"

Asher looked up, startled. These were the first words she'd said in almost half an hour, since her laughing fit in the car. She seemed more relaxed now, composed—maybe a bit intrigued by his deranged ethics lesson.

"Exactly." He followed her. When he neared, Bo scurried from under the sofa back into the kitchen area. Smart cat, Bo.

The backs of Taylor's knees were now touching the sofa. Asher was next-person-in-line-at-the-ATM distance away, facing her.

She took a step forward. He did not move. "You know what I think?" she said.

"Tell me."

Her eyelids fluttered, her tongue artfully gliding along her upper lip. "I think if you're going to make me a killer, you'd better start by making me an adulteress."

Taylor snatched his tie, pulling him closer. She made a fist around the Windsor knot, for leverage, and pounced. Her tongue tickled his teeth, her fingers fondled his ass. Asher recoiled, but could not break free. She sucked his lower lip into her mouth and bit down hard. It was just like what he had done to her in the Rainbow Room elevator—except that she drew blood. He cried out, her hands tightened their respective hold on necktie and buttock, she lurched backward, and the two of them toppled onto the sofa.

"Wait," he said, breaking away from her. His stare was intense, mad.

"What's the matter?"

"Birth control."

"I'm on the pill," she said. "Relax."

And relax he did, even though she'd had more sexual partners over the years than Menudo had members, and in 1991, people still thought AIDS could be transmitted by teardrops. (Later that year, Magic Johnson would come down with HIV, and Freddie Mercury would die from its complications.)

"Are you going to talk all day, Mr. Krug, or are you gonna fuck me?"

Traditionalist or not, Asher opted for the latter. They fucked, right there on my torn red vinyl sofa. And how was it?

"Best X *ever*," Taylor wrote in her diary the next day.

It wasn't like Asher did anything out of the ordinary; on the contrary, he wasn't remotely kinky, never deviating from the missionary position. And the length and breadth of his manhood, while porn-worthy, is not what made her feel shiny and new. It was *how* he made love that was unprecedented. When Taylor was in high school, she was having sex with gawky high school kids. By the time she got to college, she was so experienced that her subsequent lovers generally succumbed to her way of doing things. She was almost always on top, the better to impose her will on her partner. When a guy did attempt to assume control, it usually came off like Frankenstein trying to lead Ginger Rogers on the dance floor. Asher, alone among her seventy-some-odd lovers, *took her*, in the bodice-ripping romance-novel style. He made her feel touched for the very first time. That he was able to go back-to-back-to-back— and that he lasted a good half hour each time—didn't hurt. Suffice it to say, after exactly forty days—apropos, given Asher's Old Testament lecture—Taylor's dry spell was no more.

As for the pink slip, she would treat it just as she had the fall from the rope back in high school—she'd deal with it when it happened, and she'd do whatever she had to do to survive.

PART II

Cold Ethyl

CHAPTER 12

According to the National Bureau of Economic Research, the recession that plagued the nation in the summer of '91 began in July of 1990, just before the U.S. occupation . . . er, liberation . . . of Kuwait. Recessions by their nature defy rational causal analysis, but that particular economic downturn was brought on by, first, the banking "credit crunch," in the wake of the S&L scandal (a foreshadowing of our current financial crisis), and, second, a precipitous increase in oil prices, after Saddam invaded Kuwait. Or so economist Jane Katz argued in her 1999 report for the Federal Reserve Bank of Boston. While the recession technically ended in March of 1991, before Taylor had even moved to Manhattan, Katz notes that "a sluggish early recovery made the downturn seem to last much longer and kept unemployment rising—up to 7.8 percent in June 1992—even as the economy started to come back." Indeed, by late '93 things were more or less back to normal, and the economy, spurred on by a World Wide Web devised by Tim Berners-Lee the year our story takes place, took off thereafter, peaking big time in 1999.

But in the late summer of '91, Berners-Lee himself, peering through his rosiest Oliver Peoples, could not have foreseen such a drastic correction. The future looked bleak, even hopeless. Work was impossible to find. Prices were rising. The heat was unrelenting, as was the "sluggish recovery" that we referred to, at the time, as the "depression."

The rest of the news cycle was just as grim. A dark horse presidential candidate, the Democratic governor of backwater Arkansas, threw his name into the hat with the other hopeless hopefuls—Poppy Bush, holding a political straight flush in the wake of the Gulf War, looked like a cinch for reelection. And the lurid confirmation hearing of Clarence Thomas, as unqualified for the Supreme Court as Dan Quayle was for the vice presidency, introduced the nation to the jurisprudential definition of quid pro quo. On Tuesday, October 15, 1991, in defiance of Anita Hill and common sense, the Senate voted 52-48 to confirm Long Dong Silver. That was but one small detail, one tiny Fuck You from the gods, that contributed to October 15, 1991, being the worst day of my life. Up until that point, that is.

My day began early. I was roused at quarter to six by the urgent ringing of the phone. I was deep in sleep and disoriented; it took me a while to remember where I was, let alone to answer the call. On the ninth or tenth ring—the answering machine was on the fritz again—I managed to pick up.

"Hello?"

"Todd? Todd, is that you?"

The voice of this ghost shook me from my slumber.

"Dad?"

My parents divorced in 1978, when I was thirteen. For salvation, my mother turned to Jesus; my father, to drink. I wasn't keen on either option. When I left for college, my mother—I lived with her after the divorce, in a cramped bungalow in Toms River, New Jersey—married an evangelical Christian patent clerk; I rarely went back to visit. As for my old man, he wound up in a boardinghouse in Camden, where he indulged his taste for tequila and cooze. I'd spoken to him maybe a dozen times since the divorce, and had seen him exactly twice in all that time. His call, then, on this already bleak day, was a surprise.

"Son," he told me, "I've been a lousy father."

Clearly he was drunk.

"You weren't so bad."

"I was lousy," he insisted.

"Fine, you were lousy. Dad, why are you telling me this? Did you do the Forum or something?"

"Todd," he said, "I'm dying."

He'd been having these terrible headaches, was the story, which he attributed to the effects of the booze. Then his eyes started acting funny. After he fainted while taking a leak one morning, he finally went to the doctor. They did a CAT scan, and found embedded in his brain a tumor the size of a tomato. Malignant, they said. Inoperable. Six months, probably. No more than a year.

"Oh my God," I said, although I was ostensibly an atheist. "Oh my God."

"I'd like to see you, Todd. For Thanksgiving. Will you come down? For Thanksgiving? I'll pay for the ticket."

"To Camden?"

"I'm in Cherry Hill now."

I'd spent last Thanksgiving in Medford, Massachusetts, with Laura's disapproving—and, even worse, teetotalling—parents. This year there was no such option. I'd probably wind up snarfing down the turkey special at Odessa Diner and watching the Cowboys lose. Might as well share my loneliness with my old man.

"Yes, of course. Of course I'll come."

We hung up the phone, and I burst into tears. Literally, burst. I wasn't expecting to cry—he *was* a lousy father, even during the thirteen years he was around—but the tears poured out of me nevertheless. Even while I was crying, I was stunned that the news, somber though it was, could have such a visceral effect on me. Did I really love the guy, deep down? Or was this just a narcissistic opportunity to contemplate my own mortality? I would, once he passed, be the next Lander in line. Unlike Taylor, the thought of death scared the crap out of me, and no amount of intellectual sugarcoating was going to change that flavor. *My dad is dying; I'm next.* I couldn't get that simple equation out of my head.

As I got to work—a few minutes late; signal problems on the 6—I found Donna Green waiting at my cube, ample arms crossed, a familiar scowl on her plump face.

"We need to talk," she told me.

"Good morning to you, too."

I followed Donna into her cramped office. Between her mass and the boxes and loose papers and other crap all over the place, there was barely room for the two of us to sit down.

"We have a problem," she said, closing the door.

I didn't say anything.

"It's come to my attention that you've been routinely leaving work early. Up to three times a week."

Ah, yes. That. Well, I needed to be in the apartment alone, when Taylor was at work, so I could read her diaries at leisure. True, she hadn't been home much lately—after their initial congress on my red sofa, she'd been spending a lot of time at Asher's—but you can never be too careful. It would never do to get caught with my hand in the epistolary cookie jar.

Fortunately, I had an excuse prepared. "It's my teeth," I said, rubbing my jaw for effect. "I've been having problems with my teeth."

"Yes, so you say."

I didn't care for her patronizing tone. "What, you think I'm *lying*?"

"It's not fair for you to leave early all the time, Todd. It creates more work for everyone else."

"I understand that. Totally. That's why I work through lunch."

She arched an eyebrow, or tried to; the rings of ocular fat made the maneuver difficult. "I've never seen you work through lunch, Todd."

"What am I supposed to do, Donna? Sit here and *suffer*?"

She didn't say anything, just sat there staring at me. Her tortured breathing was unpleasantly loud.

"Have you ever had oral surgery? It's not pleasant."

"I spoke with HR about this. They said that I should ask you for a note from the dentist."

"A *note*? What is this, elementary school?"

This was not going to end well. Not at all.

"You know," Donna said, changing course, her tone more buddy-buddy, "I have a cavity, and I'm in the market for a good dentist. Would you recommend yours?"

She *would* have a cavity, with all those Boston cream doughnuts she shoved in her hungry maw every morning. Gout, too, probably.

"He's not taking new patients."

"I see." She shook her corpulent face back and forth—how clichéd!—her nine chins waddling to and fro. "Well, you've given me no choice, Todd. Either you produce the note, or we're letting you go."

"Letting me go? You mean you're *firing* me?"

"Not if you produce the note. Which, if you've really been to the dentist, shouldn't be a problem, right?"

I thought about forging a note, but what good would that do? They'd find out sooner or later. And it's not like the photo library was a career aspiration. Plus, if I got the axe, I could collect unemployment.

"You know what? I'm not bothering him to ask for a note. How about that? If you really think I'm lying, then fire me. You've had my number since the day I walked in the door, right?"

"I have not." Donna Green sighed deeply. She looked really upset, like she was about to cry. Maybe she didn't hate me as much as I'd thought. Maybe she really was just peeved that I took advantage of her and blew off work so often. "Have it your way. You're fired."

"Seriously?"

"You've given me no choice."

"Well," I told her, rising, "it's been real."

"No hard feelings?"

"No hard feelings." I stood up. "Hey, do you mind if I take the Cindy Crawford photo in my cubicle?"

The photo in question, of the world's greatest supermodel in a provocative pose, her curves artfully enhanced by the slimmest bikini on earth, had landed me in hot water, when one of my female coworkers complained about its display. Richard Gere is a lucky guy—or was, in 1991.

No longer nervous, Donna laughed. "Um . . . sure. Take whatever you want."

"Thanks."

And thus concluded my employment with API.

When I got home—and this was the worst part of the worst day—Taylor was in her room, packing her meager possessions into U-Haul cardboard boxes.

I was so taken aback I could hardly string two words together. "W-w-what's going on?"

"Oh, hey, Todd. I'm just packing up some stuff to bring to Asher's."

This was a disappointment, but not exactly a surprise. In the two weeks following the end of her dry spell, she'd slept at the Dakota practically every night. I saw Taylor just three times during those fourteen days, and only in passing, when she dropped by to pick up clean clothes. The lone silver lining was, her absence afforded me ample opportunity to study the older volumes of her diary.

"*Some* stuff? This looks like pretty much everything."

"It's just, you know, I'm spending a lot of time with Asher, and it's easier to have my stuff there."

Attractive recent college grads move to the city, wide-eyed and lonesome, and get scooped up by the first slightly older, vaguely charming dude who comes calling. Cycle of nature. This was how I managed to score a cutie like Laura, who was four years my junior. You gotta lock 'em down before they wise up.

"You've gone out with the guy twice, and the second time he stood you up, and you're moving in with him?"

"I'm not moving in with him. I'm just bringing some of my stuff there. That's all."

"That's not what it looks like."

"But that's what it is." She sat down on one of the boxes. "Look, I like this apartment. I like living with you."

"Then don't leave."

"Todd."

"I mean it."

"I'm *not* leaving."

"Whatever."

I wandered into the living room, dazed, like a boxer reeling off the turnbuckles. My life was crashing down all around me, or so it seemed. This was an overreaction to her packing a few boxes, I admit, but after the day I had. . .

"Todd, are you okay?"

"Well, let's see. I got fired . . . my father is dying of cancer . . . and now you're leaving. Other than that, everything's just great."

Something amazing happened then. Taylor took me in her arms, pulled me to her bosom, and whispered, "It's okay, baby," over and over and over. I think that's what she said; I couldn't really hear over the sound of my heart pounding. Never before had she held me like this, so tightly, so tenderly. I could smell her Alberto VO5 shampoo, her lavender oil, her savory sweat. How sublime that curvaceous form felt, squeezed against mine!

"I know it's ridiculous," I told the crook of her neck, "but I really thought we'd, you know . . ."

Without breaking the embrace completely, Taylor pulled back to meet my bashful gaze. Her eyes were—I swear on this, although it seems ridiculous—faraway and sad.

"You wouldn't want that," she said. "I like you way too much to put you through something like that."

Again with the *I like you too much*. What the fuck was *that* all about?

"By that logic, you don't like Asher that much."

"It's not the same thing."

"I don't see why." I crossed my arms and pouted like a five-year-old.

"I may be in love with Asher," she said. "But I'm not sure. It's hard to know with him, he's so hard to pin down. But I have to find out. And for the last time, I'm *not* moving in with him, I'm just moving some stuff there. Asher's old-fashioned. He doesn't believe in living in sin."

"Oh, for Christ sake . . ."

I protested more, but Taylor wouldn't hear of it. And she was stubborn. Once she made up her mind, forget it. The moment, if there had ever been one, had passed.

"I'm sorry to hear about your father."

"Yeah, well, what can you do. It's not like we were ever close."

"He's still your father, though. My father was a real asshole, but I was still upset when he died." She fired up a cigarette. "Wait a minute . . . did you say you got fired?"

"Yup."

"Out of the blue? What happened?"

I told her the story, omitting the key detail that my chronic attendance problem was in order to read her diary when she wasn't around.

"That sucks," she said. "The fucking cunt." (Taylor often applied the c-word to women she disliked—one of her many charms.)

"It's not her fault. She's just doing her job." Her cigarette needed ashing, so I handed her an empty can of Tab from the dresser. "Hey, do you think you could call your boyfriend on my behalf? Maybe he can hook me up with some work."

I was unprepared for her odd reaction. She wrinkled up her face in a way I'd never seen before, the way a child might when presented with a teaming plate of brussels sprouts. She held the expression for a tenth of a second, if that, and then reverted to form.

"I don't know, Todd. I'd only use Quid Pro Quo as, like, a last resort."

Absent the acute myopia symptomatic of the present tense, I now see that she was trying to warn me, to protect me. She had *some* empathy, evidently. At the time, however, desperation clouded my better judgment. Besides, how could I have guessed at the grim literality of the company's fancy Latin name?

"Last resort? I don't have a job, I didn't get any severance, the rent is two weeks late, and I don't have enough money to cover it. Even *if* you're able to kick in your share this month. Christ. What the fuck am I going to do?"

Taylor didn't say anything at first, just shook her head slowly. Only when I started to sob did she speak. "I just don't think Quid Pro Quo would be a very good fit for you, is all."

That pushed me over the edge. "You mean you don't think I'm *good enough* for them!" I cried. "Great. First I'm not good enough for my dad. Then I'm not good enough to be with you. Now I'm not good enough for some fucking *headhunter*?"

Taylor shook her head again, her eyes even sadder. "Okay," she said. "If that's what you really want, I'll call him."

CHAPTER 13

That Saturday, Asher Krug took his newly minted live-in girlfriend to dinner at Chez Molineaux. On this second visit, they took a cab—"I want to drink tonight," Asher explained—and instead of the cozy corner table, the hostess showed them to a private room off the dining hall. They entered to find Roland Molineaux presiding over a bottle of Bordeaux and two steak sandwiches.

"Right on time," said the rotund chef, glancing at a wristwatch encrusted with more gems than a Fabergé egg. "You have twenty minutes. Assuming he's on time, and he's about as punctual as the Long Island Railroad."

"Wait—does that mean he's on time, or does that mean he's always late?"

"Sorry. Metro North, then. The man is like an atomic clock."

Asher motioned for Taylor to sit; she did. Then, still standing, he snarfed down one of the sandwiches.

"What's going on?"

"The uniforms are right here," Roland said, gesturing to a pair of red jackets, white dress shirts, and black tuxedo pants on stiff hangers behind the door. "Bon appétit." And he waddled off, closing the door behind him.

Taylor had spent the last four nights in Asher's bed, but was no closer to—as she put it—pinning him down. He was intense, and polite to a fault, but he was also detached. He refused to tell her anything about Quid Pro Quo beyond what she had to know. This was starting to grate on her, no matter how fantastic the sex was.

"Come on, Ash. What the hell?"

"In twenty minutes," said Asher, between bites, "one Bill Steward, a prominent real estate developer, will be here with his wife, Amber, to celebrate his sixty-third birthday. You'd like Amber—you're about the same age. As for Steward, as my mother used to tell me, if you can't say something nice about someone . . ."

"Is this going where I think it's going?"

"Give the girl a prize."

A surge of adrenaline washed over Taylor, negating what had been a gnawing hunger. Asher hadn't mentioned her looming assignment since the day of the Lydia Murtomaki interview—he mentioned very little beyond his pompous rants on any number of pop-cultural topics—and she was half-convinced it would never happen. And now the time was at hand! She was nervous, of course, but no more nervous than she had been giving her valedictorian speech in high school. She looked at both the same way—unpleasant tasks she had no choice but to complete. She had long ago resigned herself to her fate. If Asher could live with himself after doing the pink slips—and his conscience did not appear to be troubled, given how soundly he slept at night—why should she fret? It's not like she had much of a choice. No, the thing to do was to get it over with as soon as possible. Then, as she predicted (wrongly) in her diary, she would be relieved to have the albatross removed from her neck.

She pushed the steak sandwich aside. "What's the plan?"

Thirty minutes later, Taylor, in the Chez Molineaux uniform, approached a cozy candlelit table, where nuzzled a bleached blonde of the trophy wife variety and a squat old chap with a pockmarked face and hair plugs. His hand was on her well-exposed inner thigh.

"Good evening. May I start you off with something to drink?"

"Bombay martini, please. Shaken, not stirred."

"And for the lady?"

"The same."

Taylor went to the bar, where a second bartender was setting up shop. Behind the Don Mattingly moustache and Henry Kissinger specs was the unmistakable mug of Asher Krug.

"How's it going?"

"So far, so good." She glanced around at the army of waiters and waitresses buzzing around the dining room. "You sure this isn't suspicious? I mean, none of these people know us. Won't they think . . ."

"Are you kidding? The turnover in this place is ridiculous. New people come and go. Don't give it another thought."

Asher mixed the martinis—shaking and not stirring them, even though that process dissipates the alcohol, thus defeating the purpose of drinking them in the first place—and Taylor presented them to the Stewards on a silver tray.

"Are you ready to order?" she asked Amber. You were supposed to ask the ladies first, was what she'd learned in her years in food service.

But it was Bill Steward who answered, in a gruff, but somehow effete, voice. "Porterhouse. Rare. Mashed potatoes—plain, no garlic. And I'll have the same."

"How would you like that cooked?"

"Rare. Like I already told you"—he looked at her nametag—"Meghan."

"Right. Rare. Sorry about that."

Taylor relayed the orders to Asher, who gave them to Roland Molineaux.

"I don't know if I like having him involved," she whispered, watching the portly chef tub-thump off.

"Who, Roland? No, he's cool. He's with the CIA *and* the CIA."

"Huh?"

"The Culinary Institute of America," he explained. "The *other* CIA, they call it. Relax. This is almost over."

She leaned against the bar and produced a cigarette, which Asher lit for her.

"I thought you didn't approve of smoking."

"This is a special occasion."

"I love the moustache, by the way. It makes you look like Burt Reynolds. You should totally keep it."

"Not a chance."

Roland brought the steaks out himself. Then Taylor swung by the table to make sure the PDA-happy Stewards didn't need anything. Other than a room, they didn't. She smoked another cigarette at the bar while they ate, and watched busboys clear the plates.

It was time.

Asher took a piece of flourless chocolate cake—a Chez Molineaux specialty—from under the bar. He screwed a candle into the cake and lit it. Then he produced an eyedropper and squirted a few drops of clear liquid onto the cake's triangular corner.

"She's all yours."

Taking the cake, Taylor began to sing, a tad self-consciously, the birthday song. She'd done this a million times at the restaurants where she'd hostessed, and always found it an exercise in humiliation. Those waiters who were in the vicinity joined in with poorly cloaked reluctance. Amber applauded, fake tits bouncing up and down. The pockmarked Bill Steward looked genuinely touched. He laughed, gave his wife a lingering wet kiss, and blew out the candle.

The waiters dispersed. Amber took a forkful of chocolaty goodness and fed it to her husband. Bill Steward accepted the offering greedily. Three minutes later, he collapsed into the remains of the cake, dead. His wife screamed. The place went ape-shit.

By then, the two assassins had changed clothes—Asher into the usual suit and tie, Taylor into a long floral skirt, black camisole, and denim jacket—and fled through a back door. They were milling in front of the *Miss Saigon* marquee across the street when the police and ambulance arrived, sirens squealing.

"Well," Asher quipped, as EMTs dashed into the restaurant, "*that* was a piece of cake."

But Taylor was in no mood for Bondian badinage. She'd thought she would be relieved when the act was completed, but no—the poisoning had been so simple, the execution so well-executed, that she didn't feel like she had done anything at all. "That's *it*? That was so . . . anticlimactic."

"I told you it'd be easy." He kissed her. "You were wonderful."

"I took a dinner order. I didn't do anything." Taylor watched uniformed men wheel out a gurney. A plastic sheet covered the body. "He's really dead?"

"They don't put a blanket on your face if you're alive."

"He seemed like an asshole. Was he an asshole? He seemed like an asshole."

"Asshole doesn't do justice to what a fucking piece of shit that guy was. Come on. Let's get out of here."

They walked west—briskly, but not briskly enough to arouse suspicion—out of the Theatre District and into what real estate brokers now call Clinton but what in 1991 was still, emphatically, Hell's Kitchen. Riffraff filtered up from Port Authority. Junkies worked the streets. Muggers were a-prowl. It was a little piece of Bed Stuy in Manhattan.

They banged a left on Ninth Avenue, slackening the pace. Passing a derelict bearing an empty coffee can and a cardboard sign that read HOMELESS VET WITH AIDS, Asher was visibly disgusted.

"Vile," he said. "Half a block away and I can *still* smell the guy. Christ, I need a drink. Is there a place to have a beer around here?"

Taylor pointed to a bar on the other side of the street, with a four-foot-tall statue of a smiling pig stationed at its door. "How about there?"

"Rudy's?" Asher loosened his tie as if to take it off, then decided against it. "Fuck it. Let's go slumming."

They went past the pig and the battered wooden door and into Rudy's Bar and Grill, purveyor of cheap beer and free hot dogs since the Great Depression. There was a crowd of people inside, almost all of them men, and most of them looking like they should be hauling amplifiers for the Allman Brothers. Asher—the only suit in the room—bought two bottles of beer at the bar, while Taylor found a booth in the back.

"Amstel Light?" Taylor said once Asher sat down. "They don't have anything good on tap?"

"The taps in this place probably haven't been cleaned since the Eisenhower administration," he said. "I already poisoned one person tonight. I'm not a serial killer."

"Actually, you are. Lucky for you that chicks dig serial killers. Ted Bundy got marriage proposals till the bitter end." She killed half the beer in one swig. "So won't the police want to, like, question us?"

Asher waved off this suggestion. "Pfft. The guy had a heart attack. He was fat and out of shape and sixty-three. He was lucky he lived as long as he did."

"I guess." She fired up a cigarette. "It's weird. I don't have a sense of closure about this, you know? I just . . . I don't feel like I just killed somebody. I don't feel *anything*, really. Maybe it's cuz I didn't see him die?"

"Konrad Lorenz," Asher said, nodding in that pompous-professor way of his. "Are you familiar with *On Aggression*?"

Taylor figured that this was the first time that anyone had ever mentioned Konrad Lorenz in the confines of Rudy's. She shook her head.

"Lorenz says that the more detached we are from the physical act of killing, the easier it is to kill," said Asher. "Psychologically, I mean. What makes Othello's strangling of Desdemona so powerful is its raw brutality. When you strangle someone, it's a tactile experience. You can feel the other person struggling. You can literally *feel* him die. The physicality exacerbates the mental trauma. But put a gun in somebody's hand—or an intercontinental ballistic missile—and you're distancing that person from the brutality of the murder. With physical distance comes psychological distance. That's why we use the methods we use. We want our clients complicit; we don't want them traumatized."

Asher held up his beer. He was fond of proposing toasts. "To a job well done. You, my dear, are now officially off the hook."

Taylor obliged him, raising her glass and drinking. But she didn't *feel* off the hook. She was *so* untraumatized, in fact, that she felt somehow cheated. The lack of closure gnawed at her . . . but why?

"Shall we?"

Back at the Dakota, they set about making love. This involved Asher lying on his back while Taylor, with hooker-worthy precision, slurped him until he was sufficiently swollen. (Fellatio was compulsory to their foreplay, but Asher, incredibly, never reciprocated. He was *so* old-fashioned, *so* traditional, that he operated under the deranged delusion that guys who went down on girls were latent homosexuals. I'm not kidding. When she complained about it one time, he shrugged and said, "I'm no faggot." If he were a girl, he would probably have believed that you couldn't get pregnant the first time. And *this* was the guy Taylor fell for. But I digress.) The sex itself compensated for the shortcomings of the buildup. Through intercourse, Taylor was able to feed, vampire-like, on the feeling of raw power he generated. With each fuck, he injected her (if you excuse the coarse metaphor) with the potency he had in ample supply: charisma, confidence, courage, invincibility, and so forth.

But this time, on this night, something was different. The pink slip of Bill Seward had changed her. Taylor realized—although she didn't elucidate it quite this way in her diary—that Asher, virile and vital though he may have been, was not the source of the power she felt while having sex with him. He was merely awakening something she already possessed, something that lay dormant inside her, shut off after years of neglect and abuse. Tonight, she saw that she did not need Asher to get high. She could realize her potential without him—and she had, when she killed Bill Seward.

There is no more primal expression of potency than taking another man's life. Why else would the Saddam Husseins and Charles Taylors of the world, the Hitlers and Stalins, the Caligulas and Ivans the Terrible, routinely commit mass murder, if not to feed that sense of power? The ancients knew this; human sacrifice was not just metaphorical, it was a literal attempt to sate the blood-thirst of the gods.

Most people, of course, don't have a thrill seeker's reaction to killing. Konrad Lorenz was right—killing *is* traumatic. Soldiers have post-traumatic stress disorder. Lady Macbeth washes her hands obsessively (as does Natasha in *The Lap of Uxory*). Homicides go to jail, repent, find Jesus or Allah. When atrocities are committed in chaotic lands—Sierra Leone, Kurdistan, Darfur— it is always a tiny percentage of the population, social scientists assert, that does the bulk of the killing. Had an abusive childhood left Taylor with deficient empathy? Was she born lacking it? Was it some opposition of the stars that made her the way she was? Look, I wish I could explain why she did what she did, but I can't. I can only report on what happened. And *On Aggression* simply did not apply to Taylor Schmidt. She wasn't traumatized by killing; on the contrary, she was exhilirated. There was no pang of guilt, only a rush of adrenaline. And she wanted to feel that way again. It was a dark inkling, this epiphany she had that night, while going down on Asher Krug of all things—so dark that when she finally gave it voice, she was shocked to hear the words coming out of her mouth.

"I want to do it again," she said, pulling away.

Asher gestured at the unwieldy thing between his legs, which had the bouncy look of a helium balloon tethered to the ground. "Me, too," he said. "But we need to do it once before we do it again."

"I'm not talking about sex, Asher. I'm talking about the pink slip."

His enthusiasm began to wither.

Once her desire had been uttered, it gained momentum. "I *need* to do it again."

"Don't be ridiculous."

"I'm totally serious."

"Well, you can't. One and done. Those are the rules."

"The rules? We just fucking *murdered* somebody, and you're talking about *rules*? What kind of an outlaw are you?"

"Outlaw? I never said I was an outlaw. I work for Quid Pro Quo in order to effect change. Period, full stop. I'm no *outlaw*, Taylor. I'm a revolutionary. I'm Patrick Henry. I'm Nathan Hale. I'm George Washington."

Her eyes were wide now. She was all Miranda. "Then let me be Betsy Ross."

"Taylor, I can't."

"Why not? You think because I'm a woman, I'm not up to the job? Is that it? Or do you get your jollies knowing you're special and everybody else is shit? You're a revolutionary. Great. Let me join the revolution."

"Taylor . . ."

The more she talked, the more attractive the idea seemed. Why not *her* doing the pink slips? Why not *her* arrayed in pricey clothes, flitting around Manhattan in a Jaguar, living in Yoko Ono's building? Why not *her* playing the Grim Reaper? "Talk to Lydia about me. See what she says."

Asher's face went ashen with what had to be raw fear, and his erection subsided completely. "No, Taylor. No way. The company . . . this is not something to mess around with."

"Whatever, talk to Lydia, don't talk to Lydia, but let me help you. I have to do this, Asher. I need to do this."

"You're upset. You don't know what you're saying."

Now both of them were sitting up, on opposite sides of Asher's king-size bed. In the silence, she found a smoke, lit up, and took a few drags. She smoked too much, Taylor. Not that it mattered in the long run—I guess she knew what she was doing.

"It would be fun, Asher." With her free hand she caressed his chest. "Do you know how wet it would make me, to do it with you?"

"I'm sorry, but I can't."

Asher took a deep breath and let it out slowly. Then, with the grace of a gymnast, he bounded out of bed, grabbed the remote on the bureau, and turned on the hi-fi. He pressed the volume button six or seven times, so when the song came on—it was "Do You Really Want to Hurt Me?" by Culture Club; bizarre, that Asher would like that song, but why else would it have been in the CD changer?—Boy George's voice was loud enough to wake the neighbors. Or would have been, in our crappy apartment.

He sat on the bed next to Taylor, caressed away the strand of hair that was over her ear, and whispered. "We need to be careful."

"What are you doing?"

"They have the place bugged," he explained, his voice so low she could barely hear him. "It's not safe to talk here."

"Why would they bug your apartment?"

"Lydia doesn't trust me. She and I . . . we've had some differences lately. Are you serious about joining the revolution?"

She didn't give a damn about the revolution. In fact, she had no idea what he was talking about—I had to piece it together myself later. But she would say whatever she needed to say to achieve the rush again. "Totally."

"Good. But just so we're clear, Quid Pro Quo and the revolution are two different things."

She had never seen him act this way before—frightened, almost panicky. It did not wholly shatter his cool image, but she could definitely detect a chink in the armor. "Does that mean I'll get to do it again?"

"Wait a few days, see how you feel," he said. "If you aren't racked with guilt, it's go-time."

"Oh, Asher, you won't regret this."

Although neither of them recognized it at the time, the subsequent lovemaking—which was well-documented in her diary and which I'll gloss over—represented the zenith of their relationship. It was all downhill from there.

When I came home from work the next day, I was surprised to find Taylor in. She was sitting at the kitchen table, poring over some thick hardcovers and a few pieces of paper, pencils at the ready. She looked like she was studying for an exam.

"Hey, Todd."

"Taylor. What a pleasant surprise."

But the surprise was not entirely pleasant. See, her absence had been so predictable lately, I had gotten a mite careless with her diaries, which she had had the decency to leave in her closet when she moved the rest of her stuff to Asher's. There were three or four of them on the nightstand by my bed (the sex scenes made for pre-sleep masturbatory fodder). Had she found them?

"Where's Asher?"

"Work," she said. "His hours suck."

Nothing in her tone suggested that she'd found the diaries, and I relaxed.

"You have some mail," I said. "Let me find it."

I darted into my room, collected the diaries, and jammed them under the mattress. Then I found the stack of her mail and brought it into the living room.

"Anybody call?"

"Just your mom. Here. Junk, mostly."

"Throw it in my bag, would you?"

I did what she asked, and took a seat on the couch.

"Todd," she said, "have you ever wanted to kill someone?"

Having just committed murder the night before, this was, for Taylor, a perfectly logical question. But I was not privy to her felonious activities. The diaries she'd left in the apartment covered the time between junior high and the morning after her Rainbow Room date with Asher Krug. The current installment of said diary she continued to keep either in her office or on her person. Thus, I did not discover the dread secret of Quid Pro Quo, or anything that happened subsequently, until later.

"Well, sure," I said. "Jerry Jones. Motherfucker fired Tom Landry."

"Who?"

I am from South Jersey—Eagles country—but I rooted for the Cowboys, mostly because I hated Eagles fans.

"Thomas Wade Landry? Creator of the 4-3 defense?"

Apparently they didn't watch football in Warrensburg. Taylor wrinkled her nose at me. "I'm serious."

So I gave the question serious thought. While there had been moments in my life when my ire was sufficiently piqued to fantasize about homicide—usually when I was driving—I couldn't think of a single instance of wanting to kill someone, nor could I name anyone whose demise I eagerly desired, the Dallas Cowboys owner excepted. I told her so.

Nodding, Taylor went to fire up a smoke, but found her cigarette case empty.

"When I was sixteen, I was going to kill my mother and her boyfriend," she told me. "I had it all worked out. I was going to forge a suicide note and blow their fucking heads off. I had the letter written, I had the gun loaded—Billy Ray always kept guns in the house. The preparations were all made."

"But you didn't do it," I said, hating the implicit question mark at the end of my sentence. I mean, of course she hadn't done it. Darla Jenkins was still alive and well, sucking at the teat of the State of Missouri. But there was something so intense in Taylor's expression that I second-guessed myself.

"I was pretty sure I'd get away with it, but I needed to be positive. I was still a minor, but I was sixteen—what if they tried me as an adult? The State of Missouri isn't exactly lenient on murderers, and Darla wasn't worth the gas chamber. So she lived, only to breed again."

I didn't say anything for a while. In the apartment below, Trey Parrish was playing "Down with O.P.P." on his megawatt sound system. We sat there mute, listening to the rumbling bass shake the building.

"Wow," I said finally. "That's heavy."

Though small potatoes to what she had done the previous evening, the information still jolted my equilibrium. It's like if someone tells you that they're gay, or that they had an abortion—it takes a while to fully process. Killing somebody takes a while to process, too. That's what Taylor was dealing with, although, again, I had no idea at the time.

"If you lived through what I lived through," she said, "you would have considered it, too."

"You're probably right." I decided to change the subject. Gesturing to the books on the table, I asked her what she was doing.

"Horoscopes," she said sheepishly. "I had our charts done."

"Ours?"

"Mine and Asher's."

"Oh." I rose from the couch to get a closer look. The books on the table included an ephemeris, the AFA's *Astrological Atlas*, a *Table of Houses*, and three Robert Hand books: *Planets in Composite*, *Planets in Youth*, and *Horoscope Symbols*. The charts themselves were circles divided into twelve uneven segments, like a sloppy pizza. Littered around the rims were handwritten hieroglyphics, some of them resembling automotive logos, whose meanings I could not begin to discern. "I didn't know you believed in that crap."

"It's not crap," Taylor said. Then she went into this long, rambling explanation of how Asher was a Scorpio—hence the penchant for secrecy—but with Gemini rising, which meant he was dispassionate about matters of the heart, and how his moon was in Aries—not good placement for the moon—and that he had Mars in the First House, which supposedly explained his macho, take-charge nature. Her chart contained several T-squares, creating conflicting aspects among her planets. There was also a lot of quincunx happening, whatever that was. She was a Pisces, which meant she was easily swayed, with Sagittarius in her Seventh House, hence the seventy-some-odd sexual partners. The placement of Saturn was also instrumental, but I don't remember how or why. There was also a third analysis, called a synastry grid, which compared his chart with hers, checking for areas of harmony or opposition. The whole thing was bunk—or so I thought at the time. Her foray into occultism did, however, make one thing abundantly clear.

"You must really love him," I said, masking what a blow to my own heart this revelation was.

"Yeah," she said. "I guess I do."

On the subject of free will, astrologers will tell you that the stars incline, but they do not compel. A nice enough platitude, but let's get real. For most of us, inclination and compulsion are in conjunction. We know this alliance by its trade name, Fate. Once she found out his secret—and certainly once he coerced her into homicide—Taylor should have been repulsed by Asher Krug. Instead, she was drawn to him all the more. She shouldn't have been, but she was. Was this inclination? Compulsion? Or just bad luck?

"I rented *Heathers* again," I said. "Want to watch?"

"Sure."

CHAPTER 14

Andrew Borden lived in a magnificent Tudor-style home in Short Hills, a tony Jersey suburb known for its ostentatious shopping mall. His manse was at the end of a cul-de-sac, rows of high bushes and evergreen trees insulating him from his neighbors and the street. His was a residence that afforded quiet, security, and above all privacy to its residents—and anyone who chanced to murder them.

A black Ford Explorer was parked out front, in the shadows between two streetlights. Its passengers could just see through the front window, between a patchwork of leaves and branches, where the man of the house sat in a La-Z-Boy, reading the newspaper. He had a cylindrical object in his hand, either a thick pen or a thin cigar.

Asher and Taylor sat there in the dark, listening to the sound of their breathing. Her heartbeat was so loud, there in the stillness, that she swore the beginning of *The Dark Side of the Moon* was on the stereo. But no, the SUV was off. Finally, she could bear the silence no more.

"So what, did someone flake out?"

"Something like that." Asher drew from an attaché case two .44s and a velvet bag. "This is the kind of guy we should be pink-slipping."

Closing the case, he laid the guns on top of it. "Baby boomer, investment banking executive. Contributes nothing to the world, but draws more salary than a dozen Gen Xers."

He dumped the contents of the velvet bag—a pair of magazine cartridges and two metal cylinders that might have been lifted from a ratchet set—into his hand and held up one of the cylinders for Taylor to see. "Silencer."

Asher screwed the silencers into place, inserted the cartridges, polished anything metal with the velvet bag. "I've been on so many assignments lately that have *nothing* to do with our stated purpose. I understand Heinz and Tower—we had to send a message. But Bakhtiar? Why send me to Paris to whack Shapour Fucking Bakhtiar? First of all, he's Iranian. Second of all, he's on our side."

Taylor was not listening to him, and even if she were, she had no idea who Shapour Bakhtiar was. She was examining the shiny weapon, caressing its barrel, her eyes gleaming. "Can I see?"

Asher handed her one of the pistols. "When you see red—there on the side—that means the safety's on. I'll tell you when to disengage it. Have you ever shot a gun before?"

She couldn't have been more excited. *This is more like it*, she thought. It was less than a week since the Steward pink slip, and her enthusiasm to continue had not abated.

"Have you ever shot a gun before? Taylor . . . Taylor, pay attention. Have you ever shot a gun before?"

"No."

"The thing to remember is, squeeze. Don't jerk your hand backward. Do this"—he squeezed an imaginary trigger—"and

not this"—he demonstrated the undesired jerk-back of the hand—
"Okay? Just hold it steady and you'll be fine."

"What if I miss?"

"It's a fucking .44. You won't miss. Now, put it in your purse
and hand me the Bible."

She handed him the book and stowed her weapon in her bag.
"How do we know he's alone?"

"His wife plays bridge every Wednesday night. We have very
good intelligence on this. What time do you have?"

"Quarter to ten."

"Let's do it."

They got out of the car and walked up the gravel driveway to the
front door. Her right hand was inside the bag, her fingers wrapped
around the pistol. Asher carried the Bible; his own gun was tucked
into his pants under his jacket.

He rang the doorbell. Decades passed. Butterflies were spinning round-round-baby-right-round-like-a-record-baby in Taylor's
stomach. Finally the door opened. Standing before them was not
Andrew Borden, investment banking scum, but a bird-like woman
in her late forties. She wore a bathrobe and hair curlers and carried
a box of tissues.

Obviously, there'd been a breakdown in intelligence, but Asher
seemed unperturbed. "Good evening, ma'am. We're very sorry to
disturb you at this late hour, but the Good News we've come to
share simply cannot wait." He appropriated a Rhett Butler drawl
that almost made Taylor laugh. Gesticulating dramatically with
the Bible, he said, "Could we kindly come in and talk to you for a
few minutes?"

Mrs. Borden—for the hair-curlered woman at the door
was she—scowled at them. "I don't think so. We're very busy,
and . . ."

Asher took a step forward, blocking the door jamb with his
foot. "Ma'am, there's always time for the Lord. If you forget Him
in this life, He will forget you in the next. We're only here for your
own good."

Mrs. Borden smiled condescendingly. "And I appreciate that. But we're really not interested."

"Abby?" called a gravelly voice from the next room. "Abby, who's at the door?"

"I apologize, ma'am, but we just can't take no for an answer."

"Abby? Honey, is everything okay?"

The would-be missionary let the Bible slip from his hands. Abby Borden watched it fall, instead of watching Asher smack her in the temple with the handle of his gun. She collapsed in a heap on top of the book.

"Abby? Abby!"

"Come on. Quick."

The assassins stepped into a cavernous foyer, its walls papered with an off-white damask print that matched the ceramic floor tiles. There was a settee, an umbrella stand, a grandfather clock, and, by the front door, a throw rug, on which had fallen Mrs. Borden's limp but still living body. Directly in front of them was an archway that led to the kitchen; on the left, a closet and a stairway to the second floor; on the right, the origin of the gruff voice, the living room.

Asher motioned to his accomplice, his right palm perpendicular to the ground, like a crossing guard, or Marcel Marceau half-miming a wall. "Stay by the door."

Taylor drew her gun, closing the door gently behind her, and watched Asher drag the throw rug—and by extension, Mrs. Borden—to the foot of the staircase. She became aware of an odd odor, a pungent mixture of cheap cigar and expensive perfume.

"Abby!"

Andrew Borden burst in from the living room, wearing dress slacks, polished Johnston & Murphys, suspenders, and a sleeveless undershirt. This last item afforded a view of his left bicep, on which was tattooed the words SEMPER FI. He was six-six if he was an inch, and all muscle. He glanced at Taylor, then at Asher, then at the fallen body of his wife, then back at Asher. "What the fuck . . . "

"Good evening, Mr. Borden." Asher waved the .44, taking a few steps toward the center of the room as the investment banker moved in the direction of the kitchen. The bathrobed woman now lay between the two men, crumpled on the throw rug.

Borden rushed to his wife, bent down, cradled her head in his hands.

"Get away from her."

"She's hurt. She needs help." He patted his wife's face. "Abby? Abby, can you hear me?"

Asher cocked the gun. "Don't make me repeat myself."

With his free hand, Asher wiped away all the sweat that had suddenly appeared on his brow, which diverted his attention just long enough for Borden to tackle him. Both Asher and his gun crashed to the floor, the latter sliding across the ceramic tile into the living room. The investment banker, muttering curses under his breath, landed a blow to the abdomen of the fallen assassin. Asher retaliated with an open-hand shot to the chin, which sent Borden reeling.

Asher scrambled to his feet and made for the living room. Before he could get there, Borden tripped him up. A wrestling match ensued. Asher might have been younger and a professional killer, but Borden was bigger, stronger, angrier, and an ex-Marine. In no time he had his attacker pinned to the ground.

"Who sent you?" He punched Asher's jaw so hard Taylor could feel it. "Answer me, you little prick." Another punch, this one a touch harder.

Taylor, meanwhile, had the look on her face of a Richard Kimble about to jump into the waterfall in *The Fugitive* (in 1991, Harrison Ford was still reading the script). She aimed the .44 at Borden, but she didn't want to fire and hit Asher by mistake, which, considering she'd never shot a gun before, was a distinct possibility. What was the best course of action? She glanced from the combatants to the unconscious woman to the umbrella stand. It was made of sturdy metal. A whack on the head with that and Borden would be knocked senseless—or would he? And in order to wield the umbrella stand she would have to drop the pistol. There was no way she was doing that.

"Who sent you?"

"Your sister." Asher, who had somehow freed his right hand, landed a roundhouse to the other's cheekbone. Borden toppled to his right, the momentum rolling both men into the living room—and toward the fallen gun. There was now a clear path between Taylor and the foot of the staircase.

In action movies the hero always shows great resource in dispatching the enemy—shoving an electric fan into his bathtub just before the bad guy can shoot, offing the last three terrorists with a .22 Scotch-taped to his bare back, and so forth. But Andrew Borden, despite his size and pugilistic ability, was no Auric Goldfinger, no Hans Gruber. He was just an investment banker. Taylor did not need to be innovative. She could beat him with the oldest trick in the book.

As the men continued to fight, she darted across the room and pointed her own gun at Mrs. Borden's temple. "Listen up, asshole. Leave him alone or I'll shoot her."

They continued to grapple.

"Did you hear me? I said stop it."

This seemed to work. Both of the men froze in mid-fight. The way their bodies were intertwined, they might have been playing Twister.

"Let him go. Let him go *right now*."

Borden did as he was told.

Slowly Asher rose, dusted himself off, rubbed his jaw. "That's some left hook you got there." He retrieved his pistol and cocked it.

"I . . . used to box at Princeton." For once in Borden's life, dropping the name of his alma mater did not help him. "What do you want from me?" His voice had lost its bravado.

"Stay down," Taylor commanded, "and come closer."

The investment banker did not move right away. He just looked at her, eyes glassy, and started the inevitable plea for mercy. "Let her go. Please let her go. Kill me if you have to, but let her go."

"I said come closer."

Borden took several uneasy steps into the foyer.

"Now, get down."

The investment banker just stared at her with terrified eyes.

"She said get down, fuckwad," Asher added.

Without further delay, Borden assumed the position of a Muslim at prayer time. "Please. Just let her go. I beg you . . ." He was sobbing in earnest now. "Please . . . please . . . please . . ."

Taylor inched closer to the blubbering investment banker, who, in his moment of pusillanimous weakness, inspired rage in her, for reasons she could not explain. His wails were like those of a car alarm—strident, annoying, and, ultimately, futile. She wanted them to stop, for there to be silence, like there had been in the Explorer. Dead silence.

"If you're a religious man," she said, "I suggest you start praying."

Although his theological convictions were probably questionable, Andrew Borden proved a pragmatist. He made the sign of the cross, held his hands in prayer position, and had rolled off a Hail Mary and two and a half Our Fathers before he felt the barrel of the gun at the base of his skull.

" . . . hallowed be Thy name . . ."

Asher was still on the floor, nursing his swollen jaw. He slowly clambered to his feet.

" . . . Thy kingdom come, Thy will be done on earth, as it is in Heaven . . ."

Taylor watched the man grovel. His *life* was in her hands! This was what she had missed with the Seward hit, and what she had sought with this one. The surge of power was tremendous—even more of a jolt than she'd expected. Or so she wrote in her diary that night.

" . . . give us this day our daily bread, and forgive us our trespasses . . ."

She glanced over at Asher, who had shaken off the pain. He gave her a thumbs-up.

" . . . as we forgive those who trespass against us . . ."

The *power* she held in her hands! It made her tremble and almost drop the gun. She felt like a god. Like God.

" . . . and lead us not into temptation, but deliver us from evil . . ."

Holding the pistol with both hands, to better absorb the kickback, she said, "Amen," and calmly squeezed the trigger. Almost instantly there were red splotches all over the white tile, giving the floor the look of a Jackson Pollock painting she had been unable to see at MOMA. She took in the tableau for a long time, as an artist would her ultimate brushstroke.

"You were right." She gestured to the larger-than-expected hole in what was left of Andrew Borden's head. "I didn't miss."

"Nice work," Asher said. "Very clean."

"Thanks."

The grandfather clock began to chime; it was exactly ten o'clock.

Taylor gestured toward the body at the foot of the stairs. "Is she dead?"

"Moot point, really." He raised his gun and rained bullets on Abby Borden's body.

For a fleeting moment, Taylor felt sorry for the older woman. Abby wasn't the pink slip, after all, and if her nose had not been runny, she would have been playing bridge. But the moment was just that, fleeting, soon replaced by a narcotic euphoria.

"Leave the gun," Asher told her. "We have to get out of here quick."

"What's the rush? Quid Pro Quo doesn't answer to the police, right?"

"Taylor," Asher said, "this wasn't a pink slip. This was an act of revolution."

"What?"

"I'll explain in the car. Let's *go*."

Too many baby boomers were going to live into their eighties and nineties, and work well into their seventies. They would make too much money and suck up too many jobs for too long, unless action was taken now. Starting with the financial companies in New York, and spreading to the entertainment industry—which was responsible for the pejorative way Generation X was perceived in the media—the baby boomers holding the top jobs would be executed. Slowly, methodically, completely. A genocide of bloated CEOs, of movers and shakers who didn't move or shake fast enough. This was the revolution, Asher explained, as he navigated the tortuous and poorly-labeled New Jersey highways, speeding back to Manhattan as fast as the Explorer could go. This was what he had enlisted her to help with.

Taylor was not paying attention. She didn't care about baby boomers and Gen Xers, financial companies or entertainment conglomerates. Her motive was, and always would be, visceral. She killed for how it made her feel. And she didn't like that the Borden job, a rogue action not under the aegis of Quid Pro Quo, exposed her to arrest. He should have told her. It was like lacing a joint with PCP and not saying so until after the hit. But unlike a laced joint, it killed her buzz.

If she had been in love with Asher Krug the day she was poring over their horoscopes—and I believe she was—the spell had worn off by the time they hit the Holland Tunnel. The subsequent sex, while still good, was not as good as it had been. All she could think, as he pounded away on top of her, was that his carelessness had spoiled her good time.

I can't be his partner, she wrote in her diary the next day (although I didn't read it until later, of course). *Somehow, I have to do this on my own.*

CHAPTER 15

Sometime after her mini-murder spree, Taylor did take a few moments to mention my employment woes to Asher, who consented to see me. So that Friday, two days after the Bordens bit the dust, I strode through the ornate lobby of 520 Madison, and the even more ornate lobby of the Quid Pro Quo Employment Agency. I raised an eyebrow and turned a nose at the ridiculous owl statue. I gave Mae-Yuan—who was smokingly gorgeous; Taylor hadn't mentioned that in her diary—my résumé and my own list of personal references (Taylor, Jason Hanson, Laura Horowitz). I joined a crowd of wet-behind-the-ears hipsters, with whom I didn't belong. Then I sat through Asher Krug's lecture, allowing me to study him up close for the first time.

My impression that morning was that Asher was the quintessential alpha male, a man's man, the kind of guy who would never get a shy bladder whipping it out to take a leak in a crowded lavatory. He was my age, which is to say around twenty-six, but there was nothing boyish about him. I couldn't imagine him as a boy, or an awkward teen; he must have hatched, fully formed, the way he was. He had the confidence, the gravitas, the carriage, of someone twenty years older. Not that he looked old—he didn't, not really—but he oozed maturity. He was all grown up. Ready for anything. He was the sort of man guys like me unquestionably follow. A leader of men. The dude was something else. No wonder Taylor was smitten. Hell, *I* was practically smitten.

Asher fed us more or less the same stump speech Taylor heard, right down to the jokes about Don Corleone and *The Merchant of Venice*. The audience reacted with the requisite awe.

Afterwards, I joined him in his office. I felt like I was in the room with a celebrity, like he was Redford or Brando—he had this intimidating glow about him that just about rendered me speechless. Thinking back, I might have even been a little attracted to him—and I'm not gay, not even remotely. Put it this way: I totally would have done a three-way with him and Taylor. (Then again, I'd have done a three-way with Taylor and just about anyone—Richard Simmons, Manuel Noriega, Larry "Bud" Melman—as long as I had a turn with her.)

"It's nice to finally meet you," I said when I'd found my tongue. "Taylor's told me so much about you."

"Likewise," he said, although I'm not sure I believed him.

"Nice suit. What is that, Italian?"

"Japanese."

"Very schnazzy."

"Thanks."

"I feel underdressed."

Asher regarded my flannel shirt, stone-washed Levi's, and Doc Marten boots with disapproval, but said nothing.

I couldn't place his ethnic origins. He was dark, as I mentioned, with blackish hair and olive skin, and although he was meticulously shaved, he had the sort of face on which a full beard could sprout in a matter of hours.

"Krug," I said. "What sort of name is that?"

"My grandparents were from Breslau. Please. Have a seat."

In addition to the earlier description of the office that I relayed from Taylor's diary—the martini stand, the Modigliani and Mondrian, the view—I noticed a few more details. Next to the three-ring binders and stack of résumés on his desk sat a well-worn copy of *The 7 Habits of Highly Effective People*; even the great Asher Krug, apparently, was not above self-help. There was a blue legal-sized folder on his desk, tucked into the corner of his blotter, marked RUSSELL TRUST ASSOC., and behind him, on a credenza, a silver-framed photograph of a younger Asher shaking hands with an older man whose face I recognized but whose name I couldn't place.

"Thanks for seeing me on such short notice," I told him.

"My pleasure. Any friend of Taylor's, as they say. So, she tells me you've lost your job."

"Something like that."

"Please explain."

I laid out the circumstances of my dismissal as best as I could without mentioning the fact that Donna Green fired me for leaving work early just about every day—an action that was completely justified. As I spoke, Asher nodded his head, like a professor listening to one of his pupils regurgitate his own lecture.

"What the hippies don't understand," he said when I had finished, "is that the only way to level the playing field is to level the playing field. You can't prevent discrimination against black people by discriminating against white people."

I hadn't mentioned to Taylor that Donna Green was black—I don't think I even mentioned it in these pages—so this was out of left field, although I didn't realize it at the time.

"The audacity," Asher continued, "of these so-called civil rights leaders invoking *slavery* in their arguments. How much mileage can they get out of that? Now they want the government to pay *reparations* to the descendents of slaves—as if a few more dollars could somehow erase the horror of what happened in this country a hundred fifty years ago. The nerve of those people! What the Jesse Jacksons and Al Sharptons of the world don't seem to appreciate is, if they *weren't* descended from slaves—if their conquered ancestors had managed to stay put; if there'd been no slave trade—they'd be in Africa right now, living under the yoke of some corrupt dictator, half-starved, circumcising their daughters with sharp stones, dying of AIDS-related illnesses at age thirty. For some reason, no one ever mentions this. Was slavery terrible? Without question. And so was the Reconstruction period, the Jim Crow laws, the separate-but-equal—all of it. But that time is past. Those days are over. Our generation *understands* that people are people, unlike the hypocritical baby boomers. And the truth, the unpleasant truth, is that every black person in this country, without exception, is better off here than he would be in Africa, where there's no such thing as civil rights, or rap music, or professional basketball. In Africa, there's no way out of the muck. Here, there's opportunity. They act like they're entitled, these people, but we owe them nothing. We *saved* them, plain and simple. We saved them from themselves. Even if our motives were less than pure."

I didn't, and still don't, support affirmative action. But it's one thing to favor a meritocracy; quite another to suggest, as Asher did, that African Americans are better off for having been slaves. How would Jackson or Sharpton have responded to Asher's lecture? That would have been a *Crossfire* worth watching. Me, I couldn't think of what to say, confronted with such egregious racism. So I held my tongue.

We sat there dumbly for a moment, and then, to break the silence, he moved on. "I do hope we can help you." He looked at a copy of my pathetic CV and wrinkled his brow. "To be brutally honest, Todd, I'm a bit hesitant about this."

"Hesitant? Why?"

"Your résumé is . . . well, it shows a pattern that I'm not altogether comfortable with."

"A pattern?"

"You've had seven jobs in four years. Assuming the dates on

here are accurate. That indicates a propensity for movement, an inability to hold onto a position."

"Most of those jobs were temporary in nature," I explained. "And I got laid off a couple times. The market . . . it's hard out there for a guy like me."

"I know. That's what keeps us in business. What is it that you want to do, exactly?"

"Well, I'm an actor by trade."

"Taylor mentioned that. Acting jobs are harder to come by than office jobs, you realize."

"I'd be happy with anything in the entertainment industry."

"That's not very specific."

"I'm open to every opportunity."

"Let me explain my reservations, then." He hit an intercom switch on the desk. "Mae-Yuan? Coffee, please. There is a trend," fixing his commanding glare on me, "for want of a better word, among people of our generation to slack off, to withdraw from society. There is a cynicism, a bitterness, accompanied by a snide arrogance I find most unbecoming. Do you know what I'm talking about?"

I was at a job interview dressed like Eddie Vedder. I knew all too well what he was talking about.

"I understand the compunction to stand up for our generation, to usurp the baby boomers who have made a cesspool of this country. What I don't understand, and can never abide, is the method. This business of standing down. I don't understand it, I don't think it works. I think it's lazy. I don't get why people don't vote, for example. I don't get why people don't try harder to succeed. We're *smarter* than our parents, Todd; we should be able to take over, to seize power, not just sit on our asses whining all the livelong day. This movement, this slacker bullshit, it makes me sick. It makes me want to puke. It makes me want to kill someone."

Asher showed great passion, just as Taylor described. So much so that for a fleeting—and quite icky—moment, I found myself drawn to him. I wanted him to cradle me in his big strong arms and protect me from harm, in a way that my own father never could. I wanted this, and he was my age, if not younger.

"My sense, based on your résumé and your choice of attire for our meeting, is that you are one of these shall-we-say fallen angels. If this is true, there's nothing we can do for you."

A sudden sinking feeling made me swoon—and not from Asher's raw, Brandovian sexuality. When I got shitcanned, the idea that Quid Pro Quo might help me get back on my feet somewhat softened the blow. If even the mighty Asher Krug couldn't help, I was, in a word, fucked.

"I'm not a slacker," I told him emphatically, determined to win his approval. "I don't not participate. I voted. I just had temp jobs so I could audition—that's all."

"Fair enough." Asher took a three-ring binder from the desk and leafed through it, as Mae-Yuan materialized like an apparition with two steaming cups of coffee. She presented the drinks and vanished just as ghostily.

"Something in entertainment," Asher said, sipping his joe—he took it black, of course, like a man. "There may be an opportunity at MTV in a few weeks, if you can hold out for that. There's a program they're developing . . . it might even lead to an acting gig, who knows."

"MTV? That'd be . . . wow, that'd be amazing."

"If the job doesn't blow your mind—if it's not a job to kill for—the arrangement is not going to work."

He really did say *a job to kill for.* Taylor already knew the gruesome truth, but I still operated under the assumption that this was just a figure of speech, an ironical idiom. How could I have imagined otherwise?

"It will be. Believe me."

"Good."

As he collected some forms for me to complete, it hit me who the old guy in the picture behind him was.

"Asher," I asked, "what's with Lee Atwater?"

As he turned to the photograph, a wan smile formed on his

face, and for the only time in my presence, he looked boyish. "A great American. One of my heroes."

"One of your *heroes*?" I couldn't believe what I was hearing. Lee Atwater was Karl Rove's mentor, the sleazy spin doctor whose shady dealings propelled Ronald Reagan, and then George Herbert Walker Bush, into the White House. His lack of scruples was so legendary—the Southern strategy, anyone?—that he wound up recanting on his deathbed. No one in the liberal, *Nation*-reading universe that I inhabited felt anything but contempt for him. In fact, when he'd died that past March, one of the bars in the East Village threw a little party. "You're joking, right?"

"Do I look like I'm joking?" Asher did not look like he was joking. His sense of humor, deficient as it was, didn't run that dry. "I suppose that if you *did* in fact participate in the last election, you voted for Dukakis."

"*Of course* I voted for Dukakis. You voted for . . . for Bush?"

"Obviously."

Dana Carvey's impression on *Saturday Night Live* muddled the then-president's true colors. George Bush *père* was far from the wimp the popular media portrayed him as.

"The guy's evil incarnate," I said. "He was the head of the CIA, he's in the Saudi's back pocket, he started the Gulf War for no good reason, he was in Skull and Bones at Yale . . . I even heard he was in on the JFK assassination."

"You have no idea what you're talking about," Asher said, which was true—all of my information came from an exposé I'd read in *Spy* magazine. "None. I see you're a conspiracy theorist, like so many of our coevals."

Coevals. Who talks like that? Asher's voice trailed off, but he was not done speaking.

"The Democrats," he told me, "have done nothing but fuck this country up for the past half century. Every time they come to power, they make things worse. Without exception. Beginning with FDR and his ridiculous and expensive social and welfare programs."

He didn't like John Lennon, he didn't like Franklin Roosevelt, he worshipped Lee Atwater, and Taylor was fucking him instead of me. Fucking great.

"What about Kennedy?"

"Overrated. The playboy charm and the assassination, the haze of nostalgia, they cloud the real picture. He got us into Vietnam, because he couldn't handle Khrushchev in Berlin, and he *completely* fucked up the Bay of Pigs. Cuba would be the fifty-first state by now, if his sleazebag father hadn't bought West Virginia for him in '60. LBJ precipitated matters, and this affirmative action horseshit you're so fond of originated on his desk. Remember that. Things only settled down under Nixon. He would have gotten us out of Vietnam sooner, too, if Watergate hadn't happened. What a travesty! So *what* if he bugged McGovern's headquarters? We should trash national security for George Fucking McGovern? The seventies were ruined—*ruined*—because the Democrats wouldn't just *let that go*. That turncoat Woodward and that little shit Bernstein—they were responsible for escalating the war. People blame Kissinger, but it was the *Washington Post*'s fault. But we'll have our revenge. Next time there's a Democrat in office—hopefully not in my lifetime—we'll take him down for something trivial, something stupid, inconsequential to the greater good. Like Watergate was. Then you'll understand how things really work, how presidents *should* be above the law."

This, apparently, was the end of the interview. Asher hit the intercom button. "Mae-Yuan, please escort Mr. Lander out." He rose, reached across the desk. "I'll see you October 30th for your follow-up. And wear a tie next time, would you? This is a place of business, not a lumberyard."

This went in one ear and out the other. All I could think of, as I toddled out of his office, was MTV. Fame was knocking on my door. I was going to be a star.

CHAPTER 16

Roger Gale, author of *The Lap of Uxory*, stood in the lobby of the Royalton Hotel, waiting for his editor to arrive for lunch. He wore black horn-rimmed glasses and a black suit over a black shirt and tie. In spite of all the black, he didn't come off as remotely cool, probably because of his involuntary habit of rocking from side to side, as if the floor were a surfboard upon which he alone found difficulty maintaining balance. He checked his watch—she was twenty minutes late—and rocked more furiously.

At last, Taylor arrived, spotting her author at once, even though she'd never met him in person before.

"You must be Roger."

Novelists are generally not lookers—Martin Amis is the exception; Stephen King is the rule—and right away, Taylor could see there was no threat of Roger

Gale's name being added to her list. To paraphrase Gertrude Stein, a dork is a dork is a dork.

"Hi, Taylor. It's, uh, nice to meet you finally."

Gale's hand, as Taylor shook it, was drenched with sweat. She hadn't been expecting eye candy, but then, neither had he—they worked in publishing, after all. Taylor was easily the hottest chick he'd ever had lunch with. Which only made the poor sap rock all the more.

They sat, they ordered, they drank glasses of wine (one of the Braithwaite Ross perquisites Nathan Ross had implemented but neglected to mention during his speech was the expense account at the Royalton, one of the trendier hotel restaurant/bars in the city). Roger Gale launched into a tired tale of the impetus for his novel—what his *process* involved, who certain characters were based on, how he'd used certain leitmotifs throughout the piece, and so forth. The way he went on, you'd think his Russian protagonist was Anna Karenina. If you come across *The Lap of Uxory* at a yard sale sometime, you won't be surprised to learn that, historical fiction or not, the shelves of university libraries aren't exactly teeming with literary criticism of it or its author. The whole time, Gale's left leg popped up and down like a piston, as if all his brain power were generated therein.

It was a futile exercise—Taylor was not listening. How could she, with so much to process? How, after all of her recent excitement, could she be expected to gamely listen to some pretentious pseudo-intellectual pontificate about his boring book? Asher'd taken the Delta Shuttle to Washington early that morning—something to do with his handler. It was the first time she had been alone in the Dakota apartment, and she realized, much to her surprise, that she preferred it that way.

Is it human nature to always want more? Or does satiety, as Aldous Huxley suggested, dispel excitement? Either way, one thing was crystal clear: compared to what she'd experienced with Asher Krug, the job that two weeks ago was worth killing for had lost its luster.

" . . . and the fact that the protagonist also has a sexual awakening is significant," Gale was saying, "because it is in stark contrast to the murders. There is creation *and* destruction, yin and yang. It's a Victorian type of novel, so in the end Natasha is punished for her promiscuity . . ."

"See, that's the problem I'm having," Taylor said.

This was the first piece of editorial criticism she'd offered since they sat down. Its sudden delivery silenced the author, who fell over as if he'd been bitch-slapped. "I thought you liked the last draft."

"I did. It's a really cool idea. It has a hook, you know? But the problem is that it sort of falls apart at the end. The third act is weak. Most novels have a weak third act, but yours is, like, Coors Light weak."

Gale was taken aback, so much so his entire body stilled. "Is it that bad," he said, with just a touch of snark.

"The heroine hires Madame Popova to kill her husband," Taylor explained, "because her husband was a violent abuser. I mean, he just beheaded her cat; offing the guy is morally justified. What other choice does she have? It's kill or be killed. Then she goes through a liberating period of sexual experimentation—which is nicely written, by the way—and for that, she gets killed? I don't buy it."

Gale took a long swig of his wine, the prospect of yet another tedious rewrite deflating his already-shopworn ego. His leg resumed its furious activity. "Well, what do you recommend I do?"

"I don't know," Taylor said. "That's the challenge. That's where the creativity comes in, right?"

Gale took off his glasses and rubbed his eyes. "I suppose."

"Maybe," Taylor said, suddenly inspired, "maybe your heroine—"

"Natasha."

"Maybe Natasha should kill the chick who killed the husband. You know, the assassin—"

"Katja."

"—so she can take *her* job."

Gale stopped breathing for a full minute. It was the only way he could stop from freaking out. "Like Macbeth," he said finally.

"Exactly. Like Macbeth. See, this way, Natasha is punished for her choice—the choice to kill Katja—rather than doing what she has to do. Although I'm not so sure the book shouldn't have a happy ending . . ."

And just like that, Taylor knew what she had to do. Roger Gale's book—his stupid, vapid book—had inspired at least one reader. "I've got to go," she told him, rising. "I'm late for an appointment."

"But . . ."

"Give it a whirl," she said, throwing some bills on the table. "I'll call you next week."

Taylor dashed outside, hopped in a cab, and fifteen minutes later was in the lobby of the Quid Pro Quo Employment Agency, demanding an audience with Lydia Murtomaki.

"You should speak with Asher," Mae-Yuan said. "He's your case worker. And he's not here right now, but I'll be happy to . . ."

"He's in Washington. I know. I'm here to see Ms. Murtomaki."

"You'll have to make an appointment."

"Like hell I do."

The waifish receptionist glanced over Taylor's shoulder. An unkempt hipster was lounging on one of the divans, flipping through the latest *New York Press*. "You have to have an appointment, okay? She's on a very tight schedule."

"Is she *here*? I need to see her. It's urgent."

"I told you, you have to . . ."

Taylor clutched Mae-Yuan's twig-like arm, yanked her forward. "Listen to me, Mae-Yuan. If you don't let me see her right this instant, so help me God I'll tell him." She gestured at the hipster on the couch. "I'll tell him your little secret. I swear I will."

Mae-Yuan's voice wavered ever so slightly. "That would not be wise."

"Don't think I won't."

"Please. If you'll just . . ."

"It's okay, Mae-Yuan," came a voice from the intercom. "Send her in."

Once Taylor had found her seat—and once the door, somewhat ominously, had locked behind her—she said, "I'm sorry to burst in unannounced."

"We try our best to be flexible," said the older woman, twisting a cigarette onto her trademark onyx holder. "What can I do for you?"

Both sat in the same chairs they had occupied a month earlier. This time, though, Taylor was not nervous. She was on autopilot, as sure of herself as Eddie Murphy at the first MTV Music Awards. "One of the stipulations of my agreement was that if I didn't like my job I could get a new one."

"But you like Braithwaite Ross."

"I've had a change of heart."

"Fine. Asher will show you the list, and you can have your pick of jobs. Now that you have more experience, in fact, you might get a sizeable increase in salary."

"I don't want to work in publishing anymore."

"Can't say that I blame you. Terrible business. The shit they print these days." Lydia blew a perfect smoke ring. "There are plenty of jobs to choose from, Taylor. The list is comprehensive."

"The job that I want, it's not on the list."

"What *can* you be you driving at, I wonder." Spoken as a statement, not a question.

Outside, police sirens shrieked. The sun went behind a cloud, and the room grew darker.

"I want to work for you. Here. At Quid Pro Quo."

The Director said nothing. Her face betrayed no hint of what she was thinking.

"All day I read these awful crime books," Taylor went on. "Books that are so obviously invented by people who have never even fired a gun, let alone shot and killed someone. How can you expect me to be satisfied editing *fiction*, when this place is real? The only job worth killing for, Ms. Murtomaki, is an executive position at Quid Pro Quo. Give me a chance. Take me on a probationary basis. Make me an intern. Anything."

"Our internship program," said the Director wryly, "is still in the planning stages. But I must admit, your ardor intrigues me. None of our other charges has ever evinced the slightest interest in joining our little family. Quite the contrary. Most of them want nothing to do with us ever again."

"All the more reason to take me on. This is where I want to be. This is the job to kill for. Take me on. I'll be the best executive you've ever had."

The Director's eyes were as wide as the giant Man Ray one behind her. "This isn't a nine-to-five job, Taylor. This is a marriage. More than a marriage. Quid Pro Quo becomes your life— your husband, your children, your family and friends, and any other ambitions you might have had. And there is no turning back. Once you're in, you're in forever. Like the Hotel California. There is no getting out. Ever."

"I don't want a nine-to-five job, Ms. Murtomaki. I don't want a husband, I don't want children, I don't like my family, and I don't have that many friends. This is what I want, right here. Just this."

Lydia leaned back in her chair, holding her cigarette holder like a magic wand. "Quite unprecedented."

They had traded volleys long enough. Time to deploy the overhand smash. "Another thing," Taylor said. She wanted to make damn sure Lydia knew she was talking about Asher Krug, without invoking his name. "If you take me on, Quid Pro Quo will be my number-one priority. Forever and always. You won't find me *freelancing*, that's for sure. I won't be part-time assassin, part-time revolutionary, part-time sociology lecturer, like certain people. No. I'll be totally killer."

"You have pluck, I'll give you that." There was a twinkle in the Director's eye and a broad smile on her face—just the reaction

Taylor was hoping for. "But all of this is academic, because the fact is, there are no permanent openings at this time."

Holding the older woman's gaze: "And if something were to open up?"

"There are no permanent openings at this time."

Taylor stood up, smoothed her skirt, extended her hand. "Thank you, Ms. Murtomaki. I appreciate you seeing me."

Lydia Murtomaki studied her carefully. "Wait a minute, Taylor."

"Yes?"

"How far would you be willing to go for us?"

"You say jump, I ask how high."

"This particular mission would require . . . a woman's touch."

Taylor smiled. "Nothing I haven't done before."

Lydia lit up a fresh cigarette. "If I say jump, you jump, period. You don't waste time asking questions."

CHAPTER 17

In the first half of the century in which our story takes place, America's was an industrial economy. The lion's share of the labor force still worked in factories. Most of the universal work standards that we now take for granted—the eight-hour day, the nine-to-five shift, lunch hour, coffee breaks, the punching of timecards—date from this period. See, in order for assembly lines to function, every worker had to be physically present at the plant for the same number of hours. Pay was docked and jobs were lost for tardiness, because tardiness cost money; if one cog in the machine ran ten minutes late, the entire apparatus stalled for those ten minutes.

But that was then, and this is now. In 2009, as I write this, white-collar jobs predominate—as they did well before 1991. Why, then, do so many companies cling to an antiquated business model designed for the industrial, and not the information, age? Yes, there will always be jobs that require a physical presence for a set duration of time—cooks, surgeons, receptionists, shortstops—but many more that do not. Nowadays, with the advent of the Internet and BlackBerries and cellular phones and video teleconferencing, lots of jobs are so portable that they can be—and are—performed not just out of the office, but out of the country. (In the Bush recession of 1991, there were no good jobs; in the current Bush recession, there are plenty of good jobs—in Bangalore.) Why, one wonders, does this dinosaurian business model endure?

The answer, I think, lies in the megalomania of the average CEO. Have you *seen* how much dough these fuckers make? In 1991, Stephen Wolf, the chairman of United Airlines, took home $18.3 million in total compensation. This raised eyebrows at the time, but now, the number seems quaint; Reese Witherspoon was paid about as much for her bimbonic work in *Legally Blonde 2: Red, White & Blonde*. With big money comes big attitude. Chief executives demand kingly treatment. And if there are still kings, there must also be serfs. This, I believe, is why people who, say, edit mass-market thrillers are forced to appear in an office for forty hours a week, even though they could more efficaciously labor from home. Their presence feeds the CEO's ego.

If corporate head honchos actually gave a crap about productivity, they would—get ready for this—*treat their workers with respect*. I'm no psychologist, but it seems obvious that people don't like to feel like slaves. They work harder for bosses they like, not fear. Machiavelli was well and good for despots, but he'd be a workplace hazard. CEOs who behave like Louis XVI should be beheaded.

Nathan Ross, the new publisher at Braithwaite Ross, understood this. Before text messaging and AIM and wireless Internet, he was a visionary. He treated his employees with dignity, provided them with enviable amenities, established flexible hours, and trusted them to get the job done. And what do you know? They did. In fact, they worked harder under his velvet glove than Walter Bledsoe's iron fist, even if they spent less time in the office.

Not that said office was deserted. Charles, Mike, Brady, Chris, Angie, and everyone else continued to show up pretty much every day, even though they weren't required to. For one thing, most of them wanted out of their cramped New York apartments. For another, there were video games in the break room. And free soda.

It was in this break room, on the day before Halloween, where Chris the Pirate, greasy hair pulled back in an Axl Rose bandana, found Taylor Schmidt curled up on an armchair with Roger Gale's manuscript revisions and a busy red pen.

"There you are," said Chris.

"Here I am."

"The boss wants to see you."

"Angie?"

"Nathan."

The pen froze. "Why would Nathan want to see me?"

"He didn't say why. Just that it was urgent."

Taylor put down the manuscript and made for the new publisher's corner office. The white heat of anxiety burned in her veins. She was sure he was going to reprimand her for her brusque treatment of Roger Gale. She could think of no other reason why Nathan might want to talk to her, and certainly no urgent one. She was in trouble, plain and simple.

Taylor found the publisher in front of his desk, putter in hand, attempting to knock golf balls into an overturned coffee mug from twenty feet away.

"Close the door," Nathan said, without looking up.

She did as she was told, trembling all the while.

"Are you dressing up for Halloween?" he asked.

"No."

"Me neither. Know why? Because I'm not seven."

She felt like there was a small animal in her chest cavity, her heart was pounding so hard. It was weird—she was more nervous now than she had been when she shot Andrew Borden.

"The Director wants to see you," he said, as he shot a ball into the cup. "Oh, yeah! Did you see that? I'm getting really good at this."

Taylor was nonplussed. "Angie's at lunch with Jean Naggar."

"Not the editorial director. *The* Director. You know. Lydia Murtomaki."

All the tension in her body released at once, and she guffawed, like some sort of animal. "So it *was* you who hired Quid Pro Quo! I knew it."

"Aren't you Little Miss Marple." Nathan fetched the balls from the coffee cup. "It was my father, if you want to get technical. But I fully supported his decision." He looked up at her for the first time and winked. "Union Square, two o'clock. Enter on Fifteenth Street, on the east side of the park. Take the first available bench on your left and wait. Bring a magazine or something. And Taylor?"

"Yes?"

"Don't tell Asher."

Taylor did a double take. "How do you know Asher?"

"We were both Saybrugians."

"Say what?"

"Say*brook*." And he burst out laughing. "Sorry. Yale humor."

For the first time in her life, Taylor felt relieved that she hadn't been accepted at Geek U. "Is that what they call it there."

"Saybrook was our residential college," Nathan said, after nodding his head to acknowledge her quip, "so I know him from the dorms. Interesting guy, Asher, and smart as a whip, but I've never been big on ideologues—especially Republican ideologues."

"Asher is a Republican?"

"How can you live with a guy like *that* and not know which way he votes?" Nathan said. "Maybe you're not so Miss Marple after all."

"I don't live with him," she said. "I just stay over a lot."

"You say tomato . . ." Nathan squatted down to line up the golf balls. "You'd better go. Don't want to keep Lydia waiting."

By 1991, the transition of Union Square from druggie wasteland to yuppie nirvana was well underway. The mighty Zeckendorf Towers, crowned by their hunter-green pyramids, presided over the southeast quadrant with pharaoic majesty. The Coffee Shop, an ironically named bar owned and frequented by models, had recently opened (one of the principal financiers, rumor has it, was the songstress Mariah Carey, whose hit single "Can't Let Go" was released that autumn). Still, Union Square was more outpost than omphalos, an ugly mess of broken cement with not much to recommend it save McDonald's, Bradlees, and a rundown place on the corner that sold textiles wholesale. The battleship-sized Barnes & Noble, the Virgin Megastore, the W Hotel, Diesel Jeans, and the upscale eateries that now line its western flank were still twinkles in some developer's eye. Who knew what lurked in the park's murk when the sun went down? Crackheads, hookers, crackheaded hookers . . . anything was possible. Union Square was cool, but it was sketchy.

No, Union Square was cool *because* it was sketchy. Ah, the good old days.

Taylor entered at the Fifteenth Street ingress, on the east side of the park, as per her instructions. She stopped at the newsstand by the subway entrance and bought the latest issue of *Rolling Stone*, which had a pouting Shannen Doherty on the cover. She found an empty park bench, took a seat, and waited. It was five to two.

Exactly five minutes later, Lydia Murtomaki emerged from the subway in a Yankees cap, a blue trench coat, and huge Jackie O sunglasses. Flung over one shoulder was one of those canvas bags from the Strand, black with red ovular logo, fat with books. She looked nothing like the chic dragon lady from the Quid Pro Quo offices; if Taylor wasn't looking for her, she never would have recognized her. As it was, the aspiring assassin had to do a triple take, and could only get a positive ID when the Director sat down on the bench beside her.

"Look straight ahead," said Lydia out of the side of her mouth.

"Thank you so much for . . ."

"Save it. You might not want to thank me when all is said and done." Lydia put the canvas bag on the ground, and then, with her foot, pushed it closer to Taylor. "Take the bag when you leave. Inside is the dossier and the ID cards. Your name is Roberta Anderson, and you're from Saskatchewan. But your code name is Delilah."

"Delilah. I like that."

Lydia ignored the comment. "The Yale Club is located at 50 Vanderbilt Avenue. That's between Forty-fourth and Forty-fifth Streets, across from Grand Central. At exactly eight o'clock this Friday evening, you'll meet your handler at the club's main bar, on the second floor. His name is Dan. Do what he says."

"Please tell me," Taylor said, "that the pink slip went to Yale. You have no idea how tired I am of all things New Haven." Then her heart went out like the cable during a thunderstorm. "You didn't go there, did you?"

"Edmund Walsh School of Foreign Service, Georgetown University, Class of '68," Lydia said. "The Ivy League is for wankers." She poked the Strand bag with her foot, to change the subject. "There's a photograph of the pink slip in the dossier. His name is Jan, codename Little Check. Not the handsomest chap, but very charming. He has profligate tastes, which you're to indulge."

"Understood."

"When you're through with the dossier, burn it."

That sounded like something one did with a dossier when one was through with it.

"You're not to tell anyone where you're going—especially Asher."

Taylor nodded. "What *should* I tell him? I have to tell him something."

"No you won't. He's leaving for Tenerife first thing in the morning. Special assignment." Some pigeons approached the bench. Lydia fed them crumbs of bread from her coat pocket, fully realizing the crazy-old-lady-in-the-park persona. "Any questions?"

Taylor did not ask where Tenerife was, although she had never heard of it, or what Asher might be doing there. She didn't care. She had but one question. "If this goes well, will you hire me?"

Lydia took off her dark glasses and turned to face Taylor. For the first and only time, their eyes met. "There are no permanent openings at this time."

"And if something were to open up?"

It was at this moment, with the momentous question still unanswered, that Yours Truly, bounding across Union Square, noticed Taylor sitting on a park bench. I hadn't seen her in almost a week, since we watched *Heathers*. The older woman in a Yankees cap and Jackie O shades sitting next to her on the bench—one of those New York stereotypes whose impression doesn't even register—vanished as I drew near. Never in a million years would I have imagined that in two short hours, I would be sitting across a desk from her, fearing for my life.

"Taylor? Aren't you supposed to be at work?"

"I'm playing hooky," she said. "You busted me."

"The Strand," I said, pointing to her bag. "What'd you buy? Anything good?"

Taylor cradled the bag, so I couldn't see the contents. "Stuff for work." She seemed awfully keyed up.

"Hey, are you free this weekend, by any chance? This chick from my acting class is in *Prom Queens Unchained*, over at the Village Gate, so I scored some comp tickets. She's playing Carla Zlotz, the beatnik. It's kind of a big part, if you wanna, you know, come with."

"I'd love to," she said, "but I can't. I'm actually going home this weekend."

"*Home* home?"

"It's Hayley's birthday," she said, Hayley being one of her half sisters.

Before I could press—she hadn't mentioned going home, which was odd; a Darla visit would usually come up in conversation—she said, "I gotta get back before somebody notices I'm gone."

"Have a safe trip."

Little did I know that Taylor was not going to Missouri to celebrate a birth, but to midtown, to orchestrate a death.

CHAPTER 18

While I trusted that Quid Pro Quo would make good on its commitment to me, I continued to seek employment elsewhere. Despite Asher's claims to the contrary, I was no slacker, and with Taylor pretty much moved out, I had the rent to worry about. Not wanting to try my own hand at other employment agencies, I took a job catering—par for the struggling-actor course. I worked a handful of events, including what would be my last—Marla Maples's birthday party (she turned twenty-eight on October 27). The catering company let me go after I spilled a gin-and-tonic on Tone-Lōc.

On the early afternoon of my follow-up with Quid Pro Quo—an hour before I bumped into Taylor in Union Square—I ran into Trey Parrish, our meathead downstairs neighbor. He was at one of the outdoor tables at Veselka, working on a cup of coffee. He was wearing his Delaware Lacrosse cap, as usual—I don't think I ever saw him take it off—and a Van Halen sweatshirt.

"Hey, Hot Toddie," he called. Trey and his nicknames.

"What up, big guy?"

A mistake, asking *him* that. The guy had no sense of idiom. He monologued for a good ten minutes about The Orlando Conference: Part Deux. Then he asked me if I had seen the game.

I hadn't. I'd spent all night reading Taylor's diaries.

"I know Twins-Braves ain't a sexy matchup here, but I'm from St. Paul, and let me tell you . . ."

And tell me he did, every last detail of the 1-0 game—the 126-pitch, ten-inning Jack Morris shutout, the 3-for-5 evening for Dan Gladden, the bloop hit by Gene Larkin to win it in the bottom of the tenth. Only at the tail end, when I was about to spontaneously combust out of sheer boredom, did he ask, "So, you seen Taylor lately?"

"Not since last week. She's been at her boyfriend's a lot."

"Asher Krug," he said. "AK-47."

"Uh . . . right." I was a bit surprised he knew Asher's name, but I assumed—wrongly, as it turned out—that he'd heard it from Taylor.

"I wouldn't worry about him," Trey said. "I have a hunch that won't last."

"I hope you're right."

"I usually am," he said, through a mouthful of eggs. "I'm good with hunches."

As I stepped off the elevator into the hallway outside the Quid Pro Quo offices, I was practically stampeded by a herd of buffalo-sized men in gray suits and mirrored aviator shades. One of them was on a cordless phone, issuing commands (this was before dime-bag-sized cell phones, when portable telephones were big as a shoe box). He noticed me, growled, and ordered the tallest of the well-tailored giants to shoo me away.

As they passed, I saw, in their midst, a shorter, squatter, older man; his balding head was scaly, and he spoke out of one side of his mouth, like the Penguin on the old *Batman* show. By the time I placed him, though, they were already in the elevator, the doors sliding shut.

"Holy shit," I said out loud, although no one was there to hear me. "That was the Secretary of Defense."

For a moment I thought about submitting this unusual celebrity sighting to the *Metropolitan Diary*, but I couldn't think of a good way to frame it. Nothing had *happened*, after all. Who cares if I saw the Secretary of Defense? Did anyone even know who the Secretary of Defense was? So, forgetting about my brush with greatness, I went inside, where Asher and the stony owl were waiting.

Mae-Yuan took my coat and showed me to Asher's office. Mr. Krug was in, rifling through some files on his desk. He peeked up from a stack of documents and glowered; I had disregarded his sartorial advice. "Still with the flannel, I see."

"I figure it's not an office job, so . . ."

"Forget it. Have a seat."

I sat, and he slid across his desk a manila folder marked VIACOM.

Dispensing with small talk, Asher got right to the point. "MTV is working on a new show, Todd. Something completely different. Revolutionary, they think. They've rented this loft space in Soho, and for three months, they're going to have seven complete strangers live there. Cameras will be rolling round-the-clock, to record all of the drama."

I thumbed through the pages in the folder. "What's this, the script?"

"There is no script."

"No script?"

"The producers are betting that enough will happen in those three months to fill thirteen episodes. It's all in the editing, is what they tell us."

My first thought was, that's the stupidest idea ever pitched. Who would watch a TV show that had no script? It would be incredibly dull. But I played along. "Sounds interesting."

I opened the folder. There was a picture of the industrial building where the show would take place, a list of six other cast members—Eric Nies, Heather Gardner, Julie Gentry, Kevin Powell, Becky Blasband, and Norman Korpi—and, finally, this:

> *This is the true story of seven strangers, picked to live in a house, work together, and have their lives taped, to find out what happens when people stop being po-lite and start getting real.* The Real World.

"*The Real World*?"

"That's what they're calling it. It's the next thing in programming—'reality' television. Real people living real life, in real situations. No bullshit. You'll be in on the ground floor. If you score with this show, Todd, you'll be bigger than the Sheen brothers."

Such was the seductive power of Asher Krug that anything he proposed—even an idea as ridiculous as this one—seemed a sure thing. Visions of celebrity danced in my head. "You think so?"

"You're going to be famous, Todd. Above-the-title famous."

Was he selling me on the job? Perhaps. Then again, MTV *was* cutting-edge. Everything that little astronaut dude touched, it seemed, turned to gold. How could the network that spent months promoting a contest whose grand prize was a pink house in John Cougar Mellencamp's Indiana hometown steer me wrong?

"The only drawback is, it doesn't start shooting until February." Asher tossed a fat envelope into my lap. "That should keep you in the black till then."

I opened the envelope, where twenty Benjamin Franklins winked at me. Two grand. Holy shit.

"Are you in?"

"I'm in. I'm definitely in."

"Then let's go see the Director."

And I followed him into the office next door, where Lydia

Murtomaki—without her Yankees cap and Jackie O sunglasses I did not recognize her from Union Square—sat under her giant glass-teared eye, waiting for me.

The Director chewed on her onyx cigarette holder, blowing smoke rings, and told me what she'd told Taylor: about the economy, about the baby boomers, about Prince Charles. She knew what to say, what buttons to push. She had it down to a science. Her job was intimidation, and she was damn good at her job. She was middle-aged and a twig—a few hours ago I ignored her on the park bench as if she were a homeless person—and I could have crushed her to death with my bare hands. But *she* scared *me*.

"Your generation, Mr. Lander, plays the same waiting game Prince Charles plays, on a much larger scale. Your parents and grandparents—my generation—hold the jobs you desire, the jobs that by all rights should be yours. And we are quite reluctant to pass along the torch. It's not that you cannot find the good jobs. It's that there are no good jobs to find—they're all taken."

Lydia Murtomaki let that hang in the air with the cigarette smoke, until both drifted away. "Do you realize that in my day, college graduates were uniformly hopeful and idealistic? Cynicism, sarcasm, and bitterness are unique to your generation of so-called . . . slackers."

I didn't say anything. I had no idea where this was heading—I was *still* clueless, believe it or not—but somehow I knew it wouldn't end well.

"Now. These jobs that my generation holds . . . what is the simplest way to make them available to you?"

"The simplest way? Just fire everybody."

"Not fire. You'd glut the applicant pool, and they'd get hired elsewhere. No, they need to be removed from the workforce. Permanently."

For the first time, a sense of danger overwhelmed me. I remembered seeing the secretary of defense in the hallway, with his phalanx of guards. Was it possible that I might not leave 520 Madison alive? I glanced at the windows, to see if they were the kind that open—I considered rushing and jumping out—but they were sealed shut.

"The simplest way to remove them," Lydia said, "is to kill them off. Any questions?"

But before I could ask one, she hit the intercom button, and Taylor's boyfriend appeared in the door. "Mr. Krug will assist you in the operation."

Asher dropped a Spanish olive the size of a strawberry into a martini glass the size of a fishbowl. Gin and vermouth splashed onto the bar-stand. He dabbed the wet spots with a linen napkin, lifted the glass, and handed it to the other occupant of his office, who was quite in need of a drink.

I had not said a word since leaving Lydia Murtomaki's office—had, in fact, hardly moved. When I saw my reflection in the glass frame of the Lee Atwater photo, my face was sheet-white, my eyes pale. I looked like a prop from a horror movie.

"After you sleep on it," Asher was saying, "think about it a little, you'll see. It's not as awful as it sounds."

I made a fist around the linen. "Not as awful as it sounds? Not as . . . we are still talking about murder, aren't we? Or did you change the subject on me?"

Asher leaned against the desk, his face a study in tranquility. "No. I didn't change the subject."

"Then let me make sure I have this right. The only way I can get an acting gig is by—and please correct me if I'm wrong—is by *bumping somebody off*? You're so right, Asher. That's not awful. That's just fucking *peachy*."

"We didn't create the game, Todd. We're just playing the cards that were dealt to us."

"This is crazy. You're crazy. You and Wednesday Fucking Addams in there."

"Keep your voice down." Asher glanced at the wall that separated the two offices. He appeared genuinely concerned that Lydia Murtomaki might be listening.

"Oh, and what if I don't? What are you gonna do, kill me, too?" I tapped with napkined fist the invisible bull's-eye over my heart. "Go right ahead. Saves you the trouble of *pink-slipping* me later, doesn't it?"

"We would never terminate someone who used our service," he said, without a hint of irony. "It's company policy."

"Oh, what a relief. Job security. But what if some competitor arrived on the scene? I could hardly imagine a price war."

"I don't think we have to worry about that. We've pretty much cornered the market."

The wailing of sirens interrupted the conversation. An ambulance, a cop car, a fire engine, or some combination thereof was zooming down Madison Avenue. Asher glanced out the window, although from his vantage point he could not see the street.

"I can't do it," I said. "I'm sorry, but I can't."

"That's too bad." He was by the window now, peering onto the street. "You do realize that if you refuse, we'll pink-slip your mother, your father, and the three people you listed as references? I want to make sure we're clear on that."

The magnitude of this threat stunned me speechless. The papers I turned in: three references—personal, not professional. They had me, all right . . . except. . .

"But, Asher . . . *Taylor* is one of my references."

"And you're one of hers. And you're still alive. She killed for your sake, Todd. Won't you kill for hers?"

I launched the oversized martini against the wall. Glass shattered, and gin splattered on the clean white paint. "How could you put me in this position? How could you ask me to make that choice?"

"We're here to help you," Asher said calmly, changing tack, ignoring my infantile gesture, "not hurt you. Politicians are always flapping their yaps about creating jobs, but what jobs have they created? Who do they help employ? They're about double-talk and bullshit statistics. We're about results. We create hundreds of new jobs a year, terminating baby boomers who are—let's face it—better off terminated."

Asher placed the glass on the coffee table, sat in the chair nearest mine, and crossed his legs casually, as if he were on a cruise or something. "You don't have to read Nietzsche and Ayn Rand to know that some people just don't deserve to live."

"*Who*, Asher? Riddle me that. *Who* doesn't deserve to live?"

Without missing a beat: "Charles Manson. Richard Speck. Saddam Hussein. Yasser Arafat. Fidel Castro. Idi Amin. I could go on all day. Mike Tyson." The former heavyweight champion had recently been booked for raping Desiree Washington. "The Lockerbie terrorists. Muammar . . ."

"Dictators and psychopaths don't count. Ordinary people."

"I suppose CEOs who lay off their factory workers because it's cheaper to use foreign slave labor, I suppose they don't count as ordinary? What about lawyers who make a living chasing ambulances? How about drug dealers? Rapists? Slumlords? Can you honestly tell me you want every real estate broker in this town to live to a ripe old age?"

I didn't say anything. I was still in shock. My body started to tremble. I was on the verge of having a seizure.

"No? Well, how about someone you know? Someone like, say, Donna Green? Surely you wouldn't mind seeing *her* fat ass six feet under."

This knocked the wind from my proverbial sails, if there was any wind left there in the Doldrums. I remembered the features editor Doug Schiffer, his brutal, and heretofore unexplained, murder. Had someone in my former place of employ had him taken out?

"Are you going to murder Donna Green?"

"No. You are." Asher tossed another manila folder at me. "She's your pink slip."

CHAPTER 19

The Yale Club has not made much of a dent in the popular culture, because there's nothing popular, in the strict sense of the word, about it. It is twenty-two gray-stone stories of understated elegance and Ivy League elitism. In order to walk through the door, you have to have, first, a degree from Yale, and second, enough disposable income to cough up the membership fee. A BA from Trenton State was not enough to get me past security—I wanted to tour the joint before I wrote this—so my knowledge of the Yale Club is limited to Taylor's diary entry, which wasn't terribly descriptive (she didn't even mention the paintings of Presidents Taft, Ford, and Bush *père* above the numerous fireplaces in the main lounge), the low-res pictures on yaleclubnyc .org, and the Yale Club Wikipedia entry (which is how I know about the paintings of Presidents Taft, Ford, and Bush *père* above the numerous fireplaces in the main lounge). From what I can glean, the Yale Club is similar in look and feel, if not in size, to the Quid Pro Quo offices: the stuffy sort of place to which well-heeled gentlemen repair after dinner to drink brandy and smoke Cuban cigars.

At quarter to eight that Saturday, the second of November, Taylor Schmidt, in a slinky black cocktail dress, choker necklace, and stiletto heels, waited under the royal-blue flag with the white Y that hung atop the Yale Club entrance. The stretch of East Fortieth Street where most of the city's employment agencies were head-quartered—the Employment District, if you will—was four short blocks from where she now stood, finishing the last of her Parliament Light. Just two months earlier she'd been smoking outside the offices of Fraulein Staffing, without a job or a hope. It seemed a lifetime ago.

With a final drag, she flicked the butt into the street, pivoted neatly on one heel, and strutted through the front door. She expected the uniformed doorman to stop her, but he didn't—the Yalies were smart enough to let a hot chick in unmolested. She made her way up to the second floor and found the main bar. There were plenty of people there—older men, mostly, in Brooks Brothers' best, and the occasional pants-suited older woman; not at all the company a white-trash graduate of the Missouri public school system was accustomed to keeping—but still room at the bar. She found a stool, sat down, and produced another Parliament from her silver cigarette case. The bartender lit it for her with a match from a Yale Club matchbook.

"What can I get you?"

"Bacardi and Coke," she said.

He mixed the drink with a flourish and set it down before her on a linen cocktail napkin. It was as big as three rum-and-Cokes from Phoebe's—and there was even a bit extra on the side, in a separate glass.

"Put that on my tab, Timmy," came a man's voice from behind her. "And bring me a Jameson, neat."

The newcomer slid onto the stool next to Taylor. The remains of his hair were blond and curly, and slicked with pomade. He wore a blue pinstripe suit over a periwinkle shirt and Yale necktie. He wasn't handsome in the conventional way, but there was a we're-both-in-on-the-same-joke twinkle in his eye that she found attractive. And he was young—no older than twenty-five. She had no idea, as he sat down, that this well-groomed chap was someone she already knew.

"You clean up nice, Schmitty."

"*Trey?* Holy shit. I didn't recognize you without the baseball hat." Her heart sank. The jig was up—she'd been recognized, and by our annoying downstairs neighbor, no less. Of all the bum luck, to meet this jackass—this jackass who went to *Delaware*—at the Yale Club. She took a sip of her rum-and-Coke. "Thanks for the drink, Trey, but I'm afraid I'm meeting someone."

"Indeed," Trey Parrish said. "You're meeting me." He took the whiskey from the bartender. "Delilah."

"What did you say?"

"You heard me."

This blew her away. Trey could have sprouted wings and flown out the window and she wouldn't have been more surprised. "You? *You're* Dan?"

"The Quid Pro Quo invitation you got in the mail didn't have a stamp on it," he smirked, obviously pleased with himself. "And AK-47 told you you'd been recommended. Didn't you ever wonder who hooked you up? *Moi*, that's who. And dude, you are *so* making me look good. The Director digs you big time."

She was expecting him to touch her leg—it would have been natural, especially for a guy who had been openly working her for months, and she wouldn't have minded one bit—but Trey didn't. He was all business.

"I'm glad to hear it." Taylor drained the rest of her rum-and-Coke in one stiff swallow, poured in the sidecar, and finished that, too. "AK-47. Asher Krug. Clever."

"I do enjoy the nicknames."

"Speaking of nicknames, when do I contact . . . Little Check?"

"We'll rendezvous in the Main Lounge in half an hour," said Trey, glancing at his Longines watch. "Then he'll take you to his room. Here. Take this." He handed her what looked like a tube of mascara.

"Do I need a touch up?"

"Hardly. Open it . . . but don't touch the tip, unless you're sick of living."

She unscrewed the tube and pulled out what should have been the crooked gizmo to apply eyeliner, but what was a small hypodermic needle. "What's this?"

"Ethyl dimethylphosphoramidocyanidate."

"I had to ask."

"Cold Ethyl, we call it. You know that song? By Alice Cooper?" Taylor did not know the song, so Trey pressed on. "It's a lethal nerve agent—developed in Langley, battle-tested in Iraq. One jab with that, you're dead in three to five minutes, depending on how much you weigh." He took the opportunity to admire her from toe to head. "You might be dead in two."

"Far out." She screwed the needle back into the tube. "Totally James Bond."

"More like Maxwell Smart, if you ask me."

"That makes me Agent 99."

"You put 99 to shame, Delilah. Little Check is a lucky man. In one respect, at least."

Taylor simpered. She always did, when men complimented her looks.

"He's a voracious man with voracious appetites," said Trey. "Each time we engage him, we provide him with . . . female entertainment. Like throwing the dog a bone. You're the latest—and the last—in a long line of bones. But you don't need to actually, you know, *do* anything with him. Just get him undressed. It's easier for the cleaners if he's naked."

"The cleaners?"

"These guys are the best, Schmitty. Wait till you see. When they dispose of a body, I mean, they *dispose* of a *body*. What? Why are you looking at me like that?"

"I just can't believe *you're* Dan. I mean, in the building, you're so . . ."

"Square. I know. And I apologize. Part of my cover. If I talk about the consulting firm a lot, maybe people won't realize that I spend most of the time sitting in the apartment playing *Prince of Persia*. One of the perquisites of my line of work. Lots of free time. Pink slips don't come off the assembly line, right?"

"Well, you had me fooled."

"What can I say? I'm good at what I do. Once you get him with this," pointing at the mascara tube, "knock three times on the door to the adjoining room, and there I'll be. You ready?"

Taylor took Trey's arm. He led her down a corridor and into the Main Lounge, all leather chairs and bookcases and tall windows. It was surprisingly bright, on account of the gleaming white marble walls that made it feel like the inside of a venerable bank. She half expected to see J. P. Morgan smoking a Cohiba.

"Here we are."

Taylor spotted Little Check right away. He was alone, tucked in a corner, his back to one of the windows, nursing a glass of what appeared to be scotch. He was sixty-eight years old, according to his dossier, and looked every bit of it; the armor of shiny hair on his misshapen pate, while vibrantly black, did not suggest youth. His face was pudgy and toad-like, with prominent jowls. Gin blossoms dotted his eyes. By far his most distinguishing features, however, were his eyebrows: black as the ace of spades, so large they were practically square—Ernest Borgnine to the ninth power.

Trey led her by the elbow across the room. When they approached the table, Little Check rose—the moniker did not suit him, as he was neither short nor svelte—and extended his plump paw. "Dan, my good friend."

"Evening," said Trey, shaking hands. "This is Delilah."

"A pleasure," said Little Check, his accent two parts Eton and one part Dracula's Castle. He studied her eyes for a few beats, all the while holding her hand. Then he glanced at her sideways. "You don't know who I am?"

Flushed, Taylor glanced at her handler for prompting.

"No," said Dan. "She doesn't."

"Brilliant. I'm Jan."

Little Check—Jan—pulled out a chair. "Do sit, won't you?"

Taylor, always a sucker for chivalry, plopped her ass down.

Dan did not. Instead, he said something in an unfamiliar, guttural language—probably Hebrew, although Taylor didn't recognize it. Warrensburg, Missouri, was not exactly Haifa West.

Jan contemplated what he'd been told and nodded. Then Dan delivered what she supposed were instructions. The only words she could make out were "Los Cristos."

Little Check did not seem pleased. He scowled his contact for a moment, then said, in English, "Well, if you say so."

"I say so," Dan said. "And with that, I'll take my leave. Be good, you two." And he glided off, leaving Taylor and her pink slip alone.

"Have you eaten, my dear?"

"Yes," she said. "But I could really go for a drink. What are you having?"

He gave his glass a shake. "Laphroaig," he said, and after noticing her confused look, he added, "It's scotch. From the Islay region of Scotland. Would you like one? I can summon the waiter."

"It's kind of stuffy in here." Taylor placed her hand ever so gently on his knee. "Why don't we go back to your room?"

"Thatta girl." He laughed, an almost volcanic burst of joviality. "Let me settle up."

Taylor watched him sign for the drinks. Jan was not an attractive man, not by a long shot, but he possessed an innate charisma, a magnetism as strong, in its own way, as Asher Krug's. This was a dynamic, virile man. A man of power. Which was probably why they wanted him dead.

She took his arm, and they headed to the elevator bay in the lobby.

"Are you in town for long?"

"Hardly," Jan chuckled, although there was nothing funny about this that Taylor could see. "I got here an hour ago, and I'm leaving at first light."

"Where are you going?"

"Back to the yacht."

"The *yacht*?"

"It's not as impressive as it sounds."

"I don't even have my own apartment," Taylor said. "And you have a yacht. Why are we roughing it at the Yale Club when we could be on your yacht?"

"Point taken. But at the moment, she's off the coast of the Canary Islands, alas." Jan's eyes achieved the naughty look of the child with his hand in the cookie jar. "May I tell you a secret?"

"Please."

"No one even knows I'm here. They fetched me from my yacht, and they're returning me to my yacht. Not even the crew knows I've gone."

"Sounds like quite a trip. I hope it was worth it."

He gave her a once-over that sent shivers down her spine—in a surprisingly good way. "That remains to be seen."

They were in the elevator now, just the two of them, climbing slowly and loudly to the top floor.

"Do you know why they call them the Canary Islands?"

Taylor figured it was a trick question, but she played dumb. "Because of the canaries?"

"No. Because of the dogs."

"The dogs?"

"There's a reason Spain is no longer a superpower." He laughed again, too loudly, as the elevator stopped, and they alit. "You're quite lovely, you know."

"Thanks. You're not so bad yourself."

They were now in front of a door that read HENRY STIMSON SUITE.

"Flattery," he said, with a pleasant wag of his stumpy finger, "will get you nowhere." Winking, he produced a key from his jacket. "This is us."

As soon as the door was closed, Jan jumped her, kissing her with the same urgency with which he laughed. Taylor returned the kiss with similar gusto. They collapsed onto the tastefully duveted king-size bed, pawing each other.

You might think Taylor would have been repulsed by such a grizzled, toadish man. Not so. She was attracted to his charm, to his charisma, to his money—but mostly to the fact that *in a few hours, he'd be dead*. She couldn't get that idea out of her head, and it electrified her like nothing ever had. She was not required to sleep with him, as Trey had made clear. It would have been easy to strip him down, roll him on his belly for a massage, and introduce him to Cold Ethyl before things got heated. But Taylor did not even consider not nailing the guy—even in her diary, she did not entertain the possibility. After all, it's one thing to be the first to have sex with someone; quite another to be the last. For her, the bang was part of the bang.

"I have just the thing," said Jan, breaking the embrace. He opened a sideboard. Taylor expected sex toys, or a video camera, maybe even a midget in bondage gear, and was relieved when he produced a black bottle, two glasses, a dish of sugar cubes, and a slotted silver spoon.

He held up the bottle. "Do you know what this is?"

She didn't.

"Absinthe. The stuff Van Gogh was blind on when he hacked off his ear."

Taylor had heard of absinthe from her art history class. The Green Faerie, as it was called, was big with depressed French aesthetes between the wars, but not yet with American expats in Prague. That wouldn't happen for a few more years. "I thought it was illegal."

"To make, yes. The prohibition dates to the war. Fortunately, there are bottles in cellars here and there that have survived. Quite rare, and very expensive. This is one of them."

Jan poured the bright emerald-green liqueur into the glasses, filling each about a third of the way. "You know how many living people have tasted real absinthe? Not many. Welcome to the club."

Now thoroughly impressed, Taylor reached for the glass.

"Not yet, my lovely."

Jan put the slotted spoon over the glass—it stretched across it perfectly, as if designed for that purpose—and piled sugar cubes atop it. Then he dripped Evian water over the sugar cubes, until the glass was almost full. In a minute or two, the drink changed color—the emerald hue was now a milky, whitish green. If an opal were green, it would look like absinthe.

"*Now*, we drink."

She clinked glasses and sipped. It tasted like Jägermeister—shots of which she'd consumed more than she cared to remember, back in college—but less syrupy, and it gave her an instant and unprecedented buzz. "Wow. That's nice."

"Quite."

Taylor slid closer and rubbed his shoulders, finding there more tension than she'd expected. "Hard day at the office?"

"You have no idea."

"Let's see if I can help you relax."

There was the possibility that the Little Check would be unable to perform. He was not a young man, and he'd consumed who knows how much scotch before the glass of absinthe. Or it might be that the sex would be over lickety-split. Or that his codename referred to his penis size. Or some combination thereof. But lo, Little Check proved a giving and able lover, despite his physical shortcomings. The intercourse went on . . . and on . . . and on, like some X-rated Big Red commercial. Fifty-three minutes, the guy lasted—she timed it. And Taylor enjoyed it so thoroughly that she was still raring to go fifty-three minutes later. None of his seventy-six predecessors had close to this kind of stamina. Even Asher couldn't hold out for that long.

She remarked on it, as they lay in bed, smoking a postcoital cigarette.

"I wish I could take credit," he said.

"Huh?"

"A friend of mine is a chemist at Pfizer, out at Sandwich. He developed this drug that enhances the sexual experience for men."

"Is it, like, ground up rhino bones or something? I think you can get that in Chinatown."

"Sildenafil is the scientific name. They're still working out the kinks. When they perfect the formula, they'll patent it and sell it as an impotence cure. Fountain of youth in a little blue pill, for old farts like me."

"Absinthe, sildenafil . . . you're, like, the crown prince of awesome drugs. Anything else you got behind the counter? Birth control pills for men, maybe?"

That laugh again. "That's still in development."

She sat up and reached for the nightstand, where the fake mascara tube lay next to her cigarette case. She rested her cigarette in the ashtray's groove, picked up the mascara tube, and unscrewed the top.

"I want you to know," she said, "that you are the best lay I've ever had."

"Oh, come."

"I mean it," she said. "I'm not just saying it. I mean it with all my heart."

Holding the needle in her left hand—she held it behind her back, so he couldn't see, although he was not paying attention—she caressed his face with her right hand and kissed him greedily on the mouth. When she saw that his eyes were closed, she jabbed the needle into his upper thigh.

"What the . . ." Jan swatted at the wound, as if shooing a mosquito.

Taylor moved in for a closer look.

"Who sent you?" he asked, between cries of pain he tried to suppress. "MI5? Mossad? KGB?"

"I didn't ask," Taylor said.

Then his body began to flail around, and foam drizzled from his mouth, and he was unable to speak. Sixty-three second later—she timed this, too—all movement ceased. She found this so erotic that for a fleeting moment she entertained necrophiliac thoughts—"Cold Ethyl" is a song about sex with a dead girl, after all—before remembering that there was a living, breathing man in the next room who would certainly indulge her carnal desires.

Taylor got dressed, retrieved her cigarette from the ashtray, and took a long drag. She went to the door that led to the adjoining room, unlocked it from her side, and knocked three times.

There was the sound of the lock, and then the door opened to reveal Trey Parrish, can of Budweiser in hand.

"Took longer than I thought," he said. "I was starting to worry."

"When do the cleaners get here?"

"We don't have to wait for them. In fact, it's better if we leave before they arrive. Can I give you a lift?"

Taylor gave him her best come-hither look—the prelude-to-a-kiss equivalent of a Rob Dibble fastball right down the middle. "Only if you come up for a nightcap."

He put his arm around her waist, consummating the deal. "Done."

And he drove them back to the Dakota, where they fucked, albeit briefly, on Asher's black silk sheets.

Trey Parrish was the cause of so much suffering—without his referral, remember, Taylor would still be alive, and my life would not have been destroyed—that no amount of revenge could ever make things right. Did Edmond Dantès really feel better, when all was said and done? That said, I do take some small consolation in reporting that, according to Taylor's diary, Trey Parrish was "abysmal" in bed, and—it gets better—"hung like a prepubescent hamster."

CHAPTER 20

Although I have mentioned it several times, I have not discussed at length Taylor's bouts of clinical depression. She had been on Prozac since her junior year of college—and they don't give you Prozac unless you exhibit signs of extreme melancholy, such as crying during *Ghost*. (My psychiatrist may as well have hung a GOT MEDS? sign outside his office.) All joking aside, she was really fucked up for a while there. She wound up dropping all her classes the first semester of her junior year—her friend Kim Winter had spent the year in Prague, which was part of the reason Taylor became unhinged; it was during this period that she had the three-way with her roommate's fiancé—because she had trouble getting out of bed in the morning. She just stayed under the covers, in the fetal position and in tears, listening to *Disintegration* over and over.

I mention this now because I want to paint as complete a portrait of Taylor Schmidt as I can, but also, and more importantly, to contrast her feelings of intense despair during her junior year at Wycliffe with the volcanic surge of exhilaration that greeted her the morning after pink-slipping Little Check. This was not the Cure. This was Katrina and the Waves. Taylor was walking on sunshine.

When she woke up, it was almost noon. The sun burst through the window like glory streaming from heaven above. Trey Parrish and his hamster dick were gone. Taylor bounced out of bed, put on one of Asher's dress shirts—she had slept in the nude—and made for the Mr. Coffee machine. She was startled to find Lydia Murtomaki at the kitchen table, presiding over a pot of coffee, a basket of scones, and the *Times* crossword.

"Ms. Murtomaki. What a surprise."

"'Saturn, for one,'" Lydia said. "Three letters."

"Car."

"Thanks." The Director filled in the answer, in ink. "Coffee?"

Taylor poured herself a cup. Since living at Asher's, she had taken to drinking the stuff black.

"You acquitted yourself like a pro last night, Taylor."

Taylor took a sip of coffee and burned the roof of her mouth. "Does that mean I'm hired?"

"There are no permanent openings at this time. Alas."

"Something I learned from you, Ms. Murtomaki, is how to offer the incumbent a severance package he can't refuse."

Lydia smiled, but otherwise ignored the comment. There was no reprise of the death-rattle laugh. "We know you killed Andrew Borden," she said. "We also know that you didn't realize that the Borden hit was not sanctioned by Quid Pro Quo, but was instead the reckless act of a rogue agent."

The roof of Taylor's mouth began to throb in pain.

"Don't worry about fingerprints or DNA evidence—we sent our best people to clean up the mess. And I do mean *mess*. You left the Bible there. Careless, careless, careless." Lydia picked up a scone. "Cranberry walnut. Delicious. Try one."

Taylor took the scone but did not eat it. Her eyes were glued to the Director's. Where was this going? They were pleased with her, right? If they were going to kill her, they'd have done so last night, when she was sleeping, right? Immediately, her fears were allayed.

"If you work for us," Lydia told her, "you get it all—all the perquisites of membership: the Dakota, the Yale Club, the Jaguar."

Now Taylor began to get excited. It was late in the fourth quarter of a football game she was pretty damned sure her team would win—too soon to completely relax, but late enough in the game to get her hopes up. "The Jaguar is a bit fancy for my tastes," she said.

"And forever in the shop." Lydia took a bite of the scone. "Really. Delicious." She washed it down with a big swig of coffee and took our her cigarette holder. "Understand, Taylor: we place a premium on loyalty. Nothing is more important to us than loyalty. Not even competence. The situation with Mr. Krug, this is *not* how we like to do business. The only reason we're moving in this direction—the *only* reason—is because we cannot accommodate agents with dual allegiances. Our servants cannot have two masters. It *does not work*." She gave the last three words full emphasis as she screwed a cigarette onto the holder.

Sitting down at the table, Taylor bit into the scone. "Ms. Murtomaki, are you asking me to do what I think you're asking me to do?"

"Please," said the Director, lighting her cigarette. "Call me Lydia."

CHAPTER 21

If Asher Krug kept a diary—and he almost certainly didn't; diary-keeping was too feminine a pursuit—I did not have access to it. Nor did he routinely get drunk and unburden his secrets upon me, like his girlfriend did. Thus I cannot say with one-hundred-percent certainty what was on his mind as the yellow cab whisked him from JFK to Central Park West just before midnight that Sunday night, nor am I absolutely sure of what transpired when he got back to his apartment. All I have to work with are two sparse and conflicting accounts of what went down. With that said, I hope that you will indulge my relating the scene from Asher's point of view. I have thought this through for eighteen years, mulled it over from every possible angle, and this is absolutely, beyond a shadow of a doubt, what could have happened:

As the cab coasted through Central Park via the

Seventy-second Street crossing, Asher was grumpy. Grumpy and tired. His Japanese suit was wrinkled, his hair was matted to his head, and a painful pimple was in full flower on his chin. He resented that the company had sent him to do such low-level work. Yes, Little Check was not the usual pink slip. Yes, the operation required more coordination and planning than usual to bring off. But why waste his considerable talents hauling bodies and bribing yacht crews? He was Quid Pro Quo's best pink-slipper—the starting quarterback, by God—and where was he during the Super Bowl? On the sidelines holding a clipboard. *Disposal* duty? Beneath him. He was a hit man, not a garbageman.

The taxi deposited Asher in front of the Dakota. Victor, the night doorman, opened the door of the cab for him. Usually Asher bantered playfully with Victor, but not tonight. He didn't even say thank you. He was still fuming about the Canary Islands assignment. Lydia's panties were in a twist about the Borden hit, Asher decided. She was making it personal—women were unable by nature to think dispassionately and had no business running this kind of delicate operation—and that made Asher mad. The proof was in the endgame. Who wound up offing Little Check? Some new girl he didn't even know. A new hit man? A hit *girl*? He couldn't tell which was more ridiculous.

In the elevator, Asher remembered that Taylor would be there waiting for him. Good. A blow job was just what he needed. That and a tumbler of Johnny Walker Blue would take the edge off. Hopefully she was still awake. Well, fuck it. If she was asleep, he'd wake her up. She paid no rent; let her earn her keep.

He saw her as soon as he opened the door, down the length of the hallway, sprawled out on the leather sofa. She was flipping through an *Us* magazine, listening to "That'll Be the Day" on CBS-FM, which was then an oldies station.

"You're up late," he said.

"Couldn't sleep." She got up and kissed him on the cheek. "You're home early. How was your trip? I hear the Canary Islands are lovely."

Asher dropped his valise—the corner of *The 7 Habits of Highly Effective People* was sticking out of the front pocket—just missing his Bruno Magli-ed foot. His eyes squinted, like he was looking down the scope on a rifle. "I was in Washington."

"Like hell. You were in the Canary Islands, on disposal duty." Taylor grinned like a contestant on a game show who'd just won whatever was behind Door Number Two. "I did it, Asher. It was me."

"What the fuck are you talking about?"

"I gave Little Check the pink slip," she said. There was obvious delight in saying the colorful euphemism aloud. "I went to see Lydia last week."

Asher took a deep breath, the vein on his neck pounding with fury. Molten anger flowed like lava through him. Anger at Taylor for meeting Lydia behind his back. Anger at Lydia for recruiting her to . . . to replace him? No. It couldn't be. For a moment he thought he would lose his temper—for all his passions, he was generally able to keep himself in check; the job demanded it—but he reined himself in. He grabbed Taylor by the wrist. "Outside."

"I don't have shoes," she said, grabbing her handbag.

"We can't talk in here," he whispered. Then, practically shouting: "Outside. *Now*."

He dragged her by the wrist into the hallway, slamming the door behind them, and made for the elevator doors. The night of the Rainbow Room date, when it was as hot as it's ever been in New York, he hadn't broken a sweat, but now, the first week of November, he was perspiring. Now he took her by the hand—he gripped her as hard as he could, like he wanted her bones to crack—and pushed the button for the elevator.

"Asher, that hurts."

Good, he thought, and tightened his grip.

They waited a minute in silence, watching the numbers descend. It opened, they got on. And they were not alone. A short, slim woman in enormous sunglasses was in the elevator, holding a white lapdog.

"Asher dear," she said. "How lovely to see you."

"Yoko!" Asher released Taylor from his grasp and greeted the woman. He was not one to be impressed by celebrity, but even before moving to the Dakota, he'd been a fan of Yoko Ono. "Likewise. And may I present Taylor Schmidt."

"Charmed," Taylor said. "I am a big admirer of your late husband."

"Thank you, dear."

They exchanged pleasantries—how was the heat in his apartment? It was too hot in hers. Where was he at the co-op meeting? Richard had shown up drunk!—until the elevator stopped on the ground floor. Asher supplied rejoinders when necessary, but his mind was elsewhere. His anger tempered, his brain functioning mormally, he was trying to decipher the meaning of all the activity: Taylor asks to join Quid Pro Quo, Lydia hires her. Where did that leave him? Was he being demoted . . . or pink-slipped?

The doors opened. Yoko went out first, half-running past the iron gates and into a waiting limousine. Taylor tried to keep pace with her, bare feet and all, but Asher grabbed her wrist again to slow her down.

"That hurts," she said again.

Again, he ignored her.

"So Lydia said that . . ."

"Not here," he said. "The park. Let's go."

"Asher, I'm barefoot."

"You'll survive."

They went through the gates, past Victor the night doorman, and headed east on Seventy-second Street. They crossed Central Park West—there were no cars coming, so they didn't have to wait at the light—and plunged into the jungle of the park.

Taylor would know if Lydia planned to kill him, Asher reasoned, so the idea was to get that information out of her. Fortunately, he was prepared. In his inside jacket pocket—something only a professional killer would keep on his person—was a syringe of Sodium Pentothol. He hadn't needed it in Tenerife. So: get her alone, talk a bit, inject her with truth syrum, talk some more. That was Asher's plan—one that had worked for him many times before.

Manhattan is never completely dark—the taxis don't need headlights in Times Square, even at midnight—but Central Park when the lights go down might be the exception. The buildings beyond were illuminated, but once they rounded a path, shadows were everywhere. Asher led Taylor, who would let out a grunt every other minute as she stepped on something in her bare feet, around one turn, then another. Then they stumbled into the little clearing known as Strawberry Fields, where IMAGINE is inscribed in a circle of stones. Sometimes there were homeless hippies huddled in cardboard boxes there, but tonight it was deserted. Perfect.

He released her wrist in such a way that he practically launched her onto the stones. "I told you not to involve Lydia."

"It's fine."

"It's *not* fine. You don't know what she's capable of. I wanted to keep you away from her. I wanted to protect you."

"Protect me?" She got up and came at him, crowding him like a manager confronting an umpire after a bad call at the plate. Her face was inches away from his. "I can take care of myself, thank you very much."

"You don't understand." Asher grabbed her and held her fast, each hand gripping one of her arms just above the elbow. "I love you, Taylor."

He had not planned to say this. Until he gave it voice, in fact, he had not even thought about it. Just the same, he knew that it was true.

Taylor gazed at him with her patented awestruck, almost worshipful look. "I love you, too."

And they kissed, in the darkness of Strawberry Fields, on top of the word IMAGINE. "All You Need Is Love" popped into Asher's head, the song he'd disparaged on their first date, and he realized that he liked it.

When she broke away, Asher said, in a tone both warm and calm, "Lydia is inhuman, Taylor. She'll make you do terrible things. Unspeakable things."

"Unspeakable things? What is this, *Heart of Darkness*?"

"Let me put it in concrete terms. She'll make you kill Todd, okay? If he doesn't do his pink slip, she'll make you kill him. Little Check is one thing. But how would you handle killing a friend? Someone close—someone you loved?" With one hand he caressed her cheek; with the other, he found the syringe of Sodium Pentathol in his jacket. "Shit, they might make you kill *me*, Taylor."

They were standing close together, as if slow-dancing. His head was slightly tilted, his eyes gazing so intently into hers—and his attention sufficiently focused on readying his own chemical injection—that he didn't see her unscrew the fake mascara tube. So they stood there, the two of them, half making out, half preparing to jab the other with a needle.

Ah, trust. The foundation of every good relationship.

"They would never make me kill you," she said, kissing him.

Asher relaxed a little. Best as he could tell, she was telling the truth. She loved him, she wouldn't hurt him. Maybe he could do without drugging her. Heck, maybe this bit of awkwardness would be over soon enough that he could get that blow job after all. It was the blow job he was picturing as he kissed her—picturing so intently that his eyes fluttered shut. The needle was already stuck in his neck, half an inch above his starched collar, before he realized that he'd been duped.

"I would only kill you," she said, "because I wanted to."

Asher shrieked, more in surprise than pain—the great Goliath felled by a boy with a slingshot!—as Taylor pulled away and began running, barefoot, for the street. Staggering, he reached into his jacket pocket and pulled out the Sodium Pentathol. With his remaining energy, he hurled the syringe dart-like at Taylor, piercing her left ankle as she scurried away. He heard her cry out, but her footsteps did not abate. And then the pain became too intense to listen, and the sound of his breathing echoed like thunder in his ears, and he writhed in agony on top of the IMAGINE stones, and love is all you need.

I was one weekend removed from Asher dropping the Quid Pro Quo bombshell on my lap. In those forty-eight hours, I'd gone through the gamut of emotions—denial, depression, shock, grief, and all the other crap they teach you in change-management seminars. But I found myself stuck on anger. I was really pissed off at Taylor, for so blithely sending me into the lion's den. True, she'd told me to only use Quid Pro Quo as a last resort, but come *on*. Never in a million years would I have imagined that I'd have to kill somebody—and my former boss, no less!

I'd been trying all weekend to get a hold of Taylor. I tried her mother's—this is when long distance calls were still expensive, but I was willing to pay fifty cents a minute to sort this out—but the damned phone just rang off the hook. Only eighteen years ago, yes, but with no cell phones, no e-mail, no Facebook status updates, Taylor and I may as well have been star-crossed characters from a Thomas Hardy novel, victims of a hapless inability to communicate.

That Sunday, I took a late dinner alone at Restaurant Florent, a French dinerette in the West Village that just went out of business last year, which was at the time offering a "Recession Prix Fixe" special. The economy was lousy, as I said. I ate marked-down steak frites and reread the first twenty pages of *Foucault's Pendulum* and tried to forget the shitstorm that was my life.

By one in the morning, I was back in the apartment, in boxer shorts and a Hard Rock Café T-shirt (the more obscure the city, the hipper the shirt—mine said Košice, although I doubt there was a franchise there) listening to a bootleg cassette of Andrew Dice Clay's dirty nursery rhyme routine, nursing a Rolling Rock, and attempting the same Sunday crossword that I'm sure Lydia Murtomaki had finished in an hour—I was too tapped out even to masturbate—when I heard a key in the lock.

For a minute I was scared . . . until Taylor staggered in, bombed off her ass. She looked like shit. Her eyes were bloodshot, her crooked nose beet-red. There was a bruise on her cheek and a stain down the front of her pink sweater that might have been salsa but was probably puke. Needless to say, none of this unpleasantness stemmed the blood engorging that which was peeking from the slit of my boxer shorts. Monomania is monomania.

But I fought off my sexual impulses. This was no time for love. This was time for war! Two days I'd spent preparing myself for what to say to her . . . but at the moment of truth, all I could do was shout at her incoherently, which I did for some time. Finally I mustered a lucid question: "Where the fuck have you been? I was trying to reach you all weekend."

"I told you, I was in Missouri."

"Bullshit. How could you do this to me? How could you fucking *do* this to me? You fucking *bitch*."

My anger was a flamethrower, zapping white-hot flames right at her. But Taylor's heart was made of asbestos, apparently; the fire had no effect on her. Her eyelids were barely open. She seemed not to be aware that I was upset. "Can you get me some water?"

Taylor teetered through the living room and fell onto the sofa.

"Sure thing," I said, with as much sarcasm as I could muster, which was quite a bit. "Coming right up." I made a big show of the operation, filling a glass with ice, topping it with water from the tap (bottled water was unheard of in those days), and presenting it to her like Marcel would a fine Burgundy. "Here you are, Your Majesty."

The sarcasm, like the anger, while radioactive to me, did not seem to register on her inner Geiger counter. "Thanks." Taylor took a sip and coughed violently.

Now I was *really* pissed. The only thing worse than rage deferred is rage ignored. One wrong word and I don't know what I would have done. Hit her, probably, although I've never hit anyone before in my life, much less a woman. I am not, by nature, a violent man. "Well? Talk, damn it!"

With some effort, Taylor forced her eyelids open and met my angry gaze. Her voice was a whisper, faint and faraway. "Asher and I broke up."

Forget placation—this had the effect of a horse tranquilizer. "You broke up?"

It got better.

"We broke up because of you."

"Because of me?"

"Because of you."

Instantly my anger evaporated. Everything that I had planned to say, the monologue I'd spent all week preparing, fled my brain. None of it mattered now. Not with this bit of news. Completely disarmed, I sat down next to her. My voice took on its usual soft, avuncular tone. "What happened?"

"He said if you didn't do your pink slip by the end of the week . . ." Taylor paused here for another sip of water, and again wretched violently. "He said if you didn't do the pink slip by the end of the week, I'd have to kill you."

You know the expression "my blood turned cold"? Well, mine did. Really. It felt like every ounce of hemoglobin in my veins transmuted to ice water. Not just my veins—every synapse, every nerve ending in my body was chilled to the . . . well, to the bone. "Is that why you're here? To kill me?"

"Retard." She punched me in the leg. "That's why I broke up with him. You're my best friend. You're the only person in this whole stupid town who doesn't treat me like shit. I would never do anything to hurt you."

"Why are you so drunk?"

"I'm not drunk, Todd. I'm drugged. The fucker tried to poison me."

"What?"

"He slipped me something. The date-rape drug, I think. That's why I'm so out of it. Fortunately, I realized it before I took the full dose." That explained the bloodshot and watery eyes, the heavy eyelids. "See? I'm barefoot. I didn't even have time to put my shoes on." She wiggled her toes at me. "I can't believe I fell for a fucking *psychopath*."

All things considered, the fact that Asher was a professional murderer should have tipped Taylor off to his warped psychopathology months ago, when the secret first came out, but I didn't press the issue. Taylor Schmidt was having her Saul of Tarsus moment, and better late than never. That was enough for me.

I didn't have time to savor my victory, though, because I realized that this was far from over. "But won't *Asher* try and kill me?"

"I don't think so."

"How can you be sure?"

Taylor smiled a wicked smile purloined from Lydia Murtomaki.

"You didn't . . ."

The wicked smile vanished, and her voice got curt. "I don't want to talk about it, okay?"

"Okay, we won't talk about it."

"All I did was buy us some time. Lydia *will* send someone for you . . . unless Donna Green gets her P.S., and soon."

I thought of my ex-boss, her bad clothes, her Gospel singing voice, her struggles with her weight. I didn't like her particularly, but I didn't want her dead, and I certainly didn't want a hand in her murder.

"I won't do it," I said. "I *can't* do it."

"I know that," Taylor said, "and I respect that. That's why I'm going to do it for you."

This was touching and all, in a reverse-chivalrous kind of way, but it didn't exactly solve the larger problem, i.e., Donna Green getting offed. "But . . ."

"All you need to do is keep it secret. Lydia and the others will never know."

"The others? What others? Who are the others?"

Taylor continued as if I hadn't even spoken. "Understand one thing, Todd—Donna Green is a goner, no matter what you decide to do. She can't be saved now. Your choice is simple: preserve the lives of your parents and friends, as well as your own, or don't. There is no third option."

It was like a game we used to play in college. Someone would propose two undesirables—Barbara Bush and Marilyn Quayle, say—and you have to decide which of the two you'd rather get jiggy with. Death Is Not an Option was the name of the game. In the Quid Pro Quo version, death was the *only* option.

"I understand."

"I can see your mind spinning. Just stop. There's no way out of this."

"I said I understand."

"I got you into this mess, and I'm going to get you out. Just trust me, okay? Will you do that? Will you trust me?"

There is an old adage about how you're never supposed to trust people who ask you to trust them. That old adage doesn't apply when the speaker is as lovely as Taylor Schmidt—not when the listener is Todd Lander.

"Of course I will."

"Good." Suddenly and without warning, Taylor rested her hand on my thigh, well above the knee. "I missed you, the last few weeks. I really missed you."

The stirring down below began anew. I liked where this was going. "Me, too."

"The day I moved out . . . those things you said, about us . . . about us being together . . . did you really mean them?"

"With all my heart."

Before I could say another word, she kissed me. Oh, my! As our tongues danced, her dexterous hand slid from my thigh to more exigent regions. The more we made out, the more she got into it. At last, I could hear her moaning without the sound being muffled by the bedroom door, or the whir of the pocket rocket!

Where is this going? I wondered. *Should I make a move?*

But I didn't have to.

"Todd," she said, "I want you."

In case of emergency, break glass.

It took me as many uncondomed thrusts as it took licks for that cartoon owl to get to the center of the Tootsie Pop. The thrill of consummation completely overrode any lingering negative emotions I may have still been feeling. Put simply, sex with Taylor Schmidt was the best thirty seconds of my life.

I awoke with a jolt, as if zapped by Jovian lightning. It was almost dawn—I'd been out cold for three or four hours. Taylor was still asleep, her breaths tortured. I held her closer, stilling her myoclonic jerks, hoping she'd come to. Batteries fully charged, guns reloaded, I was ready for more. I caressed her hair, kissed her forehead, rubbed her butt—did what I could short of pouring cold water on her face to wake her up—but she remained unconscious. Damned Asher and his damned roofies!

Sex and sleep, both of my preferred options, would have to wait. I was wired, plus I had to pee something fierce. I disentangled myself from Taylor's naked body—What sublime contour! Like fine sculpture!—and headed for the can. On the way, I stubbed my fucking toe on the fucking leg of the fucking sofa. In my subsequent throes of pain, I noticed the corner of a familiar faux-marble writing tablet peeking from Taylor's bag. Could it be? It was. The latest installment of her diary, right there in front of me—and its author passed out cold in the next room!

The way I looked at it, as I went into the bathroom with the diary, was that Quid Pro Quo, and her dealings with it, proved that Taylor really loved me. The evidence was all there. For *me*, she broke up with, and possibly whacked, Asher Krug. For *me*, she was going to murder Donna Green. Where most people would see a slut and a murderess, I saw a saint and a savior. *Taylor Schmidt loved me.* Surely the diary would confirm this. . .

The final installment of Taylor's diary covered everything that happened from her initial meeting with Lydia Murtomaki at Quid

Pro Quo through the final meeting with her at Asher's kitchen table that morning—everything that had happened except her final rendezvous with Asher. For all of the shocking developments in those pages, for all of the gruesomeness and death—it was like I'd popped *Pretty Woman* into the VCR, but on came *Rambo*—I couldn't help but be a tad disappointed. In the entire journal, some fifty some odd pages, there was not one mention of Todd Lander. Not one. If she really did dig me, if I were really the love of her life, it must have just occurred to her on the cab ride downtown.

A normal person would have pegged Taylor right then and there as an irredeemable maniac and fled the country. In fact, a normal person would have done so as soon as he learned the truth about Quid Pro Quo. Me? I was under her spell, no two ways about it. I was able to gloss over, and to rationalize away, the inconvenient truths. Cognitive dissonance, they call it. So what if Taylor poisoned Bill Steward? He had it coming. So what if she wasted both Andrew Borden and his wife? It's not like she had a choice. So what if Taylor was tapped by Lydia Murtomaki to assassinate Little Check? She was impressionable, my old roommate; always had been. Even her astrologer said so—she was a double Pisces, a watered-down water sign. And the Asher hit? Hey, she was just following orders.

The last entry snapped me out of my haze of lusty delusion, albeit too briefly. My eyes scanned the words in her girlish, almost cartoonish hand. The pink ink. Dying pink ink, replaced by indelible black midway through the almost Shakespearean final paragraph:

> *Three words are all you need to make a guy putty in your hands. Say I love you and he will blush, he will glow, he will cringe, he will even freak out, but what he won't do is fear you. Men say I love you all the time to get what they want. When he is at his weakest, I will strike, and the job will be mine!*

She wrote this that afternoon, before her quarrel with Asher, which meant that (a) she had, in fact, killed him, and (b) she'd *planned* on doing so, in order to appropriate his job. Tayor'd gone Macbeth on his ass! Only there was no obsessive washing of hands with her. Her conscience was clear.

A normal person—back to him again—would have made the obvious leap and asked himself, *If she killed Asher . . . what does she have in store for me?* This thought never crossed my mind.

In my defense, I'd just had sex with her, like, a few hours before. I was on Cloud Fucking Nine, my happy state of mind augmented by what we used to call PFG, or Post Fuck Glow. Rational thought had no chance in the face of such unbridled bliss. I was in la-la land, deluded to the point of temporary insanity. There's no other way to explain it.

I mean, it's not like I was *completely* in the dark, even before I read the latest diary. I knew that Quid Pro Quo was a front for a squadron of assassins. I knew that it was scary and evil and not to be fucked with. And now, I knew that Taylor was an integral part of it. I knew she'd killed at least four people—her own pink slip, plus Borden, plus Little Check, plus Asher Krug—and that my old boss, Donna Green, was next. Furthermore, I knew that Taylor *enjoyed* the hits. Or, at the very least, the hits had no discernible effect on her psyche. I knew, in short, that she was dangerous . . . except for the fact that I didn't. On some deep-seated, subconscious level, I refused to recognize the bloody writing on the wall. I was like that pope who condemned Galileo—my faith was stronger than my reason.

Faith is always stronger than reason.

And Fate is stronger still.

I replaced the diary in her pocketbook, climbed back into bed, and slept until three in the afternoon. It was after dark when Taylor finally got up.

CHAPTER 22

Sketchy as Union Square was in 1991, it was the Emerald City compared to the stretch of Fourteenth Street to the west, a Yellow Brick Road of subway stations, parking lots, wholesale clothing stores, and junk emporia hawking New York baseball hats and T-shirts and coffee mugs. Head west along Fourteenth Street, past the PATH station, and past Seventh Avenue, and you came to a nebulous neighborhood on the borderlands of Chelsea, the Meatpacking District, and the NYU environs. Here, in a building that used to be an electronics store, was one of the hottest nightclubs in town—Nell's.

With its chandeliers and velvet couches and gilded mirrors, Nell's looked like the drawing room of a Garden District mansion the morning after Lestat took possession. The eponymous owner, Laura "Little Nell" Campbell, was best known for playing Columbia in *The Rocky Horror Picture Show*—the cult classic Village Cinema played every Saturday at midnight for twenty-some-odd years. Little Nell may have been a white girl from Australia, but her nightclub, with its pulsing R&B upstairs and hip-hop on the basement dance floor, catered to African Americans, particularly African Americans celebrities. Prince was a frequent guest, as were many visiting NBA players. In 1993, Tupac Shakur—whose debut album was released in 1991—would bolster Nell's thug-life bona fides by partaking of oral sex on its dance floor.

On Monday nights, Nell's had an open mic. This wasn't the usual bit, where fops in ponytails meandered through "Blowin' in the Wind" on slightly-out-of-tune Ovations, nor was it Lach's hipster antifolk scene at Sidewalk. Nell's had a house band that specialized in reggae and R&B, and it was world-class. If you were going to get up and sing, you had to be good, or someone might take your ass *out*.

Donna Green, my former boss, had come to Nell's that Monday, as she did more or less every Monday, to strut her stuff with the band. (I didn't care for her rendition of the "Happy Birthday" song in the office, but she was obviously talented, or the crowd would have eaten her for lunch—and a plentiful bounty she would have made.) A walking tent of teal taffeta, she ended her short set with a rollicking performance of "I Will Survive"—forget Nell Campbell; Donna had channeled Nell Carter—and afterwards was sweating profusely. Her braided hair extensions intensified the heat. She needed some air. So she waddled off the stage and made for the downstairs lavatory.

Her gown cascaded behind her. There was enough material to enclose a yurt. Donna made it down the staircase, across the downstairs dance floor, and was almost to the bathrooms when the train of the dress caught beneath her squat legs and tore along the waist, exposing her ample buttocks.

"Shit," she muttered, hoisting up the skirt. "Shit."

"Everything okay?"

Looking up, Donna saw a girl in a slinky black and white polka-dot dress—a pretty young white girl with dishwater-brown hair, a crooked nose, and a Midwestern twang to her high-registered voice. There was always a plentiful supply of white girls at Nell's, but relatively few white guys.

"I tore my gown," said Donna.

"I think I have some safety pins. Let me help you."

The girl with the dishwater-brown hair and the crooked nose gathered up the excess yards of taffeta and followed the hefty diva into the bathroom.

"Stand there. By the wall."

As Donna followed the instructions, she spaced out, thinking about the performance. She had been happy with it, but was now having second thoughts. Had she hit the right note at the end? Or did it fall flat, as her voice sometimes did when she got tired?

Meanwhile the girl with the dishwater-brown hair and the crooked nose squatted behind Donna, busy with the gown. The swoosh of fabric muted the rumble of hip-hop from down the hall.

"Almost there."

And then—

"Ouch!"

Sharp pain in Donna's meaty left rump. Like a bee sting, or an acupuncture misadventure. One of the safety pins, probably.

"Oh, shit. Sorry about that."

Donna rolled her eyes, gritted her teeth, but said, "It's okay."

A few minutes later, the gown was repaired. Thanking the girl with the dishwater-brown hair and the crooked nose, but without really looking at her, Donna quit the bathroom as quickly as her dachshund legs would carry her. Once on the dance floor, her nose began running, mucus pouring like water from her cavernous nostrils. As she wiped her nose with the back of her hand, Donna felt a tightness in her chest. *Oh shit*, she thought. *I'm having a heart attack*. The room got blurry, the lights and the clubgoers fading from focus, turning into an Impressionist painting. She cried for help but her stentorian voice failed her. She was gasping for breath now. Sweat oozed like lava from her pores, and drool from her mouth, frothy, like a rabid dog. *Not here*, she thought. *Not now.* Then the nausea hit, wham! and cramps like PMS on steroids. She fought back the urge to vomit. People had gathered around her now. They realized that she wasn't dancing, that these were not choreographed moves. As Donna fell to the floor, smacking down hard like a felled sequoia, she lost control of her bodily functions. She began to twitch, to jerk, to convulse. The music stopped cold, the room, so raucous a second ago, now funereally silent.

"Somebody call an ambulance," someone said.

Her eyes went white. Bile trickled from the side of her mouth. Donna lifted up her head—it was as difficult as anything she'd ever attempted—but before she could say a word, her body went slack, her head banged against the hardwood floor, and brightness overwhelmed her.

While Taylor was out padding her homicidal résumé, I was scouring East Village jewelry shops, in the middle of a cold November rainstorm, for an aquamarine ring. See, aquamarine was her birthstone. I wanted to buy her a present, a humble token of my gratitude for the transfiguring sex that I was sure would lead to better things—something more than the mix tape I'd already put together.

I was out all evening, putzing around in my galoshes, fighting through the relentless downpour. Aquamarine is not exactly common in jewelry stores, I found out. I think it's because there are fewer people born in March.

I never did find the right ring. Finally giving up, I went to Kim's Video and, to get my mind off my troubles, rented *Silence of the Lambs* (in which Hannibal Lecter, in his iconically creepy voice, says, "Quid pro quo, Clarice."). Then I bought a coffee at Veselka and called it a day.

By the time I got home, my jeans were soaked through from the knee all the way down. With its shitty exposures, the apartment is poorly lit anyway, but on overcast days, it's like Miltonic hell in there. It was dark, is what I'm saying, and I didn't bother flipping on the light. Plus my brain was still mush—amazing the soporific effect a good lay can have on your gray matter. This explains, somewhat, how I was able to walk down the hall, through the living room, and into my bedroom, change my pants, and come back to the living room without noticing that there was someone sitting on the vinyl sofa. Someone who smelled faintly of Drakkar Noir.

"There's nothing to read in here," my unbidden guest announced, flipping on a table lamp. "*Sassy* magazine? Is this yours?"

"Taylor's. She has a subscription." I knew the voice, of course. Voices like that you don't easily forget. Especially when they belong to ghosts.

I thought about beating a hasty exit through the terrace, but decided against it; if he'd wanted to kill me, he'd have done it when I first walked in.

"I heard you were dead."

"How did Mark Twain put it? Reports of my demise have been exaggerated." Asher closed the *Sassy* magazine—I couldn't imagine any single object looking more ridiculous in his powerful, masculine hands than that glossy teenybopper rag—and dropped it on a pile of back issues stacked on the floor. "And *Generation X*?" he said, gesturing at the oversized blue-and-yellow paperback on the bookcase. "That must be yours. Taylor isn't that pseudo-intellectual."

"You're not down with Doug Coupland?"

"The book's a piece of shit. They don't *do* anything, those people, just sit around whining. Bunch of fucking babies."

"You want something to drink?"

"I won't be staying long. Have a seat." He crossed his legs and flashed a smile I can only describe as hospitable, as if this were *his* apartment, and *I'd* been the one waiting in the dark. Except that, you know, Asher Krug would never have lived in such a dive. This easy appropriation of my space should have been taken as an affront to my manhood, but under the circumstances, I meekly sat down.

"You aren't totally off base," Asher said. "Taylor did try to kill me, and she believes she was successful. Not that I'm in a hurry to correct her. No one comes looking for you when they think you're dead. It's a very pleasant arrangement."

Humor had saved me with Taylor before, so I tried it on Asher, giving him my best S.P.E.C.T.R.E. accent: "You only live twice, Mr. Bond."

He laughed—the only time I'd ever seen him so much as chuckle. Asher had many things going for him, but sense of humor wasn't one of them. He was way too serious.

"Taylor is planning to kill you," he said, which pretty much wet-blanketed my attempt at levity. "Tonight, probably. She'll wait till you have your guard down, and then inject you with a toxic agent called Cold Ethyl. She keeps it in a dummy mascara tube. She has to kill you, company policy, because you failed to execute your pink slip."

"I thought that was your job."

"Not anymore." He glanced at his Rolex. "By now, Donna Green has already joined the heavenly choir. It's too late for you to make it right, unfortunately."

I studied him intently, looking for a tip that might help me figure out his plan. It was no use. He was a professional killer and a spy; he could easily outwit the likes of me.

"Why are you telling me this?"

"So you can save yourself. And avenge my death, as it were."

So there it was. *He wanted me to kill Taylor!*

"No way," I said. "No fucking way."

"By tomorrow morning," Asher said, producing a revolver from his jacket pocket, "one of you will be dead."

Asher set the gun on the table, by the lamp.

"Election Day," I said.

"What's that?"

"Tomorrow is Election Day." I observed the gun gleaming

under the table lamp. I had never even held a gun before, much less shot one. "What's funny is, Taylor said that *you* were planning to kill me."

"Let me guess," said Asher. "She said she'd do your pink slip for you on the sly, so you'd be off the hook, but I knew the truth, so I had to be removed. Something like that?"

"Something like that."

"She told me she loved me," he said, his voice losing all trace of its usual arrogance. "For the first time, she said those words. Then she kissed me—and shot me up with Cold Ethyl."

I remembered that final diary entry:

> *Three words are all you need to make a guy putty in your hands.*

Was Asher playing it straight with me?

"Fortunately, I've been inoculated. You haven't." Asher stood up, straightening his jacket. "The gun is loaded. Keep it under your pillow, is my recommendation."

"You're wrong, Asher," I said, rising. "Taylor loves me. She didn't say so, but I know she does."

Asher shook his head grimly. "I hate to be the bad messenger," he said, handing me a thick envelope. "These were taken a few hours ago. She's a fucking whore, Todd."

He gave me a pat on the shoulder. "Under the pillow." And with that, Asher Krug took his leave.

He must have liked living under the radar, too, because I never saw the guy again.

Inside the envelope was a roll of grainy, black-and-white film, date-stamped today, showing Taylor leaving the apartment, being accosted in the stairwell by Trey Parrish, going into Trey's apartment, taking off her clothes, and . . . well, you can figure out the rest. Do I really have to spell it all out? Put it this way: the pictures were so graphic, I could see that Taylor's hamster analogy was actually generous.

My mouth went dry; my face, white (I could see it blanch in the mirror). I felt a tightness in my chest, like I was having a heart attack. I've never been more angry in my life—not at Taylor; at Trey. Displacement, they call it in therapy. I hurled the photographs at the sofa, which did little to appease my rage. They billowed in the air and came down gently, like hang gliders. I picked up the gun. I tucked it into my pants, the barrel between my butt cheeks (even in my mad state, I knew not to point a gun at my balls). Then I raced out the door and down the steps.

I couldn't get to that fuckwad fast enough. My adrenal glands were working overtime. You know how these tiny women can suddenly lift up automobiles when their kids are pinned underneath the tire? I felt like I could knock that bastard's door down with my fists. And I sure as hell tried.

"Open up! I know you're in there, you piece of shit!"

There was a New York Mets emblem on the door, another for the Hoboken Ski Club. I pounded my fists against those stickers until they were raw.

"Open the door!"

I didn't know what I would do when I saw him. Sock him one in the jaw, probably. Then kick him while he was down. He'd date-raped Taylor, was how I read the situation, and he had to pay. I'd bash his kidneys until they were tenderized. I'd stomp on his balls until he could never breed. I'd blow him so full of holes you could play him like an oboe. I'd. . .

The door opened. I reared back my fist, ready to strike . . . but Trey Parrish was not there. At first, in fact, I didn't see anyone. Then I looked down, where a shrunken old Indian woman, four and a half feet tall at the most, with a wrinkled fuchsia sari and a gold bindi where her cycloptic eye would be, regarded me with suspicion. Behind her, rows and rows of U-Haul boxes. *Moving* boxes.

"Where's Trey?"

She muttered something in Hindi.

"I said, where's Trey?"

But she didn't know. How could she know?

"Fuck!" I shouted, as she urgently slammed the door.

He must have moved out that afternoon. And in 1991, before Google and Classmates.com and all that, when someone moved, they were much harder to track down. Since Trey Parrish would probably not take my phone calls or respond to a forwarded letter—and since Trey Parrish's real name was almost certainly not Trey Parrish—it didn't matter if he'd relocated to the Upper East Side or Outer Mongolia—the guy was history.

Defeated, I went back to my apartment. Still a bundle of nerves, of potential energy, I paced around the living room, burned holes in the rug. I was trying to figure out my plan of attack. Or, more properly, my plan of defense.

It could have been that Asher was playing me—appealing to my emotions to trick me into killing Taylor. That's what I wanted to believe. Problem was, the evidence—the Trey Parrish photos, the absence of my name from her recent diary—suggested otherwise. With no better recourse, I decided that when Taylor came home, I would just pretend that everything was normal and play it by ear.

But I hid the gun underneath my pillow, as Asher had suggested, just in case.

There are many ways enlightened human beings can harness raging emotions: yoga, meditation, prayer, Nintendo. For us unenlightened types, serenity comes in a bottle. A longneck bottle.

There was a six-pack of Rolling Rock in the fridge. I drank three of them in about five minutes. Usually that would get me tipsy, but all it did that night was take the edge off. I could have done surgery, my hands were so steady. Or won a round of Operation, the Wacky Doctors' Game.

No sooner did I pop open the fourth bottle then Taylor came

home, wearing a slinky black and white polka-dot dress. She kissed me on the lips, with just a taste of tongue, and goosed my ass.

"Wow, you look great," I said.

"Thanks. Hey, give me one of those, would ya?"

I dug out a beer, twisted off the cap, and handed it over. By the time I'd turned around, Taylor had doffed the dress, and oh my. She looked so good I forgot my anxiety. Black silk panties, teddy, fishnet stockings, stiletto-heeled shoes, a garter belt. A fucking *garter belt*. I'd only seen garter belts in T&A mags. She looked like someone you'd meet in Gene Simmons's hotel room at three in the morning. She looked like . . . well, she looked like a prostitute, to be honest. This raised a red flag in my beleaguered brain—as well as something more tangible in my boxers.

"Let's drink these on the terrace," she suggested.

Taylor pivoted on one of those shiny heels and vamped her way into my bedroom, shaking her derrière all the while. Her stockings had lines on them that ran from her heel up the center of each leg—wow! When she crossed the threshold, she glanced over her shoulder, shot me a come-hither look, and coquettishly closed the door.

You might think I'd have been apprehensive, making my way to the room. No, sir. Al Toon couldn't have high-tailed it to the bedroom faster than I did (or David Meggett, if you prefer '91's Super Bowl champion Giants to '91's 8-8 Jets). The only thing that held me up was the folded-up sheet of paper I spotted on the floor by the sofa. I recognized it at once—her list! It must have fallen out of her bag. In one smooth motion I picked it up and slipped it in my pocket, for further study (it is the only piece of her writing still in my possession). Then I went into the bedroom, closing the door to keep the cat out. I was in no mood to share.

Taylor lay on the futon, on her side, chin propped up by her right hand. Her left was between her legs, holding in place a familiar whirring device.

The presence of my plastic rival only heightened my desire.

"This beats the terrace," she said.

"You said it."

I stripped down to my boxers (in '91, men's underpants were either boxers *or* briefs, hence the query put to Governor Bill Clinton on MTV the following year; the boxer short had not yet been supplanted by the dialectical boxer brief).

"Can I tell you a secret?"

"Please do."

"It's done."

"What's done?"

"Your pink slip. Signed, sealed, delivered."

Outside, tires were screeching, horns blowing, drunks screaming. As usual.

"You killed Donna?"

"No," she said, working the vibrator; this conversation was obviously exciting her. "You did."

"But . . ."

"No buts, Todd. She was dead before we even got involved. All I did was protect you, and your family, and your references. No one needs to know that you wussed out."

So many conflicting emotions coursed their chemical way through my body that I didn't know what to feel, let alone what to say. I took a sip of beer and choked on it.

"It was beautiful," she said. "I wasn't sure how it was going to go, but then fatso's dress ripped, so I was able to inject her without her even noticing."

Cold Ethyl.

"Ethyl dim-*eth*yl-phos-pho-*ram*i-do-cy-*an*-i-date," Taylor said, singsong, like a child remembering her ABC's. "It's a lethal nerve agent they're using in the Gulf. Cold Ethyl, we call it. Three or four minutes after the injection—five or six, if you're a whale like Donna—you drop dead. Coroner's report will say heart attack. Like Walter Bledsoe's. Cool, huh?"

Taylor worked the pocket rocket in and out as she spoke, muffling and unmuffling its whir. "Someday maybe you'll do one. Just to do it. It's such a fucking *rush*, my *God*."

Despite the fact that Asher was probably right, despite the fact that I was probably in grave danger, despite the fact that I felt horrible about Donna Green buying the farm, despite the fact that a homicidal lunatic was masturbating on my futon, I was, of course, hard as a rock. Because said homicidal lunatic was Taylor Schmidt, and I wanted nothing more than to supplant that stupid little vibrator.

Taylor spread her legs wide. Her pubic hair was waxed and trimmed, just a narrow racing stripe of hair down the center, an arrow telling me where to land. I'd never seen that look before—she was ahead of her time, that girl—but boy did I like it.

"You gonna stand there all night, Todd, or are you gonna fuck me?"

Talk about a rhetorical question! But I did stand there, because despite my blinding lust, there was one thing that bothered me, one thought I couldn't get out of my head.

"Why did you fuck Trey Parrish this morning?"

Taylor's face turned bright red, like a fire engine in a children's book. She closed her legs, sat bolt upright, and threw the pocket rocket across the room. "Who told you that?"

Should I tell her Asher had come to see me? No, not yet. Keep that ace up my sleeve. I spun a lie of my own. "The horse's mouth."

"That asshole." She closed her legs. "Yeah, I slept with him. I felt like I owed him."

"Owed him? For what?"

"Trey Parrish hooked me up with Quid Pro Quo."

"I know," I told her.

For a fleeting moment panic flashed across her eyes—it was like she had broken character—but she quickly regained her composure. "I suppose," Taylor said, in an affected tone of voice, like she were reading off a cue card, "that he told you *that*, too?"

The weird tone of her voice threw me, until I realized that *I* was the one who had fucked up. *I wasn't supposed to know* about Trey Parrish's complicity with Quid Pro Quo. The only reason I was hip to this detail was because I'd read it in her diary. Fortunately, she'd given me an out.

"Yeah," I said. My voice, too, sounded affected, fake. I hoped she didn't pick up on it. "The dude's got a big mouth."

This seemed to satisfy her. She got out of bed, walked over, took me in her arms. My worn-out boxers were all that separated her crotch from mine, which served to highlight what she told me: "I shouldn't have done it, but I had to. It didn't *mean* anything, Todd. I didn't care about Trey. I don't care about Trey. All I care about is you. All I want is you."

The long, lingering kiss that followed—my erection had slithered out the slit in my boxers and was rubbing against her warm skin—sent shockwaves rippling through my body that probably registered at the earthquake center at Columbia.

"Do you forgive me?" she asked, as she pulled down my boxers.

Unable to speak, I nodded.

"Why don't you lie down and I'll give you a massage."

I was unable to resist her suggestion. I was totally under her spell, like Robert Shaw in *The Manchurian Candidate*. I was going to pass the time by playing a little solitaire—even if it killed me.

"I bought some great massage oil at Pink Pussycat. Hot Hester, it's called. It's got a big scarlet 'A' on the bottle."

I fell facedown onto the futon. Just like that, the four beers went to my head, and the room began not to spin, but to rock back and forth, like the futon had been launched out to sea. I closed my eyes, fighting off the dizziness, and prepared for the thrill of her massage-oil-lubricated touch.

Taylor ran a single teasing finger down the length of my spine. "Let me get the oil," she whispered.

I heard her rummaging through her handbag, but I was too preoccupied by humping the futon mattress to pay attention. Suddenly,

I remembered Asher's warning. If Cold Ethyl was really contained in a mascara tube . . . *maybe she was preparing it right now!*

My heart began to pound like Tommy Lee's "Shout at the Devil" snare. I reached under the pillow for the gun. The handle was slippery in my sweaty palm. I opened my eyes. I took a deep breath and waited.

Waited for what? For a sign.

And I knew exactly what the sign would be.

Three words are all you need to make a guy putty in your hands.

Ready. . .

Massage oil or nerve agent, Taylor had found whatever it was she was looking for. (In retrospect, I should have asked to look at the bottle—she had even created the opening by describing the Hawthorne-themed label—but by the time I thought of that, it was literally years later. I never was good off the cuff.) She was at the foot of the futon now, on all fours, crawling toward me. I held my sweat-slick finger against the trigger.

. . . set. . .

In her high, wispy voice, Taylor uttered four words I'd longed to hear since the day she moved in. Four words that, under any other circumstances, would have heralded the happiest days of my life. Four words that instead were her death knell.

"Todd, I love you."

. . . go.

I whirled around, fired . . . and hit.

The kickback was incredible; my whole wrist went numb. Taylor, meanwhile, lurched backward, smashing into my desk and landing in a heap on the floor. As she fell, she knocked over her handbag, the contents of which fell on top of her. Outside the door, Bo let out a hideous moan, like he knew what had happened.

"Taylor? Taylor, are you okay?"

She was not okay. Not unless you're an evangelical Christian, like my mother's husband, who believed in the blessed afterlife—and even if you were and you did, what were the chances that

Taylor would end up with wings and harp rather than horns and pitchfork? Seventy-eight men had fallen for her charms, but St. Peter sure wouldn't.

"Oh, shit. Oh, *shit*."

I'd blown her face clean off. Taylor's nose—her sexy, Streisandy nose—had taken the brunt of the blow. The bullet had driven her oversized ethmoid bone into her brain, and then both out the back of her skull. Blood sputtered from the open wound, from her mouth, from her ears even. Blood seeped into the sheets, into the futon mattress, into the Oriental rug. Everything was blood.

The contents of her handbag had scattered around her. By her left hand was a bottle of massage oil; by her right, a tube of mascara. *The* tube of mascara.

Bo was scratching at the door, his meow like a foghorn.

It was all over so fast. The most significant act of my pathetic life, over in a flash, a literal flash, a single burst of gunfire.

I looked down the barrel of the gun. Another bullet in the chamber, and four more after that if I screwed up. I pressed the gun against my right temple and closed my eyes. I took a deep breath. I began to count.

One . . . two. . .

Before I could pull the trigger, there was a knock at the door. An authoritative knock, one not to be avoided. I heard voices, men's voices, deep voices. There was fumbling in the lock—someone had a key—and the door burst open, knob slamming into the wall and making a hole in the plaster.

"This way, this way!"

"Down the hall!"

"Here, here!"

There were four men in gray suits and sunglasses. The same guys I'd seen at Quid Pro Quo that day? Maybe. They had guns at the ready. They had white wires dangling from one ear. How did they get here so quickly? Who sent them?

"Drop the weapon. Drop the weapon!"

"Put your hands on your head."

"Drop the weapon, motherfucker!"

"Hands on your head, you piece of shit!"

I did what I was told.

Two of them dragged me into the bathroom, threw me into the shower—I was naked, remember—and hosed me down with cold water. They threw some clothes at me, made me get dressed. By the time I'd obliged, the other two had already wrapped Taylor's body in a thick plastic bag, the kind you see in Vietnam movies. They collected her purse, my envelope of hundred-dollar bills, the photographs of her and Trey Parrish, her diary—all the evidence, basically; everything but the list of lovers, which was still in the pocket of my jeans—in a black Hefty bag.

"You're under arrest," one of the suits told me.

"You have the right to remain silent," said another, a big square-jawed prick, "and blah blah blah."

"Her diary," I was shouting. "It's all in her diary. She was going to kill me. *She was going to kill me!*"

"I said you have the right to remain *silent*," Square Jaw said. He reared back and socked me in the temple.

Fade to black.

CHAPTER 23

Bail was set at five hundred grand—an excessive magisterial measure; it could have been five, and I wouldn't have been able to pay—so I spent the weeks after Taylor's death shuffling between rooms at the city jail. The Tombs, as said jail is called, is something of a misnomer—most of my cellmates were there for the oh-so-heinous crime of possession of controlled substances, which didn't stop them from toking up behind bars.

Jobless, more or less penniless (Taylor never did surrender her share of the rent) and desperate, I phoned Laura, my ex, whose now-fiancé Chet was a defense attorney at Legal Aid. Chet felt that representing me was a breach of ethics, or so he claimed. Instead, he pawned me off on the newest Legal Aid recruit, Elliott Gross.

Gross was a wet-behind-the-ears law school grad, with next to no trial experience, but his heart was in the right place. He still gave a shit—no small consolation, in that line of work. He genuinely loathed injustice. He did pro bono work for animal rights organizations and homeless shelters. And he was sharp. He was very sharp. Top of his class at Hofstra.

In the days that followed, I told Gross everything, every last detail, just as I've laid it out in these pages. He took it all in. He promised to do whatever it took to exonerate me. He liked me, I could tell, probably because I had more in common with him than the rest of his drug-addled clientele. As for me, I insisted on pleading innocent. I clung to the naïve faith that the truth would come out in the trial, which was scheduled for after the New Year.

"Mr. Lander is innocent of the charges," he told the vulturine press, who were, as you might recall if you read the tabloids at the time, going to town with the story. JUNIOR EDITOR SLAIN IN CRIME OF PASSION. WOMAN, 23, KILLED BY JILTED LOVER. Nothing like spilt white-girl blood to spill ink, and the truth be damned. The articles were usually accompanied by Taylor's college yearbook picture, which wasn't particularly flattering, and my API photo ID headshot, which was even less so. And the press always referred to me by all three names, Todd *Alan* Lander, like mommies reprimanding a recalcitrant child. It was one of their ways of humiliating me, along with describing me as "friendless" (the *Post*), "a loner" (*Newsday*), and "almost certainly psychologically disturbed" (the *Daily News*).

My intrepid attorney did what he could to shelter me from the media shitstorm. But the shitstorm died down soon enough. I was like Robert Chambers, yet another lesser loser in a long line of notorious New Yorkers. The Preppie Killer, however, had only himself to blame. Me, I had as much control over my fate as the dude from the "Owner of a Lonely Heart" video.

The Friday before Thanksgiving—a holiday I would not get to spend with my dying father; I would never see him again—Elliott Gross met me in one of the interrogation rooms at the Tombs. He wore a goatee, which was fashionable in New York at the time (but is no longer, although the Red States seem not to have gotten the memo), and his suit, while a suit, was somehow unconvincing, like he was dressing up as a lawyer for a high school production of *Night of January 16th*.

"Cowboys are 7-5," he said. "Looks like Jimmy Johnson can coach a little."

"We'll finish higher than the Giants," I told him. "What's up, counselor?"

There were two red plastic ashtrays and a cracked faux-wood table, and the fluorescents overhead buzzed and flickered. Pigskin small talk aside, I could tell from his demeanor he had something on his mind—something I didn't want to hear.

"I know you want to plead innocent," he began, "and I respect that decision. But the prosecution has offered a deal, and it's my responsibility to present it."

Lawyers sought plea deals because they saved the taxpayers money—that's what all the guys said at the Tombs. I saw no reason why I should spend time behind bars because some bureaucratic DA wanted to trim his budget. "Fuck that," I said.

"Listen to me, Todd. Listen. Please. You're being charged with murder in the second. Do you have any idea what that means?"

In the movies, of course, it's always murder in the first. In the real world, they save that designation for cop killers. Murder in the second was the charge. Sorry I couldn't be more romantic.

"Fifteen to life," he continued, as if I were hearing this for the first time. "If you're convicted, you're looking at, realistically, nineteen or twenty *years* before parole. If you're lucky. Years. Before parole. That's a long fucking time, Todd."

He was right; it *was* a long fucking time. I was only twenty-six. Nineteen years represented the entire interval between first grade and now.

"You plead guilty of a lesser charge—first-degree manslaughter is what's on the table—and you could be out in as little as three. Three years is a lot less than twenty, Todd."

"Seventeen, to be exact," I told him. "But the math is beside the point. She was trying to *kill* me, Elliott."

"Be that as it may, we still have to prove it. And your case is . . ."

"Is what?"

He made a wave sign with his hand.

"Whose side are you on?" I pounded my fist on the laminate that was supposed to make the table look like real wood. "She came after me with this poisoned needle. She was still holding it when she died. They must have recovered it."

"Well, they didn't."

"Her diary, then. Exhibit A. It's all there, every last detail."

"We searched the apartment," he said. "No diary."

"The police took it. I *saw* the police take it. I was there when they took it."

"That's not what they claim."

I was beside myself that the Boys in Blue had so shirked their responsibility. Police officers were *good* guys, beacons of light in a dark underworld, right? This was before Mark Fuhrman proved unequivocally that cops are as fallible, as corrupt, as the rest of us. And it did not even occur to me, gullible-ain't-in-the-dictionary sap that I was, that the first responders, the men in suits, were not New York's Finest.

Gross, who had been leaning against the wall, sat down backward on one of the chairs, like a cutup in a John Hughes movie. "I had lunch with Mike Poskevicius yesterday," he said. "You know who that is?"

I did—the Tombs guys were terrified of him—but Gross answered anyway. "He's the assistant district attorney. Nice enough guy, but tough as balls. He told me that he can prove, in court, that your story is—this is a direct quote—a steaming pile of shit."

"Well, he's wrong. Quid Pro Quo . . ."

"There is no Quid Pro Quo, Todd."

"*Yes*, there *is*."

Gross shook his head from side to side. This was to prepare for the come-to-Jesus portion of the meeting, although I didn't realize it at the time. "It's time to come clean. You want my help? Stop bullshitting me. There is no Quid Pro Quo."

"I interviewed in the offices."

"Right, the offices. Five-twenty Madison Avenue, I got that right? That's the New York headquarters of the Carlyle Group, a financial services company. They've occupied that space for years."

"Like hell."

"Poskevicius showed me a copy of the lease."

"Maybe they leased the office under an assumed name." I was beginning to lose my patience. "Did you find Trey Parrish?"

"No."

"Is he really so hard to track down? He lived in my building for years. There's no paper trail on the guy?"

"Your landlord's never heard of him."

This was not that much of a surprise. My landlord was a heroin addict who only spoke Ukrainian. "Great." Looking heavenward, perhaps for divine inspiration, I found only tobacco-stained ceiling tiles. "What about Asher Krug?"

Even before Gross spoke, I could see what was coming. Talk about wearing your heart on your sleeve—he'd have made a lousy poker player. "There's no record of him, Todd. None. We checked the phone book, police records, student records at Yale, the co-op board at the Dakota. Nothing. And frankly, his name sounds a little . . ."

Here it comes, I thought. "A little *what*?"

"Made up."

"Made *up*? You think I'm making this *up*?"

Gross shifted into his most authoritative lawyerly voice, as if he were auditioning for *Law and Order* (which began its second season in 1991). "Highly secretive employment agency. Very well financed. Offers a deal too good to be true. Everyone who passes through there has blood on his hands. Does that sound familiar, Todd?"

From his cheap briefcase, my attorney produced a copy of the bestselling novel of 1991. On its familiar green-marbled dustcover, a besuited man with a briefcase was pulled to and fro by marionette strings.

Gross held it up dramatically, like it was the lost Watergate tape. "It's straight out of Grisham. Quid Pro Quo is just the recruiting arm of Bendini, Lambert & Locke. Even some of the names match . . . Nathan Ross, Nathan Locke. And who's behind all the *evildoing* at Quid Pro Quo, Todd?" His voice took on a most unbecoming tone of sarcasm. "Let me guess . . . oh, could it be . . . *the Mafia*?"

This did not bode well for my defense.

"First of all," I told him, "I never even read *The Firm*. I think Taylor did, but I never got around to it. I'm not into mass-market stuff. Second of all, it isn't the Mafia. It's the government. The Defense Department. I saw Dick Cheney there. In the office. He was there."

"Dick Cheney?"

"The Secretary of Defense."

"Well, *gee*, Todd, why didn't you just say so? I'll just go ahead and subpoena the *Secretary* of *Defense*."

In 2009, of course, the idea of Dick Cheney being involved with a sub-rosa assassination squad doesn't seem quite so far-fetched. Witness those CIA torture centers in Eastern Europe, or the White House energy meetings no one's allowed to know about, or the fact that he shot his hunting companion square in the kisser. But in '91, Cheney's reputation was still impeccable. He was a compassionate conservative from Wyoming, a tool of the oil companies maybe, but innocuous. Most people had never heard of him.

"You think the government doesn't kill people?" I said. "The government kills people all the time."

It had only been a few weeks since Taylor's death, and in those few weeks, I was pretty much useless. Not only was I in panic mode about my future—Life in jail? Really?—but I was still grieving her loss. Whatever the prosecution claimed, it was never my desire to kill her. Grappling with these weighty issues, I had not had a chance to contemplate Quid Pro Quo itself. What was it, exactly? Why did it exist? What was its purpose? My waking mind had never considered these basic questions, but my subconscious must have been mulling them over, because I found myself speaking effortlessly, as if delivering a monologue in acting class.

"The government kills people all the time," I said again. "Americans. Our own people. The government killed JFK, the government killed RFK, the government killed Martin Luther King, the government tried to kill Ronald Reagan. And those are just the ones we know about. The dramatic ones. There are plenty more. Like those senators who died in the spring—Heinz and Tower? You think it was just a coincidence that they both died in plane crashes on successive days? Two guys who were prominently involved in the Iran-Contra hearings? No way. I'm telling you, Elliott, those were Quid Pro Quo hits."

Gross was silent for a moment. Then his expression softened, and he nodded his head. Was I winning him over?

"And Elvis Presley? I suppose that was a Quid Pro Quo hit, too? Death by peanut-butter-banana-and-bacon sandwich?"

I sprung from the chair and began to pace around the table, like a caged cheetah I once saw at the Bronx Zoo. "You really think I made all this up?"

"What *I* think is not important. It's what the jury thinks."

"That's a good one. Did they teach you that in law school?" I stopped in my tracks. "Yoko Ono! Yoko Ono knows Asher Krug. We'll get her to testify."

Gross shot this down, too. Even if she did know Asher, so what? That wouldn't prove anything, other than someone by that name existed.

"What about Donna Green?"

"She's dead, all right. A hundred and fifty people witnessed it. She wasn't murdered, though."

"But the nerve agent . . . Cold Ethyl . . ."

"The only thing they found in her bloodstream was cocaine. A shitload of cocaine."

"Donna didn't do cocaine."

"How the hell would you know?"

Touché.

I kept scrambling. "Go to this bar called Continental. Subpoena one of the bartenders, big dude with tattoos named J.D."

"What's he got to do with this?"

"He slept with her."

"With Donna Green?"

"With Taylor."

"So what?"

So what, indeed. J.D. would know bubkes.

I snapped my fingers—eureka in the bathtub!

"Bill Seward," I said. "She murdered a guy named Bill Seward. At that steakhouse . . . what was it called . . . Chez Molineaux."

"We already checked on that," Gross told me. "A man named *Bob* Seward died of a heart attack at the Ruth's Chris near Rockefeller Center, which proves what? That men who eat steak have heart attacks? Take the plea, Todd."

I ignored that. "What about Andrew Borden? She shot Andrew Borden. In Short Hills, New Jersey. It wasn't a sanctioned Quid Pro Quo hit, so there should be more evidence. We can surely prove *that*."

"Right. Andrew Borden. You mentioned that. Andrew and *Abigail* Borden. You know who Andrew and Abigail Borden are?"

"An investment banker and his wife."

"Lizzie Borden's parents. The ones she murdered with a hatchet. In 1892."

At that moment, I doubted my own sanity. I became lightheaded, like I was in a nightmare, but there was no waking up.

"Well, they obviously gave her bad information, a wrong name." I fell to my knees, clasping my hands together as if in prayer. "I'm just a pawn, Elliott. Can't you see? I'm a pawn in the chess game."

"Take the plea, Todd. I'm begging you."

"What about her job? Somebody at Braithwaite Ross has to

know something. One of the senior editors died recently. Walter
Bledsoe. And Taylor was convinced that Nathan Ross knew all
about it, that he commissioned Bledsoe's hit."

Gross didn't say anything at first. He waited for me to calm
down and sit back down. Then he said, in a softer tone of voice,
"None of it checks out. Walter Bledsoe did die recently—his obit
was in the *Times*, actually—but he was seventy-one and in poor
health. Variety of heart problems. Taylor was never a full editor,
as you suggest. She was Angela Del Giudice's editorial assistant,
making sixteen-five a year, according to her pay stubs. Also, Del
Giudice is just an editor, not the editorial director. That job is
held by someone named Lou Dravillas. Nathan Ross *is* the publisher; that's the only thing you got right. When I questioned him
about Quid Pro Quo—yes, I really did go there and speak with
him—he laughed and said it sounded like the plot of one of his
books."

"Well of course *he'd* deny it."

"Take the plea," he said. "I implore you. I beseech you. I beg
you. Take the plea."

Each statement Gross rattled off in his calm, hypnotic voice was
a nail in my coffin. I was walled up, shut in, a claustrophobe suffo-
cating. I was down to my last breath. There was but one straw left
to grasp at—the only person besides me who Taylor confided in.

"Kim Winter," I said. "Were you able to get in touch with Kim
Winter?"

"Yes. Yes, we were." Gross offered me a cigarette. For some
reason—maybe because it was a Vantage Light, the same brand my
father smoked—I took it. He lit it for me, then fired up one of his
own. "Occupational hazard. I can't seem to quit these things. But
everyone has vices, right?"

"What did she *say*, Elliott?"

He took a long drag, then let it out slowly. The smoke punctu-
ated a mournful sigh. "Kim Winter was an exotic dancer at a strip
club called Sugar Walls."

"So what? Strippers aren't reliable witnesses?"

"She *was* a stripper. We located her in a Dade County correctional facility."

"Prostitution?"

"Extortion. She tried to blackmail the owner of the club. But that's moot, because she refused to testify on your behalf. Even when I offered to cut her sentence down. She said, 'Whoever killed Taylor belongs in jail.' She was adamant."

We sat there for three or four minutes, smoking, listening to the lights buzzing overhead. Down the hall, someone was screaming. It was as quiet as jail gets.

His cigarette was smoked to the filter. He smashed it out in the plastic ashtray. The overt symbolism of this gesture made my heart sink.

"Take the plea, Todd."

I took the plea.

I was sentenced to nineteen years, but I was told not to fixate on that number.

"In three years, you're up for parole," Elliott Gross assured me. "Just keep to yourself and you'll be fine."

Up the river I went, to the Downstate Correctional Facility, a maximum-security prison near Poughkeepsie, figuring that in about a thousand days, I'd be a free man. Unfortunately, Gross's promises of clemency proved optimistic. Parole boards don't like it when pretty, young white girls have their pretty, young white faces blown off. Good behavior and all, my application was denied in 1995, in 1998, in 2001, and again in 2006.

By then, I had lost most of my illusions. I traded them in for a poorly rendered tribal tattoo around my left bicep.

You'll be curious about my time doing time—I know I would be, if I were in the comfy slippers that are Your Shoes—but my experiences at Downstate constitute a memoir of their own, and will not, for considerations of space, be dealt with here. I will say that the popular perception of prison is, thankfully, overblown. *Oz* is bullshit. The tedium, the loneliness, the stir-craziness were worse than any unpleasantness visited upon me by the other inmates. Mostly I was left alone; I was there for murder, after all, which has a certain cachet—a street cred, if you will—inside. Which was just as well. Pretty much everyone there had the IQ of a pastrami sandwich; prison, for me, was a Sartre play.

For the first year, that is. Until I met Walter Maddox.

Other inmates found Jesus in jail, or Allah. Me, I found Maddox. The guy was a revelation.

Maddox showed up in late February of 1993, a few weeks after my father died. He was a scrawny guy, his face grizzled and lined, like a carving of a cigar-store Indian, with a ridiculous walrus moustache that only a relief pitcher could pull off. Nevertheless, no one fucked with him. People seemed to be afraid of him, probably because he was something of a wing nut. Maddox was down with alternative history, the unvarnished truth of past events that is derisively called *conspiracy theory.* He'd be forever making some or other outrageous claim: the Sphinx was more than ten thousand years old, older than human civilization by far, and was the work of a master alien race that still ruled the earth. The proximity of the Roswell UFO crash (July 1947) to the formation of the CIA (September 1947) was not a coincidence. FDR knew all about Pearl Harbor, and LBJ, the Gulf of Tonkin.

We both worked at the prison library, so we'd spend a lot of time together, and Maddox never seemed to run out of off-the-wall pronouncements: L. Ron Hubbard was a CIA operative. The Church of Scientology was established to secretly test people's innate facilities for remote viewing. Tom Cruise was the greatest living remote viewer. The Mormons were collecting genealogical data for the purposes of a neo-eugenics movement, in which ethnic cleansing would rule the day. Darwin's theory of evolution was horseshit. The Federal Reserve Bank was owned by the Rockefellers and other private moneyed interests. Every cent of income taxes collected in the country went to finance those interests. Abraham Lincoln and John Kennedy were assassinated because, and only because, they tried to liberate the U.S. economy from the iron fist of central banks. Booth and Oswald were patsies. And on and on and on.

"None of this is secret," Maddox would insist, after every wild proclamation. "The truth is out there. Anybody can find it—all you have to do is shut off the fucking television and seek it out."

At first, I treated his outlandish comments with the skepticism conventional wisdom demanded. I assumed he had a few screws loose; it was a Poughkeepsie jail, after all, not Vassar. I only listened to him because, kook though he was, he was also interesting and smart, and he seemed to gravitate toward me. I never thought to ask how he had acquired his secret knowledge—probably because I never took him seriously. (So total is the establishment's control of historical narrative, so relentless is its suppression of the truth, that even a victim of conspiracy like me didn't see the light.) Maddox was a diversion, my own personal TV show, and that's all. He was the Discovery Channel, the History Channel, and A&E, all rolled into one commercial-free superstation. As long as he kept on entertaining me, making the time go faster, I didn't think to ask why he never talked about his personal life, or where he grew up, or how old he was, even.

So it went on, as the months turned to years, until one day, in March of 1995, he told me something that completely changed my perception of him. My Road to Damascus was the sidewalk to the basketball courts.

We were in the yard, watching a group of heavily tattooed inmates play hoop. Maddox looked agitated, which was unusual. He generally had this serene persona, like a hero in a kung fu movie. Being in jail didn't seem to bother him in the least. Not that day. That day, you could tell, there was something gnawing at him.

"Do you know anybody who lives in Tokyo, Todd?"

This was out of left field, but so was most of what came out of his mouth. "No. Why?"

"Chatter," Maddox said. "Big chatter. There's gonna be an attack on the mass transit system tomorrow. Poison gas. Lots of collateral damage."

I didn't believe this, of course, but I let him talk. It was that or play basketball, and while I was tall, I sucked at hoop.

"It's a coup," Maddox continued. "Japan is a prelim, an opening act. If it succeeds there, they'll open in New York."

"They?"

"The New World Order. Although they'll blame it on Islamic terrorists. No one will know the truth."

"What if it fails?"

"They'll find some two-bit doomsday cult to play patsy." He grabbed hold of the chain-link fence with both hands and shook it. "Something has to rattle the cage, bring back the thirst for blood. The sheep are complacent."

"So," I quipped, "when did they change your medication?"

Judging by the glower, he didn't find my remark the least bit funny. "If you know anybody who lives in Tokyo, have them call in sick tomorrow."

"Whatever you say, Nostradamus."

"Fuck you, Lander." Maddox balled his hands into fists. His face went red. It was the first time I'd seen him get angry—and everybody gets angry in prison. Immediately I felt like a big jerk.

"Sorry," I said. "That was out of line. But seriously, how do you know that? And don't say you read it in some book."

There was a long silence. We watched one of the inmates, a six-seven guy called Ron-Ron, burst free of his defender and dunk. The netless rim rattled relentlessly.

"Did you ever wonder," Maddox asked, "why they offered you a plea bargain?"

During the previous two years, I'd told him my entire story a thousand times, just as I've laid it out in these pages, sparing no detail. That's what you do in prison, other than smoke (I took up Taylor's old habit and Taylor's old brand) and read dirty magazines—you discuss your crime. While he always listened with patient interest, he'd never offered any insight, until now. I sprang to attention.

"Trials," I said, "cost a lot of money."

Maddox ran his fingers through his moustache and nodded. If not for the orange jumpsuit, he would have looked professorial. "Trials also bring a lot of publicity. Especially a high-profile case like yours. No, I think they offered a plea because they didn't want your case to see the light of day. I think they wanted you—they *needed* you—to admit your guilt. I think if you took the stand, and swore, under oath, that Quid Pro Quo was true . . ."

"That's just it," I said. "The assistant DA said he could prove my story was bullshit."

"Maybe, maybe not."

"What are you saying?"

"That you're the fall guy," Maddox said. "That you're Jack Ruby without the tittie bar or the dogs."

I knew that I had been set up, but the extent of the collusion had not occurred to me. If I was thinking about anything at that time, it was about Taylor, not about Quid Pro Quo. "How do you figure?"

"Let me count the ways," Maddox said. "Where to begin? Okay: You mentioned that Asher had a file marked Russell Trust Association. Russell Trust is the legal name of the Skull and Bones Society. You know, at Yale. President Bush is a Bonesman. So are a number of other prominent people."

"Asher Krug," I said. "And Nathan Ross."

"Exactly. The Little Check hit happened at the Yale Club, so there's obviously a Yale/Skull and Bones connection to Quid Pro Quo."

"But Lydia Murtomaki went to Georgetown."

"To the School of Foreign Service. She graduated in '68, you said, if I remember correctly. You know who else graduated from the School of Foreign Service at Georgetown University in 1968?"

I did not have at my disposal an alumni database of a school I did not attend.

"William Jefferson Clinton," Maddox said. "Slick Willie himself. Clinton was mentored there by a professor named Carroll Quigley, who was actually a DIA operative and a Grover."

I was starting to get lost. "A Grover? As opposed to an Oscar the Grouch, you mean?"

Maddox ignored my joke (and rightly so). "You also alluded to a statue of an owl in the lobby," he said. "There's a similar statue at the Bohemian Grove."

"The what?"

"Oh, for fuck sake. Don't you know anything?"

The Bohemian Grove, he explained, was a redoubt in the hills of northern California, where the *real* powers that be met each year to drink, carouse, and establish world policy. Membership included politicians, CEOs, and éminences grises of every stripe with sufficient dough and influence.

"So, we're talking about a covert operation," Maddox said, counting on his fingers as he spoke, "with ties to the Defense Intelligence Agency, the Central Intelligence Agency, the Skull and Bones Society, the Grovers, the Carlyle Group, Dick Cheney, Lee Atwater, Osama Bin Laden . . ."

"Wait . . . who?"

I had asked simply to clarify— even after the first WTC bombing, no one knew Bin Laden from Ben Hogan—but Maddox took my question as a challenge.

"Your friend met a really tall Arab there, right? Bin Laden is almost seven feet tall. That must have been him."

There aren't many well-heeled Arabs as how's-the-weather-up-there as Ron-Ron, I had to admit.

"Bin Laden," Maddox continued, again counting off, "Mossad . . ."

I didn't know at the time that Mossad was Israel's state intelligence department, but I played along. "Really? Mossad?"

"What kind of a name is Krug, anyway?" Maddox asked.

I wasn't sure he wanted an answer, but I gave him one. "German."

"Bullshit. Asher's one of the Twelve Tribes. You don't name someone Asher unless you're Jewish. Dollars to doughnuts he's Israeli. His parents were probably kibbutzniks. Settled there with Ben-Gurion in '48."

(Years later, I would locate Asher's birth chart, from Taylor's visit with the astrologer. Its precise natal information would confirm Maddox's suspicion. Unless he had lied to Taylor, which was possible, Asher was born in Tel Aviv.)

"So he's Jewish," I said. "So what?"

I was half-expecting him to claim that a clandestine cabal of Jews, spearheaded by the Rothschilds, ran the world, and that the Holocaust was a hoax intended to hush up the truth—in which case I'd write him off as a raving lunatic. My tolerance for crack-pottery only ran so far. But Maddox didn't go there.

"His nationality is relevant only because it establishes a Mossad connection," he said. "Or should I say, *another* Mossad connection. Robert Maxwell was a *kidon* operation, everyone knows that. And your friend Taylor did the job, so . . ."

Only then did I put Asher's Canary Islands jaunt and Maxwell's mysterious death together. The wool over my eyes was thick and clingy.

On November 5, 1991, Robert Maxwell, the British publishing magnate, fell to his death from the deck of his yacht. Said yacht was sailing around the Canary Islands at the time. For three days, CNN—the 24-7 cable news network that had made its name in '91 during the (first) Gulf War; Fox wasn't even a full-fledged network yet, let alone the Republican propaganda machine it would become—covered the story with a ferocity usually reserved for prepubescent Cuban refugees, even though most Americans had never heard of Robert Maxwell.

I had heard of him, as had Jason Hanson. Maxwell's media holdings included, among other things, the Mirror newspaper group, and, by extension, API, my shady former place of employ. At the time, of course, Maxwell's death was presumed accidental by Bernard Shaw and Company. But was it? Maxwell matched the description of Little Check—his eyebrows were black caterpillars. Asher was in the Canary Islands that weekend. Could they have whisked him to New York from his yacht—as he himself suggested—killed him, and whisked him right back? A logistical headache, to be sure, but hardly impossible.

According to Maddox, Maxwell was a Mossad operative gone bad. His death was not accidental—he'd been injected with a lethal nerve agent and dumped overboard. Successive autopsies proved only that Maxwell hadn't drowned—but the case is no longer under investigation. Buried in state in Jerusalem, in accordance with Jewish custom, his body (unlike that of our Zachary Taylor, which was dug up in 1991 to determine if Old Rough 'n' Ready had been poisoned or died of bad gas, as was originally thought) can never be exhumed. Officially, his death remains, as of this writing, a mystery.

But Maddox knew better. Robert Maxwell was born Jan Hoch in what was, in 1923, Czechoslovakia. *Jan* Hoch, please note; the same first name as Taylor's pink slip. According to Maddox, Maxwell's Mossad code name, a nod to his tall physical stature (who says spies don't have a sense of humor?) and the land of his birth, was—mirabile dictu—Little Czech. Obviously Taylor had never seen it written and spelled it in her diary phonetically.

"There's still some things I'm not clear on," I said, after all of this had sunk in.

"That's an understatement," Maddox said with a grin. "Shoot."

"Why would anyone pay money to kill Donna Green? She was the head of the photo library; they couldn't just lay her off or something?"

"She was black, and she was in her forties—that's two protected classes under Title VII right there. She'd been at the job for years, and her performance, while lackluster, was not abysmal. You know how hard it is to fire someone like that? If you don't think management wouldn't consider killing employees they couldn't otherwise get rid of, then you obviously haven't worked in human resources." Maddox ran his fingers through his moustache. "You still look confused."

"Why would Averell Ross hire Quid Pro Quo?" I asked. "I mean, he's a baby boomer, right? If the idea is out-with-the-old, in-with-the-new, wouldn't it make more sense for a middle manager—someone like Angela Del Giudice—to contract the pink slip?"

"You haven't listened to a word I've said." Maddox shook his head, his disapproval palpable. "The people who actually run this country, who control the media, who control the school system, who control the fucking House of Representatives—those are not people that get taken out. Those are the people who take out everyone else, dig? The people who have a seat on the shuttle when the planet blows up. Averell Ross is one of those people. Same with the honchos at the Mirror Group. Setting aside the fact that she couldn't afford it and would have no way of knowing about it, if Angela Del Giudice went to Quid Pro Quo and asked Lydia Murtomaki to pink-slip Averell Ross, man, she wouldn't leave the building alive. Killing your boss is the American dream, Todd, but that's all that it is—a dream."

"But why kill Walter Bledsoe at all? Is the editorial director of a small publishing house really worth murdering? I mean, he's a fucking *editor*."

"You think a book editor isn't important to the Grovers? Shit." Maddox crossed his arms and turned to watch the basketball game. "A book editor runs interference, man. The best way to cover something up is to write a book about it, or make a movie about it—*to present what is fact as fiction*. Have you caught this new show, *The X-Files*? The one about the aliens? Half the shit on that show is completely true. But if some reporter were to print the truth now, people would just say, 'That can't be true—it was on *The X-Files*.' You dig?"

I dug.

"Maddox, dude, how do you know all this?"

"I used to work for Central Intelligence," he said. "That's why the inmates leave me alone. And they leave you alone because you're with me."

The bell sounded then, and it was time to return to our cells.

"What did you do for the CIA?"

"Black ops," Maddox said under his breath. "And if you don't know what that is, believe me, you don't want to know."

The next day, events unfolded exactly as Maddox had foretold, although the damage was not as severe as he'd feared. Sarin nerve gas was released in five places on the Tokyo Metro, killing twelve people. Aum Shinrikyo, a Japanese doomsday cult, claimed responsibility. The following month, Timothy McVeigh would blow up the Alfred P. Murrah Federal Building in Oklahoma City. And I don't need to remind you what happened six years later in lower Manhattan—although I will mention that the heat generated by jet fuel is insufficient to melt steel girders, as any metallurgist worth his sodium chloride will tell you.

That Maddox, incarcerated in a state prison halfway around the world, had predicted the Tokyo subway sarin incident lent credence to his other seemingly preposterous assertions. Maybe the world really *was* run by sub-rosa alien overlords. It certainly would explain some of the shit that goes on. Advanced societies like ours have the trappings of civility, its shiny veneer; but at its core, the world is a dark, anarchic place that still holds to the law of the lawless jungle. Anything as big and unwieldy as a government inevitably crushes the occasional insect beneath its Colossus's feet.

As sarin gas seeped into the Tokyo subway on the morning of March 20, 1995, a prison guard found Maddox in the shower, bleeding profusely from the neck. They never found out who killed him. I don't think they really wanted to know.

I feared—and sometimes hoped—that whoever came for Maddox would come for me. But Judgment Day never dawned. Quid Pro Quo didn't vanish me, nor did they harm my parents or my two extant references—Laura Horowitz and Jason Hanson. I guess they didn't have to. I was an unemployed actor, a criminal of passion, and a "fucking nut-job," as Darla Jenkins remarked to the *New York Post*. I was a cipher, a nebbish, a nothing. I possessed so little threat potential that they didn't *need* to have me silenced. Jack Ruby? Please. Next to me, Jack Ruby had the moral credibility of John Paul II. They could leave me languishing in prison, a Cassandra in chains, proclaiming a truth that no one believed.

And so I languished—for seventeen years, nine months, and twenty-three days. Take the plea? My guess is, Elliott Gross was in on it, too.

Seventeen years. Nine months. Twenty-three days.

When I was finally released this past August, I was forty-three years old.

EPILOGUE

Independence Day, 2009. Eighteen years to the day after Taylor Schmidt moved into my apartment. Eighteen short trips round the sun—the interval between birth and high school graduation—and the world is a completely different place. So much technology at our disposal: cheap, ubiquitous technology. Cell phones, BlackBerries, Palm Pilots, DVD players, hi-def TV sets, iPods, satellite radio, camera phones, digital cameras, laptop computers, photo-quality printers, and, of course, the Internet, with its countless applications and conveniences. In 1991, you still had to buy your porn in adult bookstores!

On the other hand, the economy is in shambles, and we're fighting a war in Iraq for reasons only George Bush really understands. The more things change, as they say.

I am sitting at Taylor's old desk in Taylor's old room. Her futon is still here, and her dresser, and, in its bottom drawer, one of her old pink Molly Ringwald sweaters. Though faded by time, the collage of Absolut Vodka ads remains intact, still taped crookedly to the cinderblock wall, giving the room the feel of a freshman dorm. The last of her stray belongings—a forgotten hairbrush, a scrunchie, some torn pairs of pantyhose—litter the floor. I don't dare pick them up.

(Yes, I managed to keep the apartment. After my arrest, Jason Hanson became my "roommate," moving all my stuff into Taylor's old room and keeping the rest for himself. At first he had ethical qualms about involving himself in my affairs, but he came around— he'd been living in Astoria, and the only way he was ever going to score an East Village address was to take my pad. A murderer may be a murderer, but a sweet sublet is too good to pass up.)

This sacred space is where I come to reflect, to remember, to write. For the past nine months I've sat here every day—sometimes for hours on end, sometimes for just a minute or two—pecking away at the sticky keys of my old Smith Corona, setting down what you have just read.

My work is almost complete. Just a few loose ends to wrap up—the literary equivalent of a victory lap. Why do I resist beginning the cigarette-after-sex that is the denouement? Are the memories too painful? Do I fear life without the escritoirial therapy I've assigned myself? Or am I just hungry for company, however remote, however vicarious?

It could be because there isn't much left to relate. Most of the people I've told you about are either dead (Taylor; Maddox; Nathan Ross, in a single-car accident on the Taconic Parkway in 1996; my cat Bo, of feline leukemia, in 1993), missing (Trey Parrish, Lydia Murtomaki, Asher Krug, Elliott Gross), or still collecting welfare from the State of Missouri (Darla Jenkins). Even Oxana is gone, and her three-legged dog pissing on the Great Fire Hydrant in the Sky. The only person left to report on is me, and I'm not sure I can pull that off without a healthy dose of self-pity.

In my defense, I'm still living in 1991, when self-pity was a cultural hallmark. You can hear it in the song lyrics from that era: *I'm worse at what I do best. Every finger in the room is pointing at me. Sometimes I feel like my only friend. You gave me nothing, now that's all I got. I'm a creep, I'm a weirdo. I'm a loser, baby, so why don't you kill me.* Asher dismissed it as whining, but was it really that? Ours was a generation crying for help in the only way we knew how. It's no wonder that 1991's two most luminous breakthrough celebrities—Tupac Shakur and Kurt Cobain—died so violently, so suddenly, and so soon. They were embodiments of our collective pain, the poor saps. A question for Taylor's astrologer: was there some cruel portent, some opposition in the stars that made 1991 such a shitty year? It sure seems that way.

I should be happy, I realize, or at least happier. I'm out of jail. I don't need to work, thanks to savvy investing of my inheritance (my father died in March of 1992, right around the time that *The Real World* aired, leaving a surprisingly large nest egg; I bought stock in Amazon at the initial price offering five years later). I still live in the same apartment, paying an enviable rent.

None of it matters. I'm a prisoner of a memory, of a New York that no longer exists, of a relentless and insatiable hunger for forbidden fruit. I have my freedom, if you'll forgive a cliché, but I'm not free.

I will never know for sure whether or not Taylor intended to kill me on that fateful night—if she was reaching for Cold Ethyl or Hot Hester. Both options comprise their own distinct hell. If it was massage oil she was reaching for, then she *did* love me . . . and I killed her. Whoops. That's a Shakespearean tragedy right there, an *Othello* for the third millennium. It doesn't get more heartbreaking than that.

It doesn't get more heartbreaking than that, *except for the other possibility*: that she didn't love me at all.

If I had it to do again, I would *let* her make the move—let Taylor either rub my shoulders or rub me out. Love or death: either outcome is preferable to the torment of *never being able to know*.

And if that reeks of self-pity, well, too fucking bad.

Pitying myself is one of the ways I pass the time. What else do I do? I wander around the now-sanitized East Village looking for ghosts (the pretty Asian waif ducking into Sake Bar Decibel— could she be Mae-Yuan?), and I smoke Parliament Lights by the carton, and I play warped mix tapes on my shitty tape deck. I sit at my battered typewriter, and I write—deleting a word here, adding a paragraph there, as new recollections emerge, as my understanding deepens—and I remember. Most of all, I remember.

Remembering is my only job, and it's hard work. We are natural-born amnesiacs, hardwired to let go of the past, to release ourselves from history; the only way to withstand our pain is to forget our pain. We may think we don't forget, but we do. Time wears down the rough edges of our memory, sure as a stone on the river bank is smoothed by the rushing current. And like the eroding stone, the memory fades so gradually, we don't even feel it. We don't notice. Eighteen years flow by, whoosh, and we don't even realize that not that long ago, we didn't all drink bottled water, the Soviet Union loomed as a threat, smoking was commonplace in restaurants, and Bono was just a rock star.

Once in a lifetime, if you're lucky, you meet a woman who just does it for you. Mine died eighteen years ago, and despite all that's happened, I don't want to let her go. I want to savor every last detail: her crooked nose, her awestruck stare, her lavender-oil scent, her savory-sweet taste, the stubblebumps under her arms, the Band-Aids on her heels—even the blood on her hands.

What I want . . . all I want . . . is *not to forget*. But it's an uphill battle. Over time, the image blurs, the scent dissipates, the memory fades. The memory of Taylor Schmidt, object of my desire, my pity, my obsession, and—above all—my love.

G.M.O.
Highland, N.Y.
2006–2008

ACKNOWLEDGMENTS

I would like to thank the following people for their support, guidance, and encouragement: my crack agent, Mollie Glick, and the entire team at Foundry; my tack-smart editor, Jen Schulkind; Cal Morgan, Carrie Kania, Robin Bilardello, Nicole Reardon, and the rest of the Harper Paperbackers; my teachers: Joe Russo, Jeffrey Shulman, Donn B. Murphy, and John Glavin; Roberto ("Frank") Aguirre-Sacasa, Jessica Bruce, Colleen Curran, Christine & Michael Preston, Matthew Snyder, and the whole of the DEOCUS Empire—especially the insanely funny Mike Strange, whose throwaway joke back in 1993 was *TK*'s initial inspiration.

I would also like to acknowledge the awesomeness—or the *killerness*, as it were—of my entire family, especially my parents, my brother Jeremy, my father-in-law Franklin, and my lovely and inspiring children,

Dominick and Prudence, whose like-clockwork naps gave me time to write.

To Stephanie St. John, my beautiful and talented wife, I owe more than I can possibly convey in this short space. I thank her especially for never losing faith, even when I was wallowing in a self-indulgent despair that made me about as fun as a Lars von Trier double feature. This is for you, B.P.!